Queen Alpha

NYC Mecca Series Book 2

By: Leia Stone and Jaymin Eve

Stone, Leia
Eve, Jaymin
Queen Alpha

For information on reproducing sections of this book or
sales of this book go to
www.LeiaStone.com or www.JayminEve.com

leiastonebooks@gmail.com
jaymineve@gmail.com

To the Alpha in all of us. Be strong and steadfast.

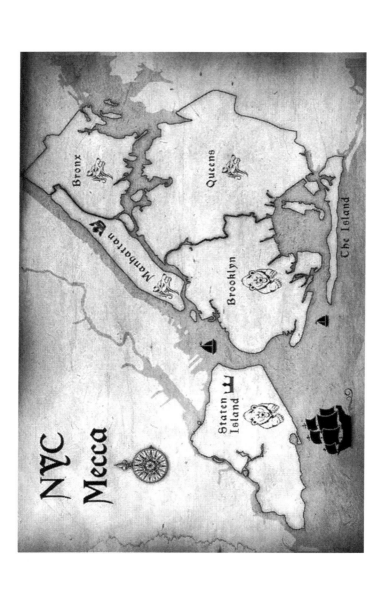

Chapter One

The first cut is the deepest.

THERE HAD BEEN many times in my life I had mourned shifters I loved. I'd mourned the idea of a father since I was old enough to realize I would never know him. I dealt with it, moved on, and decided I'd never do the same thing to my children. But that didn't mean the hole wasn't still there. It always would be. I just learned how to accept and compartmentalize it.

Then my mother. Her death had stolen the last of my childhood innocence. Despite the fact she'd always been a bit cold and distant, she was there for advice, for support. That she had been taken before knowing Winnie, my sister, was a double blow, one I wasn't sure I'd ever really recover from.

Kade had also made that list. The kiss we'd shared at the summer festival stayed with me for five years, and even though he was back in my life, there was still no chance of us ever having more than an alliance. We both ruled different shifter clans. We were allies now, but our people had been enemies for too many years for the animosity to turn into anything positive. Duty and protocol was my priority. My people would always be my focus, but that didn't mean my heart wasn't mourning for what was and what could have been. For now, I had Kade in my life as a friend, and I had to accept that was all it'd ever be.

One other death had resonated strongly with me: Jeremiah, the single father of two, who had turned to a life of crime to feed his young. I'd been an heir then, not yet the alpha of the Bronx. I'd seen his trial. The queen had him killed to prove her own strength, to show the other wolves that no one stole in her territory. I had to stand witness then, as I was coming of age. It was not an action any fifteen-year-old wanted to see, especially one who was fragile from the loss of her mother. After that I saw the Red Queen in a different light. I loved her no less, but I feared her a little more. She was brutal in a way I had no comprehension for.

That was also the day I wished to never be queen. I'd been happy being a queen heir with all of the benefits that came with it. Of course, fate had a different idea in store for me, and now I was ruler of the three boroughs in New York City, controlling the mecca, our energy and magic source.

The greatest leaders are forged in fire and trial, and this was going to be one hell of a fiery trial. I was a queen on the brink of a war, which didn't surprise me in the slightest. But I would not worry on that today. Today I was in mourning again, this time for one of my friends, dominants, and former lovers.

Derek. He had been cut down by a dark fae during the battle at Kade's home. Cut down protecting me, which he'd been doing for many years. Since becoming the alpha of the Bronx, I'd had six core dominants, the best of my people. My friends. Losing one of our own was a pain that sent roiling surges of mecca through my body. But I had to keep it contained. Mecca was powerful and dangerous; it could easily kill the shifters around me, and I was their queen. It was my duty to protect them.

"I can't believe he's gone," Monica said beside me, her voice almost inaudible. She had run her hands through her ashy-blonde hair so many times it was literally standing on end, and her eyes were rimmed in red, her hands shaking as she stared out across the mass of shifters before us.

Monica was one of my inner six – well, five now, along with Blaine, Jen, Ben, and Victor – standing with me on the raised platform. Directly across from us, on the funeral pyre, our friend Derek was going out in full warrior fashion, to take his place with the gods. The council, on the other side of the platform, were performing the last rites.

"He went out as a warrior, protecting Ari. He would not have asked for more than that," said Blaine, one of my oldest and best friends. "It is good that we honor him today, that we stand with all the shifters to honor his sacrifice."

The rest of the shifter world did not know about the fae threat yet, but they would soon. I'd finally convinced the council that we were at war, and that Derek would only be the first of many. It had taken them quite some time to accept. We'd never had to deal with the fae, the Tuatha de Danann, as a threat. Heck, they had not been much more than a fable, a folk story from the origin of shifters. They'd disappeared from Earth around the time of the first shifters. And yet … they hadn't disappeared at all. They'd gone into the Otherworld, the parallel land that shared mecca power with us, and now, since the death of the Red Queen, they'd stepped out of the shadows, and wanted control of the mecca energy.

Torine, the oldest of the council, raised his voice as he finished the death ceremony: "Dust to dust, ash to ashes. Derek of the yellow line will now take his place among his ancestors. He will rule in the next life as a warrior. We honor him."

"We honor him," was echoed back by the hundreds who were stationed around the expansive and private garden of the royal mansion. It was here that we would send my old friend to the gods.

The council turned to me then and I knew it was time for me to offer reassurance. The fact that Derek was killed in bear territory was not a great thing for our fragile new friendship. Rumors had been rife despite my initial press release about a new threat we were investigating. They thought I was covering for Kade because we were friends. Everyone wanted to blame the bears again for our troubles.

No more.

I stepped forward, my dominants remaining a respectful distance behind me as protocol dictated. "One of our own has been taken," I said, my voice strong as it echoed across the gardens.

"Brutally murdered by the same foe who killed our queen and many of our people on the night of the Summit. This was not the bears' doing. If it hadn't been for the bears, we would have lost many more that night. King Kade aided us. He forged a friendship between our people that I want to see grow and develop. For without it, we will have no chance against those who think they can threaten our people."

From the corner of my eye I could see that the council looked concerned. They probably thought I was going to drop the fae bomb on everyone right now. I knew better than that though. This was not going to be an easy sell. That information needed to start with a small group of alphas and then, very slowly, we would filter the news to the packs.

"Who attacked us, then?" someone shouted from the crowd.

Turning in that direction, I let some of my inner wolf rise up, the mecca shimmering across my skin in a purple glow of energy. I knew the mecca crown on my head would also be glowing, the stones infused with energy. I remained silent for a moment, letting them stare upon me. It never hurts to remind them that you are queen, that you are powerful.

Finally I said, "We have suspicions about who is behind the new threat. All I will say for now is that they are not enemies who will be easily countered, and until such a time I have more evidence this is all you need to know."

No one else opened their mouths, which probably had a lot to do with the purple lightshow my body was doing. Stepping across the platform, I neared my fallen friend. His body was tightly bound in a stitched cloth that displayed his yellow lineage symbol. He was handsome still, even in death, with his multicolored hair styled back neatly. But all of his vibrancy was gone; it was impossibly painful to see Derek like this, to know he was gone and that we were about to send his shell off in a warrior fire. Sucking in a few short breaths, trying to get my emotions under control, I lifted my head to the sky and shouted: "Derek, you are honored. A warrior going home to your people. Fly free, my friend. Until we meet again."

Violet, my best friend and pack magic born, stepped up beside me, and together we lifted our hands and a burst of purple flames shot up all around the pyre. I needed her help; I was a newbie when it came to mecca control. The flames smashed against us, we were so close. The heat was scorching, tightening my skin to the point it felt like it would crack, drying the tears tracing slowly down my cheeks. But I couldn't move. I couldn't leave him until he was dust and ashes. That was the way of our people.

My dominants joined me, all of us burning with our friend. Then, as one, the seven of us, Violet included, lifted our heads and let loose a long, mournful howl. My people joined in. Our cries rang out across the royal house, across the world. I let my sorrow filter out into my bonds with all shifters. Calista had sent out a press release stating the time of the funeral and asked shifters around the world to pray for Derek and to pay their respects. I felt them now, scattered about within the energy that made up my body.

For a moment the shifter packs all stood together in grief, and I knew this was the only way for us to beat the fae, as one people. But we would also need the bear shifters.

I needed Kade. It was a truth that could get me dethroned or killed, an alliance I needed to be careful with but my heart and gut told me it was the only way. Kade was going to teach me how to control and channel mecca, and then we were going to neutralize the threat against our people.

One way or another.

Chapter Two

One beary brutal beating.

I LAY ON my back panting, sweat beading my brow. The force of the mecca had just thrown me across the room and Kade was not happy.

"You need to focus!" he said, his voice firm as he reached down to pull me up. I reluctantly took his hand and stood, meeting his molten gaze.

"I am focusing! The mecca is out of control. No one can handle this kind of power." It had been three weeks since the fae had attacked us all at the king's mansion. Three weeks and over a half dozen mecca training sessions with Kade.

We were struggling to fit them all in with my new queen duties. Kade was more established within his boroughs and didn't have as much to do, so he was working around my timetable.

Kade pushed back at me again, one of the few shifters in the world who could without repercussions. "You're wrong. I can see the mecca, and although I agree it's stronger than ever, you can control it. I've never seen someone's body so responsive to the energy. Almost as if you were made to harness it."

My cheeks reddened at his reference to my body. Not only was the energy within us constantly pushing us together, the close proximity of our training was upping the sexual tension to a tangible level that was making him extra hard to resist.

Calista, my royal advisor, had been harping on about me taking a mate – at least for the short term, to kill off the rumors of my supposed affair with the king. The council was spinning it to say we were in peace talks, trying to form an alliance to figure out who had killed the former Red Queen, but rumors still abounded. My eulogy at Derek's sendoff had helped a little – I heard less talk of killing bears anyway. But one speech was never going to undo hundreds of years of animosity. Slow and steady.

"There are new rumors about me," I said to Kade after I caught my breath. "Apparently I'm sleeping my way through the bears in the hopes of conceiving a hybrid child." I shook my head at the very thought. There had never been a hybrid child. It was strictly forbidden and I wasn't even sure it was possible.

Kade snorted; his chest rumbled. "I think we need to start giving our people harder jobs. They have way too much time on their hands for gossip."

"Yep, not enough toiling going on in the shifter world. They've had it too easy for too long."

He straightened, waving his hand, which meant he wanted me to stop procrastinating and start training again. Stretching out my aching body, I let out a bit of an exaggerated sigh. As I stepped closer to him, his heat was everywhere, his scent all soil and earth and life. Dammit. Finding a wolf mate was probably the smart thing to do. It would solve plenty of my problems. But ... I couldn't, and I didn't really have the time right now to try to talk myself into it. After the battle at Kade's home, Derek's death, and the very real threat of a fae war ... well, my priorities were elsewhere.

My thoughts were cut off by Kade touching my cheek. I held my breath, barely moving.

"Eyelash," he murmured in that husky voice. As he pulled back from my face I saw a tiny eyelash clasped between his strong fingers.

"Make a wish." He lifted it closer to my lips.

There was mirth dancing in his eyes, and I knew he was toying with me. But still ... the king of bears made eyelash wishes and tended to roses. *Crap.* These training sessions were going to be the death of me. Maybe literally. We could not be together, our people would tear us apart, but that didn't mean I wasn't appreciating all the sexy that was Kade. I blew on the eyelash, sending it flying away. Kade didn't move so I cleared my throat and stepped back a pace.

"Let's do the mecca thing again," I said, trying to defuse the tension.

Still wearing that slight grin, Kade nodded and stepped back, both of us trying to get distance from the other in hopes that it would smother this burning fire that had started between us.

Yeah, right!

We were down in the basement training center of the royal home, where I had fought Selene for the crown. The wolf council begrudgingly agreed to our training sessions, but only on certain terms, and the king coming to my territory was one of them. He didn't seem to mind, and most of the time brought only Gerald and another of his guard with him. Today it was Chelle, a female bear, tall and statuesque with golden-colored hair and dark burning eyes. She did not like wolves, that much was clear, and if looks could kill ... well, the wolves would be screwed, because the way Chelle was looking at me, Selene would soon be their queen.

Selene! *Ugh.* No time to think about the spare heir right now. She was evil, and if I died in the first twelve months of my reign, she would step in as queen. If I died after a year, then another Summit would be held, as there were more shifter girls who would be of age. More queen heirs waiting in the wings.

"Focus, Ari." Kade's low voice knocked me out of my thoughts and I sucked in a deep breath, calling the mecca forward. It was everywhere, not just in the crystals or the vortex, it was life. I understood that now, I respected that. A flood of power coursed through me as I felt the mecca swelling in my veins to fill the very core of my being.

I'd been meditating a lot, working on centering and focusing my thoughts. This was part of training for all heirs, but now it was even more important.

"Now!" Kade said forcefully. He moved his body slightly, and I knew he was preparing to jump in and shield me if needed.

I aimed the energy at the tier of stacked cans we had in the corner of the room. This time, instead of throwing mecca, I just let it gently trickle out. Controlled it. It took every ounce of my focus to not let the power overwhelm me, but for the first time I seemed to be managing it. Instead of exploding in a mass, the cans tilted slightly, and then the top can toppled over, taking the rest of the stack with it. I gave a small yell of success, and then the headache hit me.

"You're holding the energy, let it go," Kade said, stepping into me again, scanning my face.

I couldn't; the headache had my focus shot and my control was lost. Calling the mecca was much easier than letting it go back. The stabbing pain in my head was increasing and I was seconds from dropping to my knees when Kade placed a hand on the side of my face, covering me from chin to temple. He stroked my forehead a few times and the headache eased, although my brain remained a jumbled mess. To be fair, not all of that could be blamed on the mecca. When Kade was this close to me, all sensible thought took a vacation. God, why was he so attractive? And his scent – smell was everything to shifters, it either dissuaded or attracted us – and Kade's scent was enough to have my wolf howling silently as need clenched my gut. I had never wanted someone so badly, and I had never wanted someone I couldn't have.

It caused an ache that I had no idea how to deal with, an ache that was strong and fierce, right in my chest. Why the hell couldn't I feel like this around any of my wolves? They were beautiful. Deadly. Powerful. But no ... had to be a damn bear.

"Want to see something wild?" I blurted out, stepping back. We needed a distraction, the mecca was trying to push our energies together, and neither one of us were fighting very hard.

Kade shook his head as if to clear his thoughts and nodded. "I like wild," he said, and I could tell from the low timbre of his voice that he wanted to say more but didn't.

Uh, crap – what was I going to show him? I'd blurted out that last sentence without thought, but ... maybe...

"Okay, so you cannot breathe a word of it to your people. Even Gerald." I would be in deep shit if the council knew what I was about to show him. But with a fae war looming on the horizon I needed another powerful ally, and I trusted Kade. If he wanted me dead he'd had plenty of chances by now.

He nodded, his head tilted in a way that meant he was intrigued. A part of me, which was clearly channeling the wolf council, was asking if I was really going to show the bear king our mecca crystal, the heavily-guarded stone that had been viewed only by a very select number of heirs and rulers.

Only people with royal blood could even get near it, which wouldn't be a problem for Kade.

He was a king, and had an extra affinity for the mecca. And he might just be able to shed some light on the mystery of the crystal. Mostly I wanted to know, if the fae came, could it be used as a weapon?

Together we walked to the outer doors, where my guards stood. Kade's were across on the other side of the room but they could still hear us.

"We're going to have a meeting in the library room," I said.

Both bear and wolf guards looked confused, as it was not a normal meeting room, but all had the intelligence not to question me. I wasn't as brutal as the Red Queen had been, but I was no pushover either. It was a thing every alpha learned the hard way – you had to be tough on wolves or they would rip you to pieces. I had no problem being tough. I was the queen alpha now, the alpha of every wolf in existence.

Traversing the halls, our guards trailing us, I was glad there were no others in the vicinity. Panic tended to ensue if Kade was spotted in our territory. When we reached the room, I opened the door, turning back to the guards.

"Wait for us here. Don't let anyone in."

Kade's two turned to him briefly and he nodded, letting them know to follow my orders. The king and I stepped inside then and he closed the heavy wooden door behind us. I crossed into the room, which had been set up as a sitting-library room – not the Red Queen's personal library where she had been killed, but a similar room on a much smaller scale. Kade was silent, examining his surroundings, before he started waving his hands before him.

"What are you doing?" I asked, perplexed.

He lowered his arms, turning to focus on me completely. "I can see the mecca in here, stronger than anywhere else I've been."

His gift was amazing. I could feel the mecca, and utilize the energy, but he could see the actual lines of power and manipulate them. It gave him a strength and control that I lacked.

"I'm going to show you right now, but remember, I'm trusting you with this, Kade. If you break that trust, I'll kill you."

My words rang true. If he did turn against me, I would kill him.

He gave me a nod. "I would expect nothing less, and you know you can trust me."

Sucking in deeply, I reached out and pulled the book down. As the secret door swung open, Kade's eyes met mine. "This is going to be interesting," he said with a grin.

I gave him my best mysterious one-eyebrow-raised look. "Not scared are you, bear?" I asked, before stepping inside and leaving him to make the decision.

His footsteps were silent as he followed me, but I knew he was there. The energy of the mecca was strong, almost suffocating on this side of the secret chamber. Whoever had designed this hiding place had definitely spelled the walls around it. This much mecca would make even alpha wolves sick if it wasn't contained.

"Well, I'll be damned." Kade towered over me, glancing over my head so he could see the stone clearly in the middle of the room. "I've never seen a mecca stone of that size."

The stone's purplish hue washed over his darkly tanned features. It was about four feet tall and two wide. It sparkled and shone with mesmerizing depth; the pull was great enough that I always feared if I stared into it too deeply I'd be lost in its depths forever.

Swallowing through my thick throat, I forced myself to focus on Kade. "The Red Queen always hinted that she had something powerful as a weapon," I said, trying not to turn back and stare again. "But none of us realized what it was."

I was really the red queen now, but no one called me that. It had been the former leader's title, and after her reign of over a hundred years, shifters weren't going to break the habit anytime soon. Which was fine by me. Rumor was they were referring to me as Queen Alpha. I like that much better than the traditional title of Red Queen.

"Your father was the king before you, right?" I was learning about bear hierarchy, mostly from bits and pieces Kade let slip.

I'd been taught to fear and hate the bear shifters who held two of the five boroughs of New York City. That was all, just fear and hate. None of their history or traditions. To the best of my knowledge, their crown was inherited, not earned as ours was.

Kade was focused on the stone, his answer slow to come. "Yes, the crown remains in the royal bloodline. Only the males receive a familiar, and are strong enough to rule, so even if daughters are born to the king, they'll never be a leader. My brother Kian was older than me, and should have been king. But he disappeared many years ago, so when my father was killed, it was up to me to take the crown."

It was kind of odd that bears appeared to be the direct opposites of wolves. In our royal lineage, only female wolf shifters could be queen; we were the only ones to get familiars. In the bears it was only males. Odd.

Right now, Finn, my huge white wolf familiar, and Nix, Kade's eagle, were off fae hunting, making sure no more of those hideous erchos were hiding in Central Park. Both of them were on high alert, and since familiars were extremely hard to kill, they thought they were the best first line of defense.

It calmed my mind to know I could check in on Finn at any time. Our mental link was strong and thrumming within me. I knew Kade felt the same way about his Nix. It was a bond that could not be replicated.

"How did your father die?" I asked, hoping this wasn't too painful for him.

Kade had been king for a couple of years, and while this was not a long time in the few hundred years we could live, he already held the respect of his people. He was a just leader, I could tell.

"I remember the queen tolling the bells and informing us that King Roland had fallen and that the bears were vulnerable, but that she would honor the peace accords. It was a hunting accident, right?"

He focused fully on me then, some of the awe from the mecca fading out of his masculine features. The power within us was so much more potent this close to the stone, our connection back in full force. I actually took a step closer to him, unable to stand my ground. Kade was all of my woodcutter fantasies rolled up in one package – dark brown, bordering-on-black hair, tousled, thick, and shiny across his forehead; neatly trimmed beard against his throat and around his full lips, showcasing a slight dimple in his cheek. His height topped out near seven feet, and that package was finished off with broad shoulders and heavy muscles. He was huge, and his bear even bigger.

The gods could have helped me out and made the bear royal line less attractive or something. A girl only had so much restraint.

He was still staring at me, and hadn't answered my question yet. I was about to apologize for my bluntness when he said, "Hunting accident was the council's spin so that no one would know we had a traitor in our own house. A king should be able to manage his guard, but he didn't. My father was killed by his friend and advisor. The traitor thought himself in love with my mother, the queen, and decided that by getting rid of my father he'd have a free run." Kade's eyes, normally bronze, were now the color of whiskey, deep and rich, filled with emotion.

"He'd never have bested my father in a normal fight of course, but the ambush was unexpected. My father trusted him above all others. He never even saw the blow coming. Poisoned my father with dinner the night before, then killed his familiar first, to weaken him before finishing him off."

To the wolves, Kade's father had been hard and cruel. He'd initiated more than one scuffle with our queen in a bid to gain territory. But when Kade talked of him, there was a sense of softness in the tone.

"And your mother..." I said.

He smiled suddenly, and I had to blink a few times to ground myself. "Still alive. Ordering me around. She's the real ruler of the bears, I just give the final order. They all adore her."

He loved his mother too. Of course he did. Was there *anything* wrong with him?

"So your father married your mother? Like mates?" I couldn't remember the last time a wolf queen had actually married her wolf mate, and we certainly didn't refer to those mates as "king." They were simply the queen's mate, one step up from a lover.

"Mates ... yes. My father met my mother when he was nineteen, at the summer festival on the Island. Declared right then and there in front of everyone that she would be his queen."

I grinned. Sounded like the man knew what he wanted in life. I could respect that. "What did your mother say?"

Kade suddenly gave a deep rumbling laugh. "My mother replied without an ounce of hesitation that my father wasn't her type. She would never marry an arrogant, over-confident, pushy man like him."

Now I was laughing. His mother sounded like my kind of woman.

Kade shrugged. "My father loved a challenge. He fought for her. Every day. Two years later, they wed."

"That's a nice story," I said, feeling soft emotions battering my body. All the feelings.

A sudden pulse of purple light had both of us focusing on the stone again. Kade stepped closer, about five feet from it, and I found myself flashing back to Breanna. The mecca power had been too much for her to handle. This had left her unfit for the throne. I could still see her seizing wolf in my mind's eye, the memory of carrying her out of here, not knowing if she would make it or not.

I knew Kade wouldn't have the same issue, but it still made me nervous.

I joined him, both of us crossing to the side of the most powerful stone in existence. It was still a challenge, like wading through very deep sand, each step more effort than the last, but we were able to make it to stand right before the pulsing rock.

"I never knew this existed until the Summit," I said. "You have to prove your strength with the mecca. When I touched this, there were images, flashes of purple. The council had never seen that happen before, and many of them were here for the last Summit of the Red Queen. My entire body glowed, almost as if I was more mecca than shifter ... for a second."

On occasion I still had nightmares, pulled from sleep with memories of this stone. The power should be feared, even though the shifters had been controlling the mecca for half a millennium. That was how long it had been since fae had ruled this energy, over five hundred years, so why the hell were they coming back now? Why was the mecca energy so out of control?

"So, does it seem as if the energy is still filtering from the Otherworld to ours?" I asked Kade. It felt like it had slowed a little to me, but there was still a massive imbalance.

"Yes and no. The filtering is still there, but much slower. Before it was like the mecca was growing in great rushes, but now it's subtle. I notice it every few days, just a slight increase in power."

So the fae had either figured out how to slow the exodus of power from their world, or whatever had manipulated the mecca in the first place was still in control and had slowed the imbalance.

"Do you think we could use this as a weapon somehow?" I asked, reaching out and gliding my hand above the stone. I wanted to touch it, badly, to see what might happen this time now that I was queen, but it was so much stronger than it was at the Summit and I was worried it'd try to kill me again. It was hard to forget the suffocation of power during my coronation, that moment I thought I was going to die, and Kade had saved me.

"Anything this powerful could certainly become a weapon if controlled." He answered my question after a slight pause, as if he had thought it over first. "We need to start planning for war, gathering our weapons, pooling our magical knowledge so our magic borns might have a chance against the fae spellcasters."

The magic born were able to touch the mecca in a way no other could, not even me and Kade. Both of us were starting to sway now; it was time to get out of this room. I started to move away, and Kade followed my lead.

"Has your council made a decision yet about the Island?" he asked as we both shuffled our way backward.

With each step, the pressure on my chest decreased until I felt I could finally breathe again. When we reached the secret door, I said, "They still won't give me an answer. They want to deal with the meeting of the alphas first. We all decided it was too risky to tell all wolf shifters about the fae yet, but we will have a meeting to speak to the alpha of each borough, and also the other leaders of individual packs. I'll tell them about the fae, and they can make sure the packs are secure without causing a major panic."

Kade nodded, not seeming surprised at all by this information. We knew it was going to be hard to convince others that a myth was now all too real and was gunning for our world. Even harder: convincing them that working with the bears was our best chance of survival. Kade and his people wanted to start preparing for battle. We were going to use the Island – shifter neutral territory – during the summer festival to work out the logistics, but the council wasn't agreeing to anything of that nature yet. I understood: one step at a time. But it was still frustrating.

"My council and bear leaders know of the threat, but we too have not spread the word to the general shifter community," Kade said, dropping a hand onto my shoulder. "I have to return to my boroughs now. Never a good idea to leave bears alone for long without their king."

We were nearing the door of the library and I could hear our guards softly talking on the other side, Chelle's short, blunt answers a clear sign that she was not warming up to my people. I would have thought for sure Blaine would have won her over; my friend was a real charmer when he wanted to be. Not to mention he was gorgeous. And very, very dominant. Chelle was a tough cookie to crack, though, which is probably why she was one of Kade's guards.

"Send Nix with word when you want to train again," I said to Kade. No matter how difficult controlling the mecca was for me, his training was helping immensely. My control was stronger; the amount of energy I could funnel through my body was increasing. Even the headaches were less frequent and intense – still terrible – but I was taking any improvement.

He gave a slight head bow. "I have to go away for a few days, but I'll be in touch. Good luck with your alpha meeting."

Then those eyes locked me down and I couldn't move. Mecca energy oozed from him, and wrapped around me with a strength that would have had my knees buckling, but I was used to it now.

"Stay safe, Ari," he said, and then with a dispelling of the energy, he was gone.

I must have been standing like that for some time, because suddenly my dominants were around me. Blaine, one of my oldest friends, with his rich, auburn hair and green eyes, blinked at me in concern.

"Your Highness … are you okay, Ari?" He was one of the worst with protocol, always forgetting to address me as the queen.

I didn't care. It was just a title. He would die for me. A title was hardly important compared to that.

"Do you think that bear did something to her?" Monica, the more cautious of the two females who were part of my inner five, said to the others.

A chuckle escaped me. "I'm standing right here, and my brain is not defective. Kade didn't do anything to me. It's just the mecca. The energy is strong and sometimes it takes a few minutes for me to get everything back into place. Mentally speaking."

This wasn't even a lie, and they all relaxed at the clear truth in my words. Still … Kade had something to do with it all. Kade and the mecca energy equally destroyed and rebuilt me. Almost like I couldn't survive now without both of them, and yet I knew I had to. Neither were mine to keep forever.

Chapter Three

Burning bridges. Scarred feet.

AFTER TRAINING WITH Kade, I showered and dressed for my royal appointments. Calista managed to get me into a dress and everything – hair up in a crown braid, mecca stone diadem on my head. First order of business was the summer festival on the Island, which was two weeks away, and apparently the queen had to be involved in every aspect of it, including decorations. Boring. But my people expected a royal touch in all aspects of the event. I was still hoping the day would have a double purpose – discussing an alliance with the bear and wolf armies so we could fight the fae as one – which was the only reason I was giving it any of my time.

I almost couldn't believe it was summer festival time again. Where had the last twelve months gone? The leaves would soon be turning their multitude of reds, oranges, and yellows; fall was on the horizon. The wolves looked forward to it every year, the festival to celebrate the last days of summer.

It was a longstanding tradition, only missed in times of full-on shifter wars. All of the wolves and bears converged on the Island for a huge two-day festival. Two days without many rules, two days to try and reinforce the peace between our people. Some of the wolves chose to stick strictly to the wolf side of the Island, as did bears on their side, but a good number of shifters did venture out and mingle together. Got drunk, played games, got in fights, made friends, and of course enemies.

Summer, a time of magic, and then after it was over we went back to our separate lives. There was really only one strict rule: no inter-mating of the two species. I'm sure it had happened – as an alpha I heard rumors – but the women were always careful to make sure no children resulted from their forbidden night with a bear. Now … kissing? There was plenty of that going on between both shifter species. It was almost a dare: "kiss a bear once before you die" type of thing. The first time I kissed anyone on the Island had been with a bear – Kade.

The knock at my door startled me from my thoughts. "Come in." I sat up straighter on my throne, adjusting my crown, preparing to receive my next royal appointments.

My guards let in two women who were wheeling a cart full of bolts of silk fabric. I tried not to groan. I liked fashion as much as the next woman, but picking out fabric all day when I had a fae war to prepare for was a complete waste of my time.

"Your Majesty, thank you so much for commissioning us to make your royal gown for the summer festival," said the one who was slightly closer to me. She was a robust woman, not fat – wolves had fast metabolisms – but short and solid. Her hair was a shade of golden brown, her eyes similar, and she smiled prettily as she bowed so low her nose was nearly touching the floor.

"Yes, thank you," the other added, as she too bowed. She was finer boned and her hair was a strawberry blonde, her eyes an arresting shade of gray. Not as pretty or vivacious as her friend, but still striking.

I had never seen either of them before, not during my coronation, or when I went through the staff of the royal mansion. Calista must have commissioned them from outside my staff, and since I already had a palace seamstress, Casey Marie, who had been custom making everything so far, I wondered why we were going out-of-house for this dress.

"Of course. You're the best." I assumed this to be true; Calista wouldn't hire any other.

They both blushed and shared a smile as if I had just made their day. "Thank you, Your Highness," golden-haired said again. "As you know, we specialize in costumes. Have you decided what you would like to dress as?"

Of course, it all made perfect sense now. Casey wasn't proficient in costume wear. Oh sure, she could have easily whipped a dress up if I needed her to, but it wasn't her specialty and the queen would be expected to go all-out on costume, especially for my first festival since my coronation. The summer festival was a time to dress up – fairy wings, masquerade masks, Renaissance dress – Violet didn't even need to change from her daily wear. Whatever you could imagine you could become. Last year the Red Queen had a beautiful peacock dress with mask and feathers.

With everything going on, it had completely slipped my mind that I'd need a costume. "Oh, I don't know. I haven't given it much thought," I said honestly. I stood, approaching them, looking at the different silks they had. The teal caught my eye, and so did a soft, sunset pink.

"Well, Your Majesty, could we make a suggestion?" This came from the petite redhead.

I smiled at her. "Please do."

She grabbed the teal silk I was running my hands across and unrolled a long piece, holding it up to me. "Queen of the water?"

The golden-haired seamstress unrolled the pink I had also been eyeing. "Queen of love." She winked.

I let out a laugh, truly enjoying their imaginations. "You know what ... I trust you. Surprise me."

Both of their mouths popped open in unison, astonishment written across their faces.

They recovered quickly though, grabbing at tape measures and paper. I held out my arms so they could measure me. I was excited for the festival, but there were too many other things on my plate for me to completely lose myself in the joy. As they ran around me taking notes, my mind wandered and I found myself thinking of what Kade would be dressed as. I should not be thinking of the bear king when I wasn't with him. Maybe I did need to take a mate. I needed the distraction, and it would be good for my people to see me in a strong wolf relationship.

But the thought of it had my gut tied up in knots, instead of the excitement I should have been feeling.

After the ladies left, I sat through three hours of royal appointments, which included catering for the summer festival, decorations, and entertainment.

After this, it was time to play referee. You know, when grown shifters need their queen to figure out their problems. Award for the most annoying of the morning went to two dominant wolves bickering about their need for another parking space. Neither of them would budge an inch, although both agreed that I should pay for it from the royal allowance.

We paid taxes in our society, all shifters did. The royal house paid the human government, and the rest of the packs paid the royal house. The shifter tax to us was only ten percent, but some shifters thought it meant they were entitled to ask for things they should be paying for themselves. A parking spot in Manhattan was a massive cost per year, and not one the crown would be covering.

Now, if these alphas had told me they had fallen on hard times and needed money for their pack to stay sheltered, fed, and clothed, then I would give it without hesitation, but a parking spot … not happening. After telling them no and dismissing them, Calista came to get me to take me to my lunch appointment.

"Please tell me my lunch appointment isn't some petty task like this morning," I huffed as Calista expertly traversed the hallways, leading me to my private dining area.

"No, I thought you might like a break from all of that," she said as she opened the door, and I was relieved to see Violet sitting and waiting for me. The magic born were a sight to behold. Even though I had known Violet my entire life, I never got used to her unique beauty or incredible talent with magic.

"Ari, you're late and I'm starving," she moaned.

Calista tsk tsked her for using my name, but I loved that Violet, like Blaine, treated me no differently now that I was queen.

I took a seat beside her as Calista scurried off to whatever was next on her list of to-do's. I was starting to think she worked a lot harder than me, a fact I was very grateful for.

I let out a breath, settling in beside my best friend. "Sorry about the delay. Very important morning. Had to be fitted for my summer festival dress, and then got into a scintillating debate about assigned parking in Manhattan," I said with as much heavy sarcasm as I could muster.

She grinned. "Sounds absolutely dreadful. I have something that will cheer you up." She leaned forward and pulled a vial from her pocket. The liquid inside was pinkish purple and dancing slowly, as if waiting to burst out the second the stopper was lifted.

"What's that?" I inspected it closer. It smelled faintly floral ... the same floral scent the fae carried on them. My eyebrow rose as I used my queen voice. "Violet ... what is in there?"

I was a combination of excited and a bit terrified of what she would say. One never knew with Violet.

She quirked one side of her mouth. "Tuatha magic," she whispered as two of the kitchen staff came through the large double doors, bringing our lunch. My heart was hammering in my chest as I waited for the silver platters to be set in front of me and for the attendants to leave. Once they did, Violet opened her palm again.

"The fae we fought at King Kade's estate came in through the water. I'm sure of it. The fae we spoke to in Astoria Park left through the water, and the ercho that attacked you in Central Park..."

"Water," I said breathlessly.

Violet gestured to the pink vial. "I cloaked myself and slipped into the council's secret spell book chambers--"

I grabbed her by the wrist. "Vi! You could have been executed if you were caught."

Wait. There was a secret spell book chamber? Why did I not know this?

She shrugged my hand off, gently, but still firm. It bothered her when even I touched her, especially with all the mecca energy inside of me. She saw too much, felt too much. In my astonishment, I'd forgotten.

"You're queen now. Nothing should be secret from you," Violet said.

True. And at least she hadn't been caught. Yet anyway.

I nodded for her to continue.

"I had heard that all the best spells and books were hidden away. Magic born talk about it all the time. It's the Holy Grail for us. I decided to see if I could find it, and you know what, it wasn't even that well hidden." She looked mighty put out by that, like the council hadn't taken her powers seriously. "Anyway, I have to say those old losers are really a bunch of horned toads, far worse than I originally thought. They've been holding out on all of us, especially in light of recent developments. They have an entire stack of fae magic books."

Those last words were declared in a rushed whisper-scream.

I sat there for a moment, trying to absorb what she was saying. How could the council not tell me about this? Now, when we could be on the brink of war and needed every weapon at our disposal. What the heck were they playing at? This next meeting with them was going to be interesting, I wouldn't stand for this secrecy any longer. No doubt this was why Torine already seemed to know more than any other about the Tuatha de Danann.

Forcing my ire down, I focused on Violet's vial. "Okay, so fae travel through water and you stole a fae magic book ... keep going."

I had no doubt I was going to have to make sure I remained queen just to ensure Violet didn't get sentenced to death by the council.

She shook the vial. "So it turns out that water is the easiest place for the fae to cast their spell and open a doorway between the Otherworld and Earth. Water acts like a mirror which reflects both sides. I haven't had a chance to test it yet, but this should close the water to any portals."

I grinned. That was definitely worth annoying the council over. Here's hoping it worked.

"Violet, you're a genius."

With a fae war looming on the horizon, this might just turn the tides in our favor.

She put a hand out. "Don't get too excited. It doesn't work on extra-large bodies of water.

Only about a hundred foot stretch, but it's enough to secure Central Park and the waterfront at the wolf estate on the Island. Unfortunately, I could find nothing strong enough to work on all the ocean which surrounds us."

So many of our homes were waterfront, prime real estate, but turns out against the fae, that's not the best for our safety. I was grateful that this magic would help with some of the smaller bodies of water; any way we could cut the fae off was a good thing. I took the vial and gave her a side hug, which she quickly returned before moving away.

"You're the best," I said, before a thought hit me. "Hey, is there any way you could make one more for—"

She dropped a second vial in my hand. "There's enough there for King Kade's Staten home and the bear estate on the Island. Nikoli will know what to do."

I could always count on my best friend to think ahead. She'd probably already told Nikoli about it. He was Kade's royal magic born and seemed to be almost as powerful as Violet.

Almost.

I put the two vials in my pocket before picking up my turkey and bacon sub. I'd just opened my mouth to take the first bite when Violet spoke again.

"So what's with you and King Kade?" Her tone was relaxed, almost uninterested, but those white-blue eyes were locked on me, watching with intensity. I opened my mouth before closing it again. What could I say about Kade and me? It was ... I didn't even understand it.

Her next words were even softer. "When he looks at you Ari, it's like ... it's like I can see the energy between you both. More than anything I've seen before. Even in true love pairs."

I sucked in a ragged breath. Damn Violet, leave it to her to not ask a word about us for weeks and then drop this. I set the sandwich down and cleared my throat. I couldn't keep it bottled up any longer, and I trusted my oldest friend.

"You know that bear I kissed on the Island when I was fifteen?"

Some of her seriousness faded, and a smile of remembrance crossed her face. "Scrawny guy? You talked about him for weeks."

I sighed. "That's Kade."

Now it was Violet's turn for her mouth to pop open in surprise. "Holy shifter," she breathed. "Girl, he is so not scrawny."

I chuckled. "Yeah, he's not now. So yeah, we have this history, and then he was in the garden at the Summit and he remembered me. He kissed me. It's ... I'm the queen of the wolves and he's a bear king."

I let my words trail off and Violet's eyes darkened as she read some emotion across my face. She reached out a hand to lightly touch mine before pulling away; she didn't say anything more. We both knew there was nothing either of us could do or say. No matter the attraction Kade and I shared, we could never be. After this we ate in companionable silence, both of us lost in our own thoughts.

The next day, the wolf council lined up before me. We were in the basement area, preparing for the alpha meeting. All eleven were dressed in their full robes, arms crossed over their stubborn chests. I was meeting with them first, before we opened the doors to the alphas of the boroughs, and the lesser leaders of the smaller packs. These leaders had come from far and wide to learn of my news.

Finn sat at my feet. He said that all was quiet in Manhattan right now, but I could still sense the tension thrumming in his huge body. His worry was bleeding over into me, but I couldn't focus on that. I had a bunch of ignorant shifters to deal with.

"You can no longer keep secrets of the Tuatha from me," I said for the third time since we started this meeting. "Torine … you should have told me about the magic books. We should be researching everything we can to learn of a weapon to help us in this war."

They just continued staring at me, eyes glittering, expressions hard and unyielding. "You weren't there," I said, some of my composure fading away, anger leaking into my words. "It was a single fae and he cut through us no problem. Ka … King Kade and I barely managed to take him down, and we have the mecca at our command. What do you think will happen if an entire army comes through?"

Unease filtered through them then. Some shifted where they stood, and Glenda, my old teacher, stepped forward to address me directly. "Queen Arianna, you must understand that the magic information within those walls is beyond our knowledge. Beyond any wolf shifter's knowledge. Most of the books are not even in a recognizable language. So while there's a chance you would find some information inside to help, there's an even bigger chance that whomever read the books would be destroyed, or would discover a power to destroy our packs. It's too large a risk for us to let that information out."

Well, I already knew Violet could read them, and so far no one was dead. So far. I hoped my friend knew what she was doing.

Finn shifted closer to me. *Tell them, Ari. Force them to understand. This is going to come to us whether we are ready or not.*

I ran my hand over the wolf, and the rumbles shaking his huge body calmed somewhat. *I'll make them understand, and if they don't, I'll figure out a way to make sure that all of the shifters are ready. I don't need them. It would just be easier with their help.*

I tilted my head slightly up so my voice would project with strength. A tip from Calista's many years of training. "It's not your place to decide who gets to do what in this house. I am the queen. I want to know everything that is happening with my people."

I never wanted to start my rule at odds with the council. They were wise in history and tradition, but they continued to force my hand. They had left me with no choice.

Torine cleared his throat. "It was the Red Queen's desire that we seal away all books pertaining to knowledge of the fae."

What? Why on Earth would the Red Queen do that? I tucked that piece of information away for another time. It was another part of the puzzle that made up the former wolf queen. Hopefully

I'd have a full picture soon of who she was. Which might also lead me to how she ended up dead at the hands of the fae.

My voice was filled with steel when I addressed the council this time. "Well, it's my wish that you unseal them and allow my palace magic born to look them over. Times of war require us to take some risks. We may all die either way, but it's better to stand true and fight than to cower in ignorance and hope for the best. You will show me this room after the meeting, and I will do as I see fit with the information within. Do I make myself clear?"

I let the mecca energy leak from me, and that, teamed with the pure command and arrogance of my order, had the council looking very uncomfortable. Some even took a step back to distance themselves from me. I hated playing the dominating queen, but I was starting to see that a firm hand was required at times. Especially with the council. They were old and powerful, used to having all the knowledge and manipulating things behind the scenes. Not happening on my rule any longer.

Despite a few dirty looks, no one argued with me again, so I moved on. "Next thing on our agenda is the alpha meeting. How much do you think it is wise for us to reveal to them? What actions are we going to request from them? I agree it's not time to tell the general shifter population yet, but the leaders should know almost as much as we do. I expect them to start training their shifters to see and understand the signs of the Tuatha de Danann. Water is an issue. We must have guards assigned to large bodies of water around our packs. Our magic born need to be recalled to the royal mansion. They'll have to start working with me and the bear king. We need to take action now before it's too late."

Torine addressed me, his features without any expression: "You said there were fae who would stand with us. How are we to know the difference between those who are our enemy and those who are our allies?"

Good question. My knowledge of the Tuatha de Danann was practically nonexistent, but I had been reading as much as I could about the history of fae from the book Kade had given me. It let me in on a few of their secrets, and after meeting that fae in Astoria Park I had to believe that some of them didn't want us dead. She had come to warn me, and said she'd be back when she had more information.

"The Otherworld is apparently divided into two main sections, each of them ruled by a king or queen, and they are each in possession of a treasure ... or weapon ... which they use to control the mecca and rule their people. They battle among themselves, trying to take the other's power. The Otherworld is much smaller than Earth, a landmass akin to the size of America. We have met only one side. They call themselves the light fae, which I'm coming to understand is the court of summer. The dark fae are from the court of winter. There are smaller courts within those, the Spring Court and Fall Court. I have no idea of their power, or whether they have weapons also. At the moment it looks as if the dark court is trying to destroy us and the light is our ally. How to tell them apart ... I have no idea."

"What are these weapons?" one of the councilmen asked, seeming intrigued.

I shook my head. "We don't know for sure. The history vaguely suggests that a spear and sword are two of them, but this may not even be true."

"Why are they attacking us?" Glenda asked, her voice ringing out, wavering with intensity. "I truly don't understand what we can offer them. They already have equal mecca power on their side of the veil. Why now? Why kill the Red Queen?"

Intensity was good. It meant they were finally starting to believe me, to believe it was the fae who killed the Red Queen and not some sort of sneak attack the bears were trying to foist off onto another enemy.

Before I could answer her, a low voice cut through the room. "The mecca is compromised." The basement area fell silent and at first I wondered which of the council had spoken, until I realized it was none of them. Finn started to growl low and menacing, and if I had been the stranger in our midst, I'd have been very nervous. My familiar slid his massive body around until it was before me.

A huge male stepped up out of the shadows and I wondered how long he'd been there. I recognized him straight away: Seamus, the male magic born of our packs. His hair was pure white, like his skin, although he seemed to have a little more color than many of the others. His icy-blue eyes cut through me and a shiver traversed my spine. He was powerful and determined. I could see that in the way he strode across the room.

"The mecca is visible to my eye now. It was never this way before the Red Queen fell. The balance is no more and the fae will come for the power. They will destroy us all to get it."

I didn't like the way he had crept into our meeting, but magic born had a way of doing that. Ignoring my instinct to reprimand him, I turned back to the council. "Seamus is right, the power is no longer balanced. This is what the light fae told us. She said that the dark now want to rule Earth, and they plan on taking it soon."

Returning my gaze to Seamus, I let hard eyes linger on him for a few extra seconds. My power was judging and assessing him. I saw nothing of concern, but I would remain on guard. There was an offness about him. Even Finn felt it.

My next words were lower, contemplative. "What I don't understand is why the queen's death changed the mecca. It was the catalyst for all of this. What was she up to in those days before she died? What did she see or know which caused the Tuatha to send out a hit on her and all the heirs? In the Otherworld, the light and dark battle all the time, but we have never been part of it."

"Which tells you…" Torine prompted, seeming to know I had more to say.

"Which tells me that there may be a weapon on Earth, something the queen figured out in the days before her death, and which somehow the Winter Court also discovered. The Winter Court wants the weapon. They know it could tip the odds in their favor. Maybe the Red Queen used it just before she died, maybe that is why the power is coming to us."

Not everything in my theory made perfect sense, but it felt like the right place to start.

"Have you searched her private stores? Through her papers?" Torine asked me. "You should have started your investigation there."

I gritted my teeth just slightly. Did he think I'd just been relaxing and drinking cocktails on the beach since my coronation? I had been pretty busy in the few weeks I'd been queen.

"It's next on my to-do list. She had thousands of boxes filled with her personal effects. I'll begin in the library where she was murdered, and work my way back from there."

Seamus strode closer to me and I was again captured by the unique beauty of the magic born. "I would like to help you. I came today because the mecca imbalance can no longer be ignored. Now that I know more, I believe it is magic born who'll be the most help to you. Especially regarding the fae magic books and a possible weapon."

Okay, so he'd been listening since the very beginning. My temper started to get the best of me then. We should not have lax security at a time like this. The council must have agreed. They burst into loud reprimands.

"You cannot sneak into private meetings! You will be punished for this!"

"Silence!" I shouted.

It took a few minutes, and some pushing of my power, but eventually I could be heard again. "I need you to go and find Violet," I said to Seamus, ignoring the council. "I will deal with your lack of respect later. You do not run this world, that's my job. But I agree that the magic born will be instrumental in our preparations. You're going to be on the front line of this war."

He bowed his head low, especially for a magic born. "No disrespect intended at all. I just know that what we are told and what is truth are not always the same. I wanted truth this time."

Before I could say anything more, he turned and in a flash was gone from the room. Damn magic born.

Chapter Four

I am queen. Hear me roar.

THE ALPHAS FILED into the room. First were the two who ruled the other boroughs: the current queen heirs Selene and Chelsea. Selene was technically the spare queen, but I liked to think of her as an heir. Still, she was alpha of the Bronx. Chelsea was alpha of Queens.

Chelsea of the yellow clan had turned sixteen last week, and as was her birthright was now an heir and alpha of that borough. I had not spent much time with her, only the brief meeting when she came of age. But from what I had observed, the tall, willowy brunette was mature beyond her years. She did not speak without thinking, and her dark brown eyes were always assessing, keeping an eye on the shifters she ruled. She was a fit queen heir.

Selene was still a bitch. Just looking into her smug, overly made-up face was enough to send my mood into the pits.

I focused on the rest of the alphas filling the room. There were about fifty in here now, those who ran smaller packs within the boroughs and outside of New York City. Some I knew well from my time in the Bronx and Manhattan, others I had never met before. Calista had given me a large dossier on all leaders, with their names, photos, and other basic information. So for the most part all their faces were familiar.

I took a seat upon my throne. It had been moved here for this meeting. A queen needs her throne if she is to impose the right level of authority. My throne was littered with small chips of mecca stone; much larger ones made up my crown. I was literally thrumming with energy.

My skin even had a slightly purple sheen to it, which all helped to ensure no one would doubt my power.

Finn was still at my side, his head height well above the arm of my chair even though he was seated on the ground. Standing back a little and on either side were my dominants. Blaine was closest, the black and red uniform emphasizing his strong physique. His auburn hair was military-short over most of his head now, with just a little length on top for style; his focus was sharp as he observed the room.

The fierce way he protected me had a hot lurching sensation hitting me in the chest. He'd been like that for most of my life, looking out for me and Violet. But now that I was queen – and especially after losing Derek to the fae – his focus and protective instincts had increased dramatically. I prayed every day that wasn't the thing that got him killed. His was not a death I could live with.

Monica was on my other side, her wise eyes just as focused as Blaine's, but with a little less fierceness in her gaze. She was my assessing dominant, always calculating odds and anticipating events. Jen, Ben, and Victor were back further again, off to the left. Blaine and Monica were on point. I hadn't replaced Derek yet, so we were at five. I just couldn't bring myself to fill his spot in my inner six dominants just yet. I wasn't ready.

I felt the stares of the council, even though they were across the other side of the room. When I glanced at them, I was hit with a wall of grim expressions. It had taken me some time to calm them down after learning that Seamus could just stroll in like that. Oh, and they still weren't on-board with the unsealing of the fae magic room for the magic born to delve into. I had no idea if they would come around anytime soon, and really I had far too much else to worry about to dwell on their ire for long. Either way, it would happen. I had ordered it, and Violet could break in at my command if needed. I could only do what I thought was best for my people – trusting that I wasn't a megalomaniac yet – and I hoped to always see reason if it was presented to me.

"Your Highness..." A petite female alpha from outside of the boroughs captured my attention. She bowed to me. I took a long look at her, impressed that she'd been the first to find the courage to approach me. The dossier popped into my mind and I placed her immediately: Katy of the yellow shifter line. She ran a small pack in California, which explained the bleached blonde hair and casual beach dress she was wearing.

"Welcome, Katy. Thank you for coming on such short notice," I said.

She straightened from her bow. "We're most interested to hear your news, Queen Arianna. Thank you for the invite."

She left, and made her way across to join whomever she had brought from her pack. Others followed her lead then, each seeking to greet and bow to me. Some of their actions were about respect, but for the most part it was more to do with cementing their favor with the queen. I knew it, I'd been there before when I was an alpha. Just never thought I'd be the queen to which it would happen.

Eventually, the seats in the room were all filled; a few of the males stood in the back. Only females are heirs and alphas, but some males do run the smaller packs if they are dominant enough. They have the strength to lead the wolves, but if a female alpha moves into that pack, she would fight and take over. Female wolf shifters are just born with something extra, an extra toughness needed to survive.

Sitting straighter in my chair, Finn followed my movements by standing. I knew more than one eye was on my giant familiar; he was a legend in our world, but to me he was so much more than that. He was the other half to my soul. We had been bonded when I was five years old and my life would be nothing without him.

At that thought, I shot a dark look toward Selene. The spare heir was looking a little too smug in her spot, front and center. Red curls artfully pinned atop her head, her deep brown eyes glinted as they locked onto me. She wore her purple silk shirt with its large symbol of her house on the front. Thankfully, Larak was nowhere to be seen. Her snake familiar had tried to kill Finn, and if he was seen in my vicinity again, I would figure out a way to have him destroyed. She knew that, which is why she was keeping him hidden away.

I wished there was an easy way for me to strip her of her heir and spare queen rights, but for now I had no options. There were old laws that even the queen was bound to, and nothing in my power could change this unless Selene screwed up. No one wanted a sixteen-year-old, just-appointed queen heir running the wolf-shifter world if I died, no matter how mature she was.

Calista had spies in all the boroughs trying to dig up dirt on Selene, and I had a lot of loyal shifters in the Bronx pack. But so far there had been nothing I could use against her. She'd screw up eventually, though. I had to believe it. She was as slimy as her snake.

Dismissing her with a cold throwaway glance, I focused on the rest of the room. The mild chattering faded away immediately. Mecca swirled in arcs around me, I could feel it, and judging from the expressions of the others here, they could too.

"Thank you all for coming on such short notice," I said, my voice low and steady. "I would not have called for you in this manner unless it was of incredible importance. What I am going to say to you in this room cannot be shared with any others. Not yet. This is the reason you all signed the spelled confidentiality papers on the way in, so that our magic born will know if you reveal this, and we will punish you accordingly. There is no wavering on this order. I will not have anarchy in my kingdom, not when there are other ways to go about this."

Telling the general shifter population of a suspected impending fae war would cause chaos, which would only make it easier for them to divide and conquer us.

A mixture of confusion and anger spilled across the faces before me. They didn't like their rights being stripped from them, but they knew better than to argue. Not with their queen.

How they'd feel once they knew everything ... well, we were about to find out.

"The Tuatha de Danann have returned to our world..."

I did not let my voice waver. If there was even a single seed of doubt in my tone, they would jump all over that hesitation and never let go. I needed them to believe me. I needed them to start preparing.

Their initial reactions were less intense than I expected. A few shifted in their seats and some wore confused faces.

"I have recently learned that the fae are at war with each other. In the Otherworld, the Summer and Winter Courts have battled for power, for land, and for control of the mecca for generations. It seems some of this battle is spilling over into our world now. We believe..." I gestured to the council members, "that it was fae who killed the Red Queen. I was also recently attacked by a member of the dark fae court, and we barely escaped with our lives. One of my dominants was killed, along with other pack members, and some of King Kade's bears."

The intensity was coming now. More than one alpha was out of their chair, and noise built in the room as they started to question me. I held up both of my hands. "I understand your confusion. We never speak of the fae. We learn nothing of their history. But this ignorance can stand no longer. They know about us. They have attacked and tried to weaken us already, in the hopes that soon they can walk through to our mecca and take it from us. We cannot let this happen. To take the mecca would be to take the very thing that makes us powerful.

"It's time to start preparing our people for war. Shifters need to be trained, sources of magic collected and given to our magic born so they may prepare. I need your help. We all need to work together or they will cut through us with ease."

I paused, letting my message and energy fill the space. I was not at all surprised when my dominants crowded closer to me; the alphas did not look happy. In fact I would go as far to say that we were about five seconds from a riot. I shifted my head to the council and gave them a nod. It was their turn to step in. I was a new queen, and while I had the power, respect and trust would take time. The council, on the other hand, were well trusted by the people.

Torine stood, and his deep voice cut through the confusion. "The queen speaks truth on this. We have seen the evidence."

Some of the noise died down as he went on to explain everything that had happened over the past few weeks. He skimmed over the bears' involvement in all of this, which was the path we'd all decided on earlier. I already knew my people would have trouble accepting the truth of a fae war. No need to make it even harder by bringing up the enemy they did actually believe in.

When Torine was done, a sort of stunned silence descended across the room. Most of the alphas had sunk back into their chairs, eyes wide and mouths slack. We had torn their safe world apart with our revelations, but I was sure that most of them would come to the realization that it was better to know, to be prepared.

I spoke again, my voice even but firm. "I know you're in shock right now. That we even have this sort of enemy out there is not something any of us have had to consider in our lifetimes. But ignorance does not stop the fae from attacking. It only gets us killed without even having a chance to put up a fight. It's time for you all to head to your packs and start preparing for this war. But you cannot tell them everything yet. Mass panic doesn't help anyone. I'm doing as much as I can behind the scenes. I want every one of you to know that I'll be doing everything in my power to fight them … but I am going to need your help."

More than one head nodded. Some of their shock and fear was being replaced by anger and determination. We were a resilient species; we protected what was ours. Our people. Our packs. Our power. The fae would not take us unawares. We would not die off like the witches and warlocks.

One woman stood. She had long jet-black hair and carried herself in a way that told me she was a great and well-respected leader. A quick mental scan of the dossier provided me with her name: Bianca, Boston's alpha. Word on the street was that she went out of her way to help other packs – a version of the nice cat lady who took in strays, but who could also kill you with her bare hands. The other alphas loved her. I could see it in the way they looked at her now, waiting for her reaction. I held my head high, ready for whatever response she had.

"Long live the queen!" she roared, holding her fist high. I breathed a sigh of relief as the others chorused their agreement. My people were with me.

The meeting broke up soon after as the alphas prepared to return to their packs. The council gave them all one final warning of secrecy, and some information about fae security and increased patrols for all bodies of water around their territories, and then they were gone.

When it was just me and my dominants in the room, I let out a deep breath. My body almost caved forward as the tension eased itself from my tightly wound chest. Finn rested his head upon my leg, and I curled over so I could wrap myself around him.

This queen thing is so much bigger than I expected. How am I going to be enough of a shifter to do everything required of me?

A rush of warmth caressed me, and I closed my eyes at the sensation of his energy mingling with my own. *You're already enough. You're giving your people everything you have. No one can expect more than that of you. Bringing in the alphas is a sign of the true leader within you.*

Delegation is important. Letting go of control and trusting in others is one of the hardest steps all leaders take. I admire your strength, and I'm so proud of you.

Have I told you lately how grateful I am that you chose me as your heir? I leaned back and kissed him on the nose.

I chose well. I chose my equal.

Well, if that wasn't enough to give a queen her daily confidence boost, I don't know what was. Finn was incredible, and for him to say that meant everything to me.

"You okay, Princess?" Blaine stepped in closer, still looking all guard-like, but some of the tension was gone from his handsome face. I sat back from Finn, reaching a hand out for Blaine to pull me to my feet. Then I surprised us both by wrapping my arms around him and hugging him close.

"Thank you for being my friend," I murmured against his chest. "All of these years you have protected me, even before I needed guards." The room was empty now except for my dominants. I would never show this much affection in public – even Monica, Jen, Victor, and Ben were at the far wall, giving us privacy.

His arms tightened then, and suddenly I was completely pressed against his hard muscles. His familiar scent and warmth wrapped around me and it almost felt protective, like Blaine was somehow a blanket I could crawl beneath to hide from the scary horrors of the world.

"You're my best friend, Ari. I would die for you without even thinking about it. I've always known you would be queen, and I knew that there was no one worthier of the role. You're different from the other heirs. You're … more."

I pulled back. My brow rose as I gave him my "what the heck" look. "You couldn't possibly have known I'd be queen. The Red Queen stood for over a hundred years. And how am I different?"

Blaine tilted his head down to see me better; his light green eyes were glimmering, the color depthless. I stood on tiptoes to get close to him; he was much taller than me.

"When you were five and had just bonded with Finn, I had a dream. It was strange, this kaleidoscope of changing colors and scenes. The last one, which stayed with me right until I woke up, was a beautiful woman with white hair standing on a grassy hill. The grass was so green that it hurt my eyes, her dress so red it was beyond any color I knew. Upon her head was a crown of purple mecca stones."

I was clutching at him now, my nails surely digging into his biceps, but he didn't flinch.

"I had that dream for months. After some time, I started to realize it was you, that I was seeing you as future queen. It was almost like someone wanted me to know you were going to be queen and that I had to protect you. I had to make sure you would have the chance."

My breath was coming out in fast little huffs as I tried to process this. "Only magic born see visions in their dreams," I said in a whisper. "How is this possible?"

Blaine shrugged. "I have no idea. I never told anyone for fear that I'd be thought crazy, or worse, that it was a true vision and would be seen as a threat to the Red Queen. My great-great-grandfather was magic born. Maybe I inherited some of his gift."

Was that possible?

"Thanks for telling me," I said.

I realized this was the first time in a long time I'd really looked at my friend. Really saw him. He had sacrificed so much of his own life to serve me. "Thank you for everything."

He hugged me again, and it was only when a throat cleared that we pulled apart. I turned to find Calista in the doorway, tablet in hand and a half-smile on her face.

"Sorry to interrupt, but I'm going to need her highness for a few minutes."

Blaine stepped back and I let all the softer emotions inside of me swirl around for a bit before I tucked them away. It felt as if things had changed slightly, as if there was a depth to our friendship that had not been there earlier. It was a nice feeling and I was surprised by it.

Shaking this off, I crossed the room to reach my advisor. She handed me her tablet, only remembering at the last moment that electronics and queens did not go well together. She snatched it back, holding it up so I could see. She then started flicking through the pages.

I read as quickly as I could; it was an entire webpage dedicated to Kade and me, like a memoir of our love story or some crap. Only we didn't have a love story. Dark, stormy emotions crashed within me as I read through the information. Most of it was taken out of context, some completely made up, but teamed with a multitude of pictures – including one from when he'd saved me during my coronation and had his hand spread across my chest as he funneled the mecca energy out of me – well, it all looked pretty convincing.

Calista's face was creased with concern, her eyes sad. "I have the technology department staff dealing with it. We've taken the site down multiple times already, but it keeps popping up. Some of your people have seen it, and already there are discussions across the message boards. It's being contained right now, but I just wanted to let you know."

I nodded, too angry to say any more. I had not crossed any lines with Kade since becoming queen, and before that it was nothing more than a kiss or two. It was beyond frustrating that not only did I have to ignore my attraction to the bear king, but now I had to defend myself for actions I didn't even take.

"Figure out who created the site and bring them to me," I said from between gritted teeth.

Calista nodded. We were walking now, my dominants trailing behind me. Within ten minutes, I'd left the basement and was back in my office. My crown went back into its special wooden box, then I let myself sink into the plush office chair behind my new oak desk. My new office furniture was perfect. I loved running my hands across the grains of wood and leather inlay. This place relaxed me, but unfortunately I had business to attend to first. I had to deal with Seamus – and all magic born, really. I loved Violet, but sometimes she did act above me, and I couldn't allow that in my home.

Calista was the only one in the room now, so I said to her, "Print up a new royal decree. All magic born are forbidden from cloaking themselves in the presence of the queen. Punishable by..."

I would have to follow through with whatever I said here, and it would be stupid to kill a magic born over something like this. They were treasured and important, but they did need to learn their place. How dare Seamus spy on my private council meeting. The mere thought of it had my wolf howling inside of me.

"... banishment," I said.

That was an order I could follow through with. If you were banished from the boroughs you were a disgrace to your pack and family. If you tried to reenter any of the five boroughs, you would be killed on sight. The closest you could live would be the Island. Not that I would allow Seamus to live in my Island house.

Calista nodded her approval. The first year as a queen was the hardest. If you let any wolf get away with anything, the entire race would walk all over you. Word would spread, and the last thing I needed were rumors spreading that I was weak. Especially with all these Kade rumors already floating around.

Plus, banishment was quite fair. The Red Queen would have boiled Seamus alive for what he did. The only one who would get around my new ruling was Violet, which was okay. I often needed her to cloak herself, and I trusted that she would never spy on me.

"Anything else?" Calista asked.

"Yes. Plan something fun for my dinner tonight. No business."

She smiled and nodded. When I was just an alpha and heir I'd had time to relax. Now I had inherited an entire race and their drama was my drama. Rising from my desk, I crossed the room. I'd had enough for today. No more work.

The moment I opened my door, my five dominants were there, standing at attention. The sight of them always reminded me that Derek was absent. The pang in my heart was strong, but I never allowed it to linger long. I couldn't dwell on his death, I had a war to prepare for, which was in part justice for Derek's murder. He was a victim of the fae as much as the Red Queen. That was how I would honor them.

My guards followed me down the curving halls into the elevator, which took us up a few floors, and then out to a series of storage rooms. We walked in silence. They could tell I wasn't in the mood for conversation. My focus was on the Red Queen, my aunt by blood, and the woman who I was starting to think I knew nothing about. The fae at the park had said to look to my queen for answers.

So that's what I would do.

"Wait for me out here," I said to the five dominants, before entering the large storage room. Normally, they'd check out a room like this, make sure no one was waiting to ambush me. But for some reason I felt the urge to explore in here alone and thankfully my people were learning to accept my commands. Not to mention things were always a little more relaxed within the royal estate; I was powerful enough to take on most attackers, the mecca at my call and all.

Flicking the light on and closing the door behind me, I surveyed the boxes. There must have been over a hundred in here, all neatly stacked and labeled. It would take me days to go through them all, time I did not have. I quickly read the labels, trying to see if anything jumped out at me. Clothes, shoes, files, jewelry, royal trinkets. As I walked closer to a stack of boxes I felt a small pull of mecca energy. It started like a tingling of awareness along my spine, strengthening the closer I got. Kade's lesson came to me then: *The mecca is conscious, a living breathing entity. If you can learn to listen, it can be used for your benefit.*

I scanned my hand along the boxes until the tingling became unbearable. *Trinkets.* What mecca trinket were you hiding, Red Queen? Pulling the medium-size box down, I wasted no time tearing it open. The second the lid lifted I was assaulted by the floral fae scent, which I both recognized and hated now. It was faint, but definitely of fae origin.

Digging through the items, I tossed aside a few small ornaments, a pair of bronze ballet slippers, and some other pieces that didn't interest me. Right near the bottom was a wooden box. My hand hovered over it and my heartbeat picked up speed. This was important; the box was practically vibrating with mecca energy.

Slowly I lifted it out and contemplated calling Violet to help open it. Now that I knew how powerful the mecca was, I feared it. The fear had started during my coronation when the energy had almost killed me, pressing in on me until I thought I would be crushed beneath it. It was reasonable to fear power like that. But I wouldn't let the fear control me.

The second I had that thought, the mecca energy within the box lessened, almost as if it sensed my fear and wanted me to know it was safe to open. Okay, then ... here goes nothing. Lifting the lid slowly, I blinked a few times as the object came into view. It was a beautiful, falsely vibrant, blue flower on top of a photograph. The flower glowed, the hue of the petals so deep and rich that I knew it was not of this world. Not to mention it was inside of a box with no water and no sun and still it lived.

Touch it or don't touch it? As if against my will, my hand snaked out and closed around the stem of the flower. The second it was in my palm, my hand glowed the slightest bit purple, like when I touched the mecca crystal. Acting on instinct, I pulled it up to my nose and inhaled the scent of grass, sea water, and a sweetness that lay under the floral tones.

I was about to lower the flower from my face when I heard a crash. *What the hell?* Realizing it had come from the blossom, I pulled it closer to my ear and almost dropped it at the distinct sounds of waves, and birds chirping. In a rush, I set the flower down and backed up a few steps. Could this actually be possible? Was this some weird freaky fae mecca flower that was a connection to their world?

Why did the Red Queen have this? How did she get it? Could someone in the other world hear me now if I spoke?

I couldn't think about that. I stepped forward again, planning on slamming the box shut and having Calista lock it in my jewelry safe, when I noticed the photo it was perched on. I stared at it for a moment, a surge of emotions tightening my chest and throat. As I reached out for the old weathered photo, a smile spread across my face; a war of both joy and sadness were fighting within me. It was my mom and the Red Queen.

As I traced my fingers along my mother's face, I was surprised to see both her and the queen were pregnant in this photo. I recognized the surroundings and clothing style enough to know this was taken when my mother was pregnant with me. I couldn't recall her ever telling me that her sister had been pregnant at the same time. This must have been one of the times the Red Queen miscarried. If my memory served me correctly, she had more than a few losses in her quest for a child. It was one of those sad stories in our royal history.

I brought the photo closer, really seeing my former leader. The Red Queen looked radiant, healthy and happy. She had her arm around my mother, holding her tightly. I never saw this side of my aunt. She was always so cold and distant to me and others. Maybe the multiple miscarriages did that to her. I didn't know much about babies or pregnancy, but her belly was quite distinct here, which meant she lost the baby late in pregnancy. I couldn't imagine such a loss.

It was one of the few times that the Red Queen ever failed: producing an heir. Luckily my mom had had Winnie and me to carry on the red line. Slipping the photo into my pocket, I closed the wooden box, trapping the flower inside. Anything to do with the fae was dangerous. I would not open that again until we knew more about what we were dealing with. Hopefully one of the magic born would find some useful information in the secret fae spell book room.

When I exited the storage area I tried to school my features so that none of my dominants knew I was bothered. I was bothered though – a fae flower in my home, in the former queen's personal items. Did any of us truly know the Red Queen? Even the council?

I traversed the winding halls until I was back at my private quarters, exhaustion crushing in on me. Emotional stress was actually worse than physical activities. I needed a long hot bath before my dinner plans. I just wanted to wash this day away. As usual, Blaine and Victor searched my apartment for any intruders while I waited at the door with my other guards.

Blaine let out a shout. "What the hell?" And before I could think, I was running into the apartment, even though Monica tried to hold me back.

I'd never heard Blaine shout out like that. Generally he handled everything without a worry. Monica finally caught up to me, yanking me back hard so she could position herself in front of me as we skidded around the corner into my bedroom. I was so relieved to see Blaine, his body rigid, and before him ... Violet.

"Violet! You scared me half to death!" Blaine cursed a few more times, running his hand over his hair, making it stand up.

That was it. That was all I needed to lose it in fits of laughter. Everyone looked at me as I laughed so hard tears streamed down my cheeks.

I had been so stressed lately that when I finally had reason to laugh my body was just on overdrive with emotion.

Blaine shook his head, the slightest of grins lighting up his face. "Sorry if I scared you, Princess. She appeared out of thin air. I almost stabbed her."

His sword was still out in front of him, the tip a few inches from Violet's navel. My best friend was watching me, her face drawn, eyes dropping at the corners. She looked exhausted, her voice low as she said: "Well, Ari made a new royal decree that I couldn't cloak myself in the royal house, so naturally I had to come disobey her just to shake her day up a little."

I shook my head at the magic born. "My day is well shaken, thank you very much. Is that all you came for? To scare me and nearly get stabbed by Blaine?"

Violet nodded. "Pretty much. Anyways, I actually have some work to get to, so ... see you tonight at the thing. Bye." Then just like that she vanished.

"The thing?" I asked, and everyone shared a look that made it immediately clear they were keeping some information from me.

My wolf rumbled in my chest; still no one answered. Letting out a deep breath, I pushed my beast down inside. I knew they wouldn't keep anything too serious from me, and for now I had neither the time nor the energy to beat it out of them, so I let it go. Probably Calista planning a poker night, or some other gambling-style activity.

I shooed everyone out of the room. Monica and the rest of my guard just chuckled as they went. Blaine was the last one left, and it didn't look like he was leaving just yet.

He quirked his lips into a wry grin. "You know, Princess, if I'm checking your apartment for intruders and I yell ... you're supposed to run."

"Never!" I didn't even hesitate in my response. Our eyes were locked on each other, strong electricity charging the air, a spark I'd never noticed before.

I cleared my throat, stepping back so I could sit on the bed and take my shoes off. "Thanks for looking out for me ... I'm just going to take a bath now before my dinner plans."

Blaine's green eyes shot through with darkness for a brief moment, before he lowered his head into a half-bow nod. "Right, I'll just be outside keeping guard."

As he left the room, I had to smile again at Violet taking him by surprise like that. She was such a pain, but she was my pain and I wouldn't change her for anything. Blaine too. I was blessed to have such amazing friends.

Discarding my clothes, I strode into the private bathroom, which was literally the size of my old apartment. Stepping under the warm water, multiple shower heads directed spray at me from all sides. One perk of being queen was the best shower in the world.

Closing my eyes, trying to relax, I couldn't stop the multitude of thoughts crashing through my mind. The most prominent was of a giant, dark-haired, amber-eyed shifter. Kade had said he was going away for a few days, and a huge part of me wanted to know where he was. Why was it so difficult to keep my mind off of him? I should be stronger than this. I should be able to control myself. The fact that I couldn't was a bad sign. A very bad sign indeed.

That night, I dressed semi-casual in skinny jeans, gray suede ankle boots, and a red silk sleeveless top. My guess of a poker night was definitely out – Monica had told me to dress for a night out on the town. Her advice had my body thrumming with excitement. I hadn't been out in forever, pretty much under lock and key since the Summit.

There was a knock at my door and I had no idea what to expect. When I opened it, I was taken aback by the three handsome shifters awaiting me. Victor, Ben, and Blaine looked stylish and magnetic, each wearing regular civilian clothes, dark wash jeans and nice button-up shirts. Their hair was styled and they were all freshly shaven.

Blaine offered his arm and I took it.

"My, my, what a lucky girl I am," I said.

Ben winked as Victor grinned and said, "We're the lucky ones."

"So, are you going to tell me where we are going?"

Blaine just held on to my arm and shook his head. "Then it wouldn't be a surprise."

As he turned to leave the room, I noticed a glint of steel sticking out of Ben's back pocket. Ben was known for having peculiar weapons; he and Violet often stayed up late designing them. He'd craft the steel in his workshop and the magic born would infuse them with magic. He'd had more than one shifter try to buy a blade from him, but he was very selective about who got one. I had three; they were kept in a box that had been specially constructed for them.

As we walked down the halls, I whispered to Ben. "What's your latest creation?" I gestured to his pocket.

His grin was pure excitement as he pulled out a small and menacing-looking half-circular blade with four round holes on the underside. When he slipped his fingers into the holes, I realized it was some sort of sharp-bladed brass knuckles.

"Holy crap," I breathed, and Ben laughed.

"I also have a serrated wire in my boot – can behead a man in seconds," he said, all casual-like as we reached the elevator.

Of course he did. I winked. "I'll stick close to you tonight, then."

Blaine let my arm go as we entered the elevator. As the doors rolled close I had to work hard not to bounce on the spot. I hadn't been this excited in a long time. Were we actually leaving the royal home? And if so, where were we going? The anticipation was killing me.

Chapter Five

A whole new world.

TWENTY MINUTES LATER, as my private car pulled up in front of a plain-looking brownstone on the Upper-Westside, I had half an answer. There was no one around, and despite hearing muffled music, I didn't see any cool raging clubs.

I looked at my guys. "What's this? Some house party?" Maybe the boys knew some shifters who lived here and we were doing a poker night?

Blaine smiled and produced a small, intricately detailed brass key from his pocket. "This, Ari, is apparently the most highly regarded secret in the shifter and human world. We're pretty much as in the dark as you, but it's supposed to be an once-in-a-lifetime thing."

I looked closely at the key and saw that the head of it was made of swirls that formed an artsy shape of a wolf head. Ben jumped out of our vehicle first, surveying the quiet street before opening my door. Once I was standing on the sidewalk, he leaned in to whisper: "I've heard this place is so secret it doesn't even have a name. The only way to get in is to get a key. They have no bouncers and there is no cover charge. It's invite only, and it's owned by some old wolf who has kept the club in his family for generations. Rumor has it that even the Red Queen was never invited."

Now all of my dominants were around me and I was staring at the black door in shock. "How did we get a key?"

Blaine was the one to answer: "Calista. She didn't say how she knew this old wolf, just that they were friends from the past. Gave us two keys. Violet, Monica, and Jen are already inside, scouting for danger. If there is any trouble, they'll be at the front door. There's no way for us to contact them once they're on the inside."

Okay, then. Let's do this. If there was one thing I really loved, it was top secret, exclusive places. Oh, and surprises. This just happened to be a bit of both.

Snatching the key from Blaine's hand, I charged up the stairs for the front door. Victor let out a low laugh as he and the other boys followed me. There was no way to know what awaited me on the other side. Would it be a normal house entrance, or a club with a dance floor, or a bar with pool tables? Whichever it was, I was dying to know.

Slipping the key into the lock, I twisted once and it clicked. At the same time, a wash of energy descended across us, and suddenly I was staring at an old, dark wooden door that was intricately carved with what looked like magic symbols. We were all blinking; the magical disguise was completely gone and there was a purple haze hovering over the old door, like this brownstone was filled with mecca and it was leaking out. The muffled music that had barely been audible before was blaring now. I placed my hand on the intricate knob, and just as I turned, Blaine's hand dropped over my wrist, stopping me.

"Let me go first," he commanded, and despite the fact I was his queen, I didn't have a problem with him taking charge then. It was his job after all.

Blaine stepped in front of me, shielding my body with his as he opened the door. Cold air wafted out from the opening, and two stimuli hit my senses. One: mecca magic was everywhere; this place was crawling with it. Two: there was a faint floral scent, which meant a fae was either here, or had been here recently.

My boys must have failed to notice the fae scent, because they didn't mention it as we stepped into the darkened entryway. I also didn't mention it, because if there were fae in here with my people, I wanted to know about it.

Blaine went first, a dagger in his hand. Ben, with one set of his bladed knuckles, was on my left. Victor held a small shank on my right. My head spun as we moved further through the house; the mecca was pulsing to the music, surging and falling with the deep drum and bass. My heartbeat was keeping time with it also. Hopefully, I wouldn't be so overwhelmed by power that I accidentally lost control of the energy inside of me. Using the skills Kade had taught me, I breathed with the power, letting it filter through me. This was the best way to keep the buildup inside to a minimum.

The entrance hallway was long and dark as we strode along the hardwood floors toward a black velvet curtain at the end. Blaine parted the curtain and looked around. "Holy shifter gods," he said, letting out a short burst of laughter.

I couldn't see, so I shoved my big mountain of a guard to the side and peeked out.

What the…?

"Are we still in New York?" I asked, my voice wavering as awe spilled out.

There was no way this was inside a brownstone building in the city. I had expected a home that had been renovated into a nightclub. *Nope ...* it was a garden. One of the most beautiful gardens I had ever seen. The space looked half the size of Central Park, unnaturally spanning out into the distance. Green grass squished under my boots as we moved out from behind the curtains and into the first part of the outdoors area. The night sky twinkled overhead, and there had to be thousands of tiny string lights draped from trellises. Vines dripped down from trees with full blooms of blue and pink flowers. This wonderland was crawling with magic. How was it possible?

"Ari!" Violet's high-pitched shriek came from my left, and I turned to see her barreling toward me holding two pink, glowing drinks. Shifters moved around us laughing and dancing wildly to the beat. The flowers, I now saw, were pulsing to the music.

My guards made a half attempt to stay around me, but I could see they were at a loss. Their defensive poses were out of place; it was weird, but there was no actual threat, so they weren't sure what to do.

Violet reached me and I wasted no time asking her: "What is this place?"

She seemed at ease here, which was not usual for the magic born, so I was guessing she knew more than me. Monica and Jen appeared then also, both looking less at ease but still relaxed. They joined the formation of my confused guards.

Violet grinned. "Isn't it wonderful! I've never seen such intricate and concentrated magic in one place."

"Magic? Whose magic?"

Only the magic born and queen could access mecca like this. But there was no way any of the magic born were throwing secret raves. They were far too busy for one thing. So who was this old wolf Calista had trusted enough to lead us into their magical lair?

"Mine," a voice said, and everyone but Violet jumped. Ben was in front of me in an instant, both fists raised, blade held at the ready.

For a second I wondered if somehow I'd managed to drink a few of the pink drinks in Violet's hand and was already drunk. *Is he for real?* Standing before me was a handsome older wolf who looked like he could be Violet's uncle or father. He was pale white, definitely a magic born. He stood about my height, short for a male shifter, but that didn't diminish his visible power one bit. He wore an old-school tux, with skinny purple bowtie, and a half bowler top hat. His eyes were the usual white-blue, but there were shimmery streaks across them, almost like silver lightning bolts. This was one eccentric, powerful, weird shifter, and he had been under the Red Queen's nose this entire time. How was this possible? We had only four magic born and he wasn't one of them. I inhaled deeply. He was definitely a wolf. A wolf magic born who lived in hiding?

"You think I invite people into my home to harm them?" he casually asked Ben.

Violet stepped forward, shoving Ben to the side. "Queen Arianna, this is Sir Baladar."

A bemused smirk crossed my lips. My best friend wasn't usually so formal. And what was with the "sir" thing? We didn't have knights in the shifter world.

He moved closer and I offered my hand. He took it, kissing the top before gracing me with a warm smile. "It's my pleasure, Your Highness. Would you walk with me?"

Blaine and the others were quick to sound their disapproval to this idea, but before things could get out of control, Baladar put his hand up. "If I wanted to harm the queen, I would have already, and the likes of you would not be able to stop me."

"That sounds an awful lot like a threat," Ben said through gritted teeth.

The man smiled, warmth oozing from him again. "I'm much too old for threats. I simply speak the truth. It's easier."

For some reason I was inclined to believe him, and I appreciated his honesty. If I was being honest myself, I was dying to have a chat with this man and know more about him.

"I'll be fine," I said to my dominants as I began to walk with Baladar. There were no more objections, but my guards did remain close behind us, Violet following as well.

As we walked further into this weird indoors-outdoors garden, I surveyed everything closely. It was hard to remember, when standing within an area so natural, that we were still in the city. My wolf loved it though; she was howling with joy, trying to get me to shift and run.

Shifters were everywhere. Some were dancing, others lying in the grass looking at the sky; some were kissing. This place was definitely magical. Baladar walked silently beside me, content to wait until I was ready to speak.

"So, you're a magic born."

It was a question-statement of sorts. This close I could feel his power, and instinct told me that his would match my own. I trusted that Calista wouldn't put me in danger, but I also wondered if maybe she had trusted too easily. Here was a very powerful magic born that I had not known of. What if the fae didn't kill my queen? What if this man did?

"I'm magic born, yes," he said. I noticed the music was muffled now so that we could speak without shouting. When he said no more, I figured I was going to have to do all the talking, so I opened my mouth, but then he surprised me.

"Do you smell the fae?" he asked as he scanned the group before us.

I hid my worry as best I could. "Yes, from the moment I walked in."

He nodded as if he wasn't surprised by this. "I wonder what they want."

This man was very intriguing. "Well, you must have given them a key, right?"

He gave me a sidelong glance and a half smile. "No, I would never invite a fae and my queen on the same night."

So that meant other nights he did invite fae?

"Who are you? I mean, I know you're a magic born, but... why does no one know of you?" I might love some secrets, but definitely not ones which could threaten my people. And something told me Baladar could be a huge threat if he chose to go against me.

He seemed to consider my questions. "I'm the keeper of knowledge. The oldest wolf alive, I suspect. A living library of our magical history, some would say."

I stopped walking and faced him. "Why haven't I ever heard of you?"

The oldest wolf alive. A magic born. Surely this was a fact every queen should be told. Did the Red Queen know? She'd certainly never mentioned it to any of her heirs.

His eyes twinkled. "Your Red Queen preferred that I not be public knowledge. She banished me here in her first year of ruling. She and Sabina made it so that I couldn't leave this place, so I spent my days making it beautiful and inviting people to come spend time with me so that the pangs of loneliness wouldn't overtake me."

My heart clenched at that very honest confession. I was also surprised by his answer. Clearly the former queen had known about him, and she had feared him. I wondered if she had true reasons to be so cruel. Was he a hidden threat?

If the Red Queen magically banished him here in her first year, that meant...

"You've been here a hundred years," I noted as we continued walking.

He nodded. "I've had a lot of time to create this oasis as I call it. And found lots of friends to keep me company."

This day had just gotten majorly weird.

"How do you know Calista?" I couldn't imagine my prim and proper advisor hanging out at this place on the weekends.

His face changed; his eyes lit up for a second before that sparkle was swallowed by sadness. "She was the love of my life," he said, his voice low, his face flat.

My feet stumbled briefly. I hadn't expected that answer. "What happened?"

I tried to keep the curiosity from my voice, direct some sympathy toward him. In reality, I normally wouldn't ask someone I barely knew such a personal question, but I was dying to know.

"Duty called," he answered. "Calista was born to be an advisor, and I was unable to leave this home." I suddenly felt sick. I know it hadn't been me alone. Calista had been an advisor to many heirs, but the fact I had contributed to her loss of a partner hurt my heart.

Baladar must have sensed some of my guilt and pain. "You mustn't worry about it," he said in a fatherly tone. "It was the right decision. I knew you were special and that Calista could bring you to your full potential as an heir."

Great. Sounded like it was her advisor role with me that had ended their love affair. Calista had never spoken of him, but I knew she used to live in Manhattan before I was born. How did I not know about the love of her life? Or was this more one-sided, and Calista had not been hurt the same way as Sir Baladar?

Speaking of... "Why are you referred to as a 'sir?'" I asked him.

His eyes twinkled then, those shimmers of lightning growing brighter. "I'm old enough to have been part of the royal army for her majesty, the queen of England. Before shifters were so segregated from humans, I was honored with knighthood, and have always kept the 'sir.' I like it. Gives me character."

He winked. *Okay* ... well, he had plenty of character, that was for sure.

We had reached a secluded part of the garden now. Some shifters were soaking in a natural bubbling spring hot tub, drinking and talking. It looked amazingly relaxing, and I was trying to think of the last time I'd stopped and relaxed like those here in Baladar's oasis. One thing about being a leader, there was very little downtime. It was not a nine-to-five job.

When we paused, I faced him fully, trying not to get lost in those mesmerizing eyes. Magic born eyes capture you and never let go. "How is it that you are an information keeper? At your word, you have been exiled here for a hundred years, and yet I feel as if you haven't missed a single thing in the shifter world."

He smiled and gestured to the people around him. "I offer my friends and companions a fun time in a safe environment, and in return they give me knowledge. My powers allow me to discern truth from lie, so I always know what is happening."

Just as Violet could. The magic born were great at finding truth in all information.

Sir Baladar was clearly powerful. Age alone would have provided him with a plethora of knowledge that would be valuable to many. So why would the queen banish him? And if he was such a threat to her, why did she not banish him out of New York City, away from the boroughs so he would not get powerful surges of mecca energy?

Sucking in deeply, I decided to push my luck. I had already asked him too much for a friendly first meeting, and if this was Calista's ex-lover I didn't want to offend him ... but I had to know. This man seemed so well connected that if anyone knew, he would.

"Do you know who killed the Red Queen?" I asked, keeping my voice low so as not to cause an uproar.

His eyes darkened. "This is not a question I have the answer to. I suspect things, but I do not know, and speaking of it might actually end my life. My instincts tell me that the truth will be revealed in due time."

I was shocked into silence, and reminded of Bethany, the Red Queen's advisor, who I pressed for an answer on who murdered the Red Queen. Bethany had tried to tell us something, and some sort of spell had triggered, killing her instantly. I never did learn what she was going to say either. *Damn those fae.* They were always one step ahead of me.

Baladar distracted me then by producing an item from his pocket. He held it for a moment, before reaching out to give it to me. I opened my palm and a heavy metal object landed in it, a solid gold key with the House of Red emblem marked on it.

"The keys your friends have will expire tonight, but this key..." Baladar gestured to my hand. "Will never expire. You're welcome in my home anytime, and I look forward to more conversations with you. Bring your bear friend. I would like to speak with him too."

How did he know about Kade? That stupid website probably. He'd basically told me that all shifters came to his house with gossip on their tongue. There'd be no bigger story than that of an affair between wolf queen and bear king.

Tucking the key in my jeans pocket for safe keeping, I said, "Thank you." There were a thousand questions burning a hole in my tongue, but before I could say more, Baladar bowed deeply.

"I promised Calista you would have fun tonight. So eat, drink, and be merry." He looked around and inhaled again. "I don't think the fae wishes you harm. Once I leave, they will come out and find you."

I was starting to see why the queen had locked him away. He saw and knew far too much, and clearly she had been the keeper of more than a few secrets. Feeling the heavy gaze of unknown sources, I spun around, scanning the bright lights and shadows beneath the trees, trying to figure out if a fae was stalking me.

My dominants were standing guard about six feet from me. Next to them was Violet, pounding pink fizzy drinks like it was her last day on Earth and she needed to get rip roaring drunk. But no fae. When I turned back around, Baladar was gone. Typical magic born. Didn't he get the memo? No cloaking in my presence. Oh well, I was starting to see that he was in the same realm as Violet – kind of outside my rule.

My guards approached me now that the older shifter was gone.

"Who was he?" Blaine asked, after he gave the proper protocol bow.

"An old friend of Calista's. He is bound to this home, and has made it a private sanctuary."

Blaine nodded but he didn't relax. He remained rigid, his focus constantly shifting around the party. He was uneasy, and I raised my own awareness levels to make sure that this didn't end up being a bad situation for us all.

Suddenly there was a pink drink thrust in my face. "Spelled drinks!" Violet's words were a little slurred. "They take the edge off, but if you feel you're in danger or need to drive home, you just say the magic word and you're instantly sober."

Shaking my head, I reluctantly removed the glass from her before she spilled it everywhere. The pink was sloshing dangerously close to the edge. Bringing it closer I smelled it: lemon, strawberry, and a mix of a few alcohols. Shifters were governed by rules based on European society. We could drink alcohol at eighteen; most started even earlier than that. As queen it was frowned upon for me to ever drink to excess. If a war broke out and I was impaired, I would let my people down. But one or two wouldn't hurt, especially if there was a sober-up switch.

"Prove they're spelled," Monica said, watching Violet sway to the music.

"Purple pixies!" the magic born shouted, and immediately the dazed look on her face vanished; her eyes were clearer, and she stopped swaying. "See," she groaned, "I'm perfectly fine." As if to prove her point, she touched a fingertip to her nose, pulled it away, and brought it back again. She sighed. "Of course, now I'm going to need more drinks."

Somehow she had another drink in her hand then, and she raised her eyebrows at me. I knew she was silently asking if I was in or out of tonight's debauchery. Staring at the fruity cocktail in my hand, I decided that maybe just for tonight I could forget my worries. I knew my boys wouldn't touch the drinks; they would stay completely alert the entire time we were here. Monica, Jen, and Violet would drink with me though and it would be fun. Without another thought I tipped the whole thing back, letting the fizz roll down my throat. The sweetness overwhelmed me at first, but then as I got used to the taste I immediately craved more. Once the glass was empty, I noticed tiny writing on the bottom, two words. *Lovely lilacs.* There was my undo spell. I took mental note and handed the glass to Ben.

Shifters have fast metabolisms. It's almost impossible for us to become overweight or get drunk, but whatever was in these fruity numbers was clearly laced with more than human alcohol. One drink and I felt amazing. My muscles relaxed; my head felt light and airy. So much of the heavy burden I'd been carrying for weeks drifted away and I felt like a twenty-year-old for the first time in a long time.

Grabbing Blaine's hand, I tried to drag him to a nearby open dance area. He resisted me at first, and no matter how hard I yanked, there was simply no moving him if he didn't want to be moved.

"I'm your guard ... which means I need to guard you," he said, shaking his head at me as I danced around him.

"Dance with me!" I shouted, throwing my hands up before diving toward him and trying to nudge him over to the dance floor.

I could hear chuckles around me. Violet was laughing madly, clearly happy again under the pink drink's influence. Blaine tried to remain stoic, but eventually I got him to smile.

"One dance, then I need to keep watch," he said, leaning over so I could hear him better, his deep voice tickling my neck as he spoke into my ear.

"Yes, sir!" I fist pumped, the way we used to as kids when we got our own way. He shook his head at me again, but the smile was bigger this time. Genuine.

The music picked up as Blaine and I ended up in the middle of a hundred dancing bodies. I lifted my arms, spinning around, moving with the beat, brushing against my dominant as we moved to the music. He was watching me with stone-like eyes, far too serious. He needed a pink drink. This was the worst sort of relaxing I'd ever seen.

A flash of white to my left caught my eye. Violet was there dancing around us and giggling. Nothing was funny at all, and yet I felt the need to giggle too. This drink made me feel amazing, not drunk just ... relaxed. Loose. Carefree. I laughed harder as Violet leapt with her arms out like she was on Broadway. This was exactly what I needed, a night of living like I was just a normal young shifter in New York City. I was just spinning around to look for Monica and Jen when the floral fae scent hit me, stronger than I'd smelled since stepping into the brownstone. They were close.

"Lovely lilacs," I said quickly.

Immediately the buzzed carefree feeling was gone and I was focused. Blaine reacted to my hesitation, going into guard mode, scanning the area. Both of us saw her at the same time, near a beautiful purple-flowered bush – the lioness familiar in her full glory. No Labrador illusion for her today.

"It's okay. She's a friend ... I think," I said to Blaine as I began to walk toward the lioness.

I wished I had Finn with me now. Maybe he'd be able to communicate with this other familiar, find out what she wanted from me. I heard Violet mutter some words behind me and then she was at my side, eyes clear, ready to throw down if needed. All of my guards had fallen into line. It was a shame my night of fun had come to a halt so soon, but it was far more pertinent that I ask that fae from the park more questions.

Once we were five feet from the lioness, she began to prance away. I walked fast to keep up and we ended up in a high-hedged labyrinth. Baladar was either the best mecca user in existence, or he had, like, a hundred million dollars in property here. This place was beyond huge.

The second I stepped into the entrance of the labyrinth, the music vanished, leaving behind silence. Not a single sound could be heard, not a bird, bug, or bee.

"I don't like this," Victor said from behind me.

"It's okay, there's no reason to be alarmed at this stage," I said. My guards knew I had met a fae with a lioness familiar before, but they still didn't like it.

We wound through the labyrinth, until finally turning a corner to find a tall and striking male. I had a moment's pause. I'd been expecting that same woman from before. But as the lioness walked to the male, nuzzling into his side, it made perfect sense. The female fae had said she wasn't very powerful; she couldn't have been an heir. The lioness was not her familiar. It was this man's.

He looked to be around my age, but age was probably impossible to judge on a fae. He was well over six feet tall, with a strong, wiry build, and long silky blond hair pulled back into a ponytail, except for a few braided strands that hung at the side of his head. He had deep green eyes, slashed through with gold threads. He was probably one of the most beautiful males I'd ever seen, but there was no mistaking his otherness. His ears were slender and pointed; he wore no illusion to hide his fae heritage.

Crossing his left arm over his chest he gave me the slightest of head nods. "Your Majesty."

I didn't know this man, but I didn't want to offend, so I decided a slight nod in return was appropriate. "Pleasure to meet you," I said.

My guards were at my back fanned out in an arc and the fae eyed them. "I'm Caspien, one of the princes of the Summer Court, and I would like to speak with you in private."

"No!" Blaine stepped before me and gestured to the prince's weapon. "There is no way we'll let our queen go off alone with an armed fae."

Prince Caspien nodded and unsheathed his blade, placing it on the ground before his familiar. "You have my word that no harm with befall her at my hand."

Violet stepped in beside me. "I'll accompany the queen," she said, clearly not convinced.

It looked like my best friend didn't completely trust this person, and I thought that was wise. This could be a ploy to kill me and weaken the mecca, weakening the shifters so they were ripe for the killing.

Caspien did not look worried. "As you wish, magic wielder."

Violet and I shared a look at this unfamiliar term. Blaine, Victor, Ben, Jen, and Monica looked less than happy as we walked away, leaving them to stand guard over his weapon and familiar. I was calm though. Few beings could rival Violet and I together, and I sensed Baladar would also come to my aid if needed.

Violet was at my left, a few paces behind me, and the prince was on my right. "Dalia sends her warm regards," he said formally.

Dalia? Oh ... that must be the name of the woman I met in Astoria Park.

I nodded. "Thank you. Please return those regards. So what brings you here?"

He didn't hesitate, which I liked. "Things are reaching crisis point in the Otherworld. We sent

Dalia across to try and warn you after your queen's death. This was the catalyst that has set the Winter Court off on a destructive path. Why, we do not know, but they are determined to take over both sides of the veil."

"Why send Dalia before and not just come yourself?" The prince was clearly far more powerful, and a leader in his own right.

"The less powerful the fae to cross over, the less ripple effect. We were hoping the Winter Court would not know she had come. But, as this escalates, we felt it was imperative that I seek your council in person. My father is the king of the High Court of Summer. From here on I'll be the direct liaison between our two courts. Now more than ever we need this alliance. We have information to share, and hope you'll do the same."

Whoa. The son of the king of the Summer Court. I felt a little in awe, even though I was an actual queen. Something about the Tuatha de Danann had that effect on me, an ethereal otherworld energy and power. I nodded that he should continue.

"The mecca is weak in the land of fae. Ever since your late queen fell, our world has begun to die."

I was no longer walking. I didn't want to miss a single word. "Dalia did mention there was an imbalance. What happens if the Otherworld dies? Would Earth also perish?"

His expression shuttered. "Right now we have no idea. Everything requires a balance, so there is a very real risk that your world will fall with us, but we cannot know for sure. Maybe, because the mecca is stronger here now, Earth would survive.

"Even more pressing, the Winter Court has stolen a precious item of ours, a power object that promotes energy and fertility. Without that object or the mecca empowering our lands, our food, and eventually our people, will die off. This means that time is running out before war spills into your land. We are weakening. We cannot hold them off for much longer."

"What can I do to help? How do I fix this?" I would not let an entire race die because of some imbalance my queen had created.

I knew it had started with her. I just had to figure out what she had done to make it so. Plus we needed all the allies we could get, especially since the Winter Court was gunning to take us out.

The prince's skin glowed then, almost as if happiness was bleeding from him. He gave me a slight nod. "Thank you. Very few leaders offer to help. My father made the right decision in trusting you. The Winter Court believes the only way to survive this imbalance is to destroy all shifters. Then they'll return to Earth and reclaim the mecca. My father believes you can fix it, that you can send the mecca back to the fae lands and restore the balance. If the mecca is returned, we'll gain much-needed strength to not only retrieve our object of power, but push back against the Winter Court. We have more numbers than them; the Spring Court is on our side, and they are numerous. We need the power back though."

Well, great. "Okay, and do you know exactly how I am supposed to do this?"

Of course, give me another impossible task when I already have ten to get through this week.

He nodded. "You're the queen of mecca now. You have the full force of the Earth side power at your disposal."

"I don't understand what happened, what my late queen did in the first place to offset the balance. To be honest, I was raised without any knowledge of the fae or your world, so the chance that I can somehow send the mecca back there is very slim."

"Slim?" He looked confused.

I tried not to groan in frustration. I needed to brush up on my Shakespeare.

"Not happening," Violet clarified. "Difficult. Impossible. A true pain in the butt."

The prince frowned. "Oh, right."

Some of his glow dulled. I had to offer some hope. I needed them to keep fighting the Winter Court until we figured this out, because he had just all but told me that if I didn't fix it, his kind was going to make my kind go extinct.

"I know an expert in the mecca and I'm training with him. So I'll do everything in my power to find a way to fix this. I make no promises, but if there is a way, I'll figure it out."

It was the right thing to say, because his eyes softened and his posture relaxed. "How much time do I have?" I asked him.

Please don't say a week or something crazy like that.

"If I can get the Sword of Light back from the Winter Court, it could buy us a few weeks."

"A few weeks!" I said loudly, losing all queenly composure.

He put out a hand to calm me. "In fae time. That would be ... one or two seasons here."

One or two seasons. So three to six months. Okay, I could deal with that timeline. *Right?* Violet must have noticed my panic, because she stepped in to finish the conversation.

"How can we contact you to see how things are progressing?" she asked him.

Prince Caspien looked at Violet, his brow furrowed. "You're a magic wielder."

Violet let out a frustrated wolfy growl. "We're not taught your ways or your magic."

This was the exact reason I was going to open up that locked room of fae magical books. We would know everything by the time my reign as queen was done.

Prince Caspien reached out and gently caressed a nearby flower. "When you're lost, always look to nature. You'll find you can communicate with us through the plants and other things of this kind. It's the reason we can cross in bodies of water. Nature joins our two lands." In a flash, he plucked two of the bright purple flowers, bringing them close to his face. Then he pulled out one of his hairs, laying it inside of one of the flowers, before handing it to Violet.

Her face lit up. "Of course! Why didn't I think of that?"

She reached for one of my hairs, but must have decided it wasn't completely safe to link me to the Otherworld, and pulled out one of hers instead. Laying the hair inside of the other flower, she held both in her closed palms. Then she pressed her lips to her hands, spoke an incantation, and her palms glowed purple for a few moments.

The prince watched her closely. "You're powerful," he said. "Most fae have some mecca affinity, but for the more complex spells we use specialized and highly trained magic wielders. Lucian, the palace magic wielder, could not have linked those flowers so quickly."

Violet shrugged off his compliment and handed him the flower that once held her hair. He nodded and placed it in his pocket. I was immediately reminded of the flower in the Red Queen's trinket box. It had to be the same thing, a communication device. But for who? Who had the queen needed to communicate with in the Otherworld? I wondered if there was a spell Violet could do to trace the link.

Prince Caspien faced me and I was blasted with the full force of his beauty, and that subtle glow which seemed to dim and brighten on and off.

"We are well met, Your Majesty," he said formally. "If a war begins, you have an ally in the Summer Court."

"Yes, we are well met," I offered back, unsure of the protocol. I had so many more questions, but he seemed to be in a rush to go. As if he read my thoughts, he gestured behind me.

"If I spend too long in this realm, my people weaken further. In my world, royalty are linked to our people. We feed them in a sense, with power, magic. If my father, brothers, or I leave, the court weakens. With the mecca already fading, it's best I return quickly."

"Yes, of course. It's the same here with the queen and her shifters. I'm sorry that your people are suffering, but I *will* fix this," I declared boldly, catching a raised eyebrow from Violet.

The green deepened in Caspien's eyes. "I believe you. The moment you were crowned, the sky lit up in my lands like it was mid-summer."

I had no idea what that meant, but I offered a small smile. As he brushed past me to go back to where his familiar and my dominants were waiting, he paused, before moving closer and leaning into my hair. He inhaled deeply, and unsure of protocol, I simply watched him, wondering of course what the hell he was doing.

Our eyes met. "An interesting development," he said, a strange expression on his face. "You're going to be one surprise after another, Queen Arianna." Without another word he turned and strode off.

Interesting? What did that mean? I smelled my hair to make sure I had remembered to shower today before hurrying after him, needing to ask him what he meant, but he was already gone.

I turned on Violet. "What does 'interesting development' mean?"

She shrugged. "No idea. He was cryptic the entire time. I'm starting to think that's just the way the fae are. But, girl ... he was hot."

She fanned her face and I couldn't help but chuckle. "Good to see that none of this dire situation has you concerned. Your focus is exactly where it shouldn't be ... on the fact that he's hot."

Violet shrugged. "I kind of like that whole pointy ear thing."

Yeah, I got that. I really did.

The enormity of his message, and my promises, hit me hard then. "Oh, Vi, what am I going to do?"

A wicked look crossed her face. "You're going to go talk to your mecca expert and fix this whole thing, right?" She trilled this in a singsong voice. Damn me and my bold statements.

Why? Why had I said that? One thing was for sure, I did need to find Kade. Now more than ever he needed to know what was going on, because I was pretty sure I'd just promised something I couldn't deliver.

Chapter Six

Kisses aren't for forgetting...

THE NEXT MORNING I sent Finn to Kade's with a message. I had barely slept knowing that I'd stupidly promised to try and save an entire world with powers I didn't even know how to use. Normally when I sent Finn, he returned with the king, but this time he was alone, with a note in his collar.

Come to me, was all it said. Well ... okay, then. I guess I couldn't expect him to come at my beck and call every time I wanted.

He was very busy. Some drama with his people, Finn offered.

Sometimes I forgot that Kade had his own people to rule and care for.

After informing my inner guard and Calista that I would be traveling to Staten Island, and listening to them complain and say no, I eventually brushed them all aside and went with Violet, Finn, and Monica as my protectors.

When I was finally out of the royal house, away from a multitude of over-protective wolves, I breathed a sigh of relief. I was getting a little sick of reminding everyone that the bear king was an ally now, and that Violet and I were more powerful than him. If he didn't bring one of his magic born along, of course. Semantics really. The bottom line was that I was not afraid of Kade. No matter what, he would never hurt me. I knew it in my gut, the place which had served me well for most of my life as heir, and so far as queen.

I chose not to tell the council I was going, against Calista's wishes. What else was new? It felt like my advisor and I were agreeing on less and less lately. She'd been quiet around me ever since I returned from the party at the brownstone. I still hadn't had time to interrogate her about her past with Baladar, but I was dying to know every detail. He'd called her the love of his life ... that was deep. Did she feel the same way?

As I stepped onto the Manhattan vortex disc, about to merge with the mecca energy to travel, I heard a faint whisper. It was that familiar voice again.

Arianna ... protect the...

The voice cut off as I stepped off the disc in a jump. My arms wrapped around my body as I fought the chills encasing me. Breathing rapidly and ragged, I turned to the girls: "Did you hear that?" I couldn't stop my head from swiveling around as I tried to see more of the room; chills continued to creep up my arms.

Violet and Monica shook their heads. Both looked confused as they stared from me to the vortex disc and back again. I swallowed hard, trying to fight the urge to run. I'd traveled the mecca a thousand times before. Why was this happening now? What had the Red Queen done to the mecca?

The voice was familiar, but I couldn't narrow it down to who it exactly was. All the vibrations of energy were warping the tone.

I heard nothing either, Ari. Finn sounded concerned, brushing his huge head against my side. At his touch, some of the creepiness eased and I was able to breathe deeply again.

There's this voice in the mecca. It's trying to tell me something. Both times they've used my name.

I felt his concern and worry for me. *Weirdness is definitely afoot. Feels like this has something to do with the imbalance the prince mentioned. Still, there's nothing you can do now but try and figure out how to send the energy back.*

He was right, there was nothing I could do. Maybe the voice was trying to help me, or maybe it was an enemy that wanted to lure me to do their bidding. For now I would reserve judgment until I had more evidence.

"Are you okay, Your Highness?" Monica broke protocol to brush a hand across my arm, clearly sensing I needed the comfort.

Giving her a nod and forcing a smile across my face, I stepped back onto the disc. No one said anything more as I reached for the energy and we all traveled to Staten Island with ease. This time there was no weirdness. No voices. Almost like I had imagined the entire thing.

When we arrived, I was pleased to be greeted by Gerald, Kade's war councilman.

"Your Highness!" He bowed deeply.

I smiled and clasped a hand on his shoulder. "You don't need to bow to me anymore, Gerald. We're friends now."

He smiled hugely and nodded. "Queen Arianna, you caught King Kade on a bad day, but he's going to be very happy to see you."

Violet and Monica shared a look and I cleared my throat. My stomach was doing weird flips at the very *happy to see me* part.

"Well, I have official news, so..." I couldn't really say more in public; this news needed to be given to Kade first, and he could decide what he wanted his people to know.

"Right." Gerald began walking away and I followed him to the curb, where a black Range Rover sat waiting. There was a driver inside and four large royal bear guards on motorcycles waiting around it. Kade had sent his best to protect me and I didn't even try and hide my smile.

"You're blushing," Violet whispered as I climbed into the seat.

She was right, I could feel the heat in my cheeks, and I tried my best to calm the torrent of emotion inside of me. I hadn't seen Kade for a few days and ... dammit, I missed him. Despite the fact he had my nerves shot and my stomach tied up in knots whenever we were around each other, the friendship we had built was comforting. He was someone I felt I could share the inner workings of my life with, the burden of being queen. Who else could understand better than another leader? It was not something I'd expected, but Kade had become as good a friend as many of the shifters I had known my entire life.

I sat forward in my seat now as the SUV roared to life, and then we were off, heading in the same direction as the last time I was here. From my peripherals I could tell that Violet was still watching me. I narrowed my eyes on her, telling her silently to leave it alone. Of course, when was the last time my best friend had listened to anything I told her, silent or not?

"I love that color on you, Ari," she said, her voice fakely happy. "Nice shade of rose pink. Really brings out the aqua in your eyes."

My *eyes* were probably narrowed to thin slits, and there was no way Violet wasn't getting my message to shut the heck up. Of course, as she dissolved into laughter, I just shook my head. Only a true best friend would find such humor in my misery. She reached over and grasped my hand, briefly, but the effort was noted. Her gentle ribbing was no doubt her attempt to lighten the air, add some humor back into my life. For once, it wasn't working. My world felt like it was shrouded in darkness on every angle, which made it very difficult for the light to shine. Violet had the right idea though, I had to try to figure out how to ease some of the burden or I would be crushed by the sheer weight of my responsibilities.

Gerald straightened and turned to face us, drawing our attention. Monica sat forward, as if she were about to be called on for some task.

He started slowly: "So, we're aware that the website formerly titled 'Royal Secrets' is now reappearing as 'Karianna: the royal scandal.' Kade has members of his staff tracking down those who are responsible. We will not let your good name be sullied, Queen Arianna."

My blush was back in full force now. Sullied … if only. The couple name was kinda cute though. "Starting to think I might as well forget about protocol. One should at least be getting some action if they're going to be referred to as 'Her Highness, the royal traitor whore.'"

Lots of throats cleared and I had to internally chuckle as the occupants of the car tried to figure out what to say. Did they think I hadn't bothered to check out the site? I wanted to know what my enemies were saying about me and Kade. I needed to know what I was fighting against.

I think everyone was relieved when we arrived at Kade's Staten Island estate. Looking out my window, I eyed the path outside as we pulled up to the mansion. The beautiful brick exterior and romantic wraparound porch were even more lovely in the daytime. I had only ever been here at night.

When the vehicle stopped, Gerald opened my door and extended his hand, helping me out, Finn was right on my heels. I thanked him, then he led us all up to the porch, stopping to speak with a few guards.

The closest of the guards, a male who was probably a brick building in his spare time, said: "He's just finishing up his meeting with the council. He wishes for Arianna to wait for him in the garden by her favorite tree. He said she would know what that meant."

He looked toward me and I smiled. Kade was perceptive, always watching and noticing things. That old fae treeling that had been in his garden for hundreds of years was from the Otherworld. I'd had a conversation with it right before the dark fae assassin tried to kill me. The fact that I talked to a tree should probably give me a moment's pause, but hey, I was starting to get used to all the crazy. Nothing had been the same since I became queen of the wolf shifters, in charge of the powerful magical mecca. I was pretty sure nothing could really shock me at this point.

Gerald nodded to the brick building guard, and he turned and opened the door, going back inside. From my position I could see the foyer and grand double staircase beyond it. When the door opened I could hear muffled commands. It was Kade and he sounded enraged.

"...no debate here! You're my council and if I want your opinion, I will ask for it. Until then, keep your thoughts to yourself and follow your leader!"

Damn! He wasn't shouting, but the strength and fierceness of his voice had even me taking a step back. Kade didn't need to shout to make sure everyone was petrified of him.

If I ever spoke to my council like that, they would plot to have me de-throned. But I could handle some plotting, right? The way he spoke to them made me question my own actions. Why did I tolerate my council requesting that I tell them every little thing? Demanding to have long meetings about things I didn't want to debate. I was the leader, not them. For too long the wolf queen has had half her authority undermined by eleven others, who were outdated and seemingly predisposed toward their own gains with every decision they made.

The funny thing was that in the normal wolf world no one really knew that. They thought the queen was the supreme power, not one who had to puppet herself to the control of others. I had sort of known it from my time as an heir, but only now was I truly starting to understand the full extent of it. Understand and resent it.

The door was closed by Gerald. Clearly he'd decided we'd heard enough of Kade's reprimands. Stepping back off the porch, it took no time for us to be in the beauty of the lush garden. Even though I could no longer hear the king and his council, some of the unease must have still shown on my face, because Gerald turned kind eyes on me, looking far less fierce than was normal for Kade's war advisor.

"The council thinks we should fight the fae separately, not join forces with you and your people."

I nodded, not at all surprised. No matter how much control Kade had over them, it was difficult to undo hundreds of years of animosity and mistrust. "Mine think the same. Stupid if you ask me. A sure way to get us all killed."

Gerald chuckled, giving me a nod. "I agree," he said.

That admission had me relaxing. One only had to spend a small period of time with Gerald to know he had a military mind like no other. It was he who had orchestrated much of the battle that had saved Kade's people when the fae first attacked us all, the night of the Red Queen's murder. Kade had told me all about it, giving me a completely new insight into Gerald. I respected him a lot in regard to these things. If he thought our two shifter races working together was a good idea, it made me feel better about my decision to push this angle.

Gerald bowed to me when we reached the middle of the garden – close to the faeling tree. "I'll leave you here. I have to attend to some other duties. The king will be by shortly."

Violet and Monica spread out then, giving me privacy and also scouting the garden for another dangerous razor-wielding fae. My gaze was drawn to the spot where Derek had lost his life, and I had to swallow down a huge lump in my throat.

Finn brushed against my leg, distracting me, and I took hold of his fur, stroking him softly. Without thinking, I placed my hand on the tree to support my weight and suddenly I was filled with that tingling feeling of mecca and life.

Hello, young Queen, the treeling said to me.

Hello again…

You don't smell your usual self. You smell of the Summer Court fae, the treeling said in its deep, multiple-trilling-voice.

My eyes widened. *Well, yes, I met with one just last night.* I sniffed my armpit. What was it with these fae and their sense of smell? Wait … how could a tree smell anything. Did it have a nose somewhere?

The treeling was silent for a moment and I wasn't sure what to say or if I should just pull my hand off.

Can I tell you a story of old? it finally asked, just as I was about to remove my hand.

Yes, of course. Story time with an old fae tree. Totally normal.

When I was first planted here, there were many shifters of both bear and wolf origin that lived here.

Okay... *Like spread out in the mecca?*

No, no, here in this house. The king was bear, the queen was wolf, and they had a mixture of each in their staff.

Chills trickled down my back. *That's not true!* No way our kind used to mingle like that. The tree must be confused.

It is true. The wolves and bears were always meant to work and live together. Only greed and misinformation tore you apart.

I yanked my hand off. I couldn't hear anymore. What he said was blasphemy. Treason. And ... exciting. Was it possible that any of that story was the truth? Surely someone would have known if bears and wolves existed together. It would have been passed down through our storytellers, especially if at some point bear and wolf shifters did not only coexist, but actually ruled and bred together. If that happened, where were their offspring? How did they cover it all up? Was there anyone alive, besides the treeling, who knew about this?

"Sorry to keep you waiting," Kade said from behind me, startling me. I jumped, and so was already half in the air as I spun around to find him right behind me. My breath went very shallow and all I could see in my head were the images the treeling had painted. Bears and wolves ruling together. It was like seeing Kade in an entirely new light.

Sure, he looked the same as always, strong, sexy, deadly, the epitome of a woodsman. His huge muscled body was coiled and lethal, just waiting to spring into action. Where had the usual warning gone, the one that generally flashed before my eyes when I was around him, slamming me with the reality of our situation – there could never be anything between us? Damn that tree. It had given me a brief glimpse of a life that I'd die for – bear-wolf children running and playing in this amazing garden, of Kade lifting babies up and spinning them around. My heart was literally bleeding as I stood there, stunned.

"Ari?" Kade stepped even closer to me, blocking out the sun. "Is everything okay? You seem distracted."

I shook my head in a jerky motion, trying desperately to pull myself together. It wasn't real. It couldn't be. And even if that had happened in the past, we lived in the present, and there was no chance for Kade and me. For us.

"No, I'm fine. Thank you for asking. Just been a long day. You know what I mean."

He ran his hand through his tousled hair, those amber eyes tearing me apart, but thankfully he didn't push me. "I understand perfectly. Today was one of my more trying since taking the crown." He leaned in closer to me then, with a mischievous glint in his eye. "So Gerald tells me you're ready to have this affair, earn the title our people are bestowing on us." His half-smile grew, the depth of his eye color deepening. Clearly he found this amusing, and I couldn't hold in my own laughter.

"You wish," I said playfully.

His face went dead serious in a millisecond. "Every day, Arianna."

I was pretty sure I stopped breathing then. Heat sizzled down my body and settled into my core. "The fae prince of the Summer Court visited me!" I blurted out, desperate to change the subject.

Kade's face turned lethal. "When? Why didn't you call for me? Are you okay?" He scanned my body as if looking for injuries.

I hugged my arms to keep from touching him. Why did this have to be so hard? I didn't want to feel this way forever. It was too much.

"I'm fine. He gave me a warning though."

"A warning?" Kade's voice was husky as he awaited my reply.

I nodded, bobbing my head like a creepy doll. "I need to fix the mecca and send the stolen energy back to the Otherworld, or the Summer Court and all their people and food will die off. If that happens, the Winter Court will come to Earth, kill us all, and take over."

He forced a smile, but it was more bared teeth. "No big deal, right?"

I huffed. "Right! So I'm here, with my mecca expert, asking for help."

Kade's eyes twinkled. "Mecca expert, huh?"

I shook my head at him. "Don't let it go to your head. I had to say something to convince him there was a shot at keeping his entire race from dying out. At least now the Summer Court is still holding onto some hope that we can fix this, which means they continue to battle our enemy and slow their takeover of Earth."

I bit my bottom lip, which was a bad habit from when I was younger. Kade's eyes darkened as he followed that movement. *Crap.* I knew there was a reason to not bite my lips, it created cliché moments like this where kissing that damn bear was all I could think about. I needed to squash this before it could heat up and get us both into more trouble with our people.

Freeing my lip, I said in a rush, "Just forget that kiss, okay? It was a mistake." The words hurt more than I thought they would, and when his face hardened and eyes went flat, I wanted to take them back.

"Arianna," he said slowly, "for as long as I live, I will *never* forget kissing you."

Then, for some stupid hormonal idiotic reason, my eyes filled with tears. The hard planes of Kade's face softened and he reached for me, but knowing if he touched me I'd completely break apart, I shook off some of my agony and schooled my face, faking a coughing fit. I ran for the house.

Finn was right with me. *What are you doing?*

I took a hard right, and through pure luck found the bathroom right off the sitting room. Finn and I snaked inside and I locked the door as a new wave of tears fell down my face.

I huddled closer to my familiar. *I have no idea what's wrong with me,* I wailed through our mental connection. *I think it's the stress. I didn't think being queen would be this hard.*

My best friend peered up at me with wise yellow eyes.

If you're being truly honest, it's not being queen that's much harder than you expected. It's falling for the bear king.

I let that truth settle into my head and heart. He was right in some ways. I definitely liked Kade – he was gorgeous, funny, a good kisser, and powerful. But so were Ben, Victor, and Blaine, and a lot of other guys – wolf-shifter-guys who were available to me. I just needed to focus my flirting and energy on a man I could actually have. Damn that treeling for giving me even one second of hope. Hope was a strange thing. Once it found its way into your heart, your soul, it was almost impossible to get it out. But it was a false hope and I'd do well to remember that.

"Arianna, open the door."

Kade's heavy fist fell against the bathroom door. I could sense his impatience and worry. He banged again, the heavy wooden door rattling on its poor abused hinges.

"Hang on," I said, with a bit of snarl. I would not fall apart in front of him again. Walking to the sink, I washed my hands and splashed water on my face, before patting it dry with a clean, folded hand towel.

Once I was satisfied that my face looked like I hadn't been crying, I knelt and looked Finn in the eyes. *No more talk of caring for the bear king. I will not be remembered as the queen who chose a fling over her duty and people.*

Because I was starting to think that's what the Red Queen had done, and look where that had left us all – completely screwed and at the mercy of a race far stronger than us. I would not let this thing with Kade become anything real. I was done. Today. Now.

I tore open the bathroom door to find Kade standing right on the other side. He had not moved an inch from when he was banging. The intensity he was exuding almost knocked me on my butt.

"Are you okay?" he asked, not backing up even an inch. His tone was all business, but his eyes were not. They were warm and caressing.

"I'm fine. Just had an attack of allergies."

He didn't move. This was it. Now or never, I had to choose: my heart or my people. The next words came out in a strangled rush. "Kade, there's something I need to tell you."

He didn't move, and his expression didn't change, but I sensed wariness in him. "You can tell me anything."

Do it, Arianna. Now! I told myself.

"I'm taking a mate."

Kade's hard expression remained. Just the slightest twitch in the corner of his eye gave away a deeper emotion. His reply was slightly glacial. "Congratulations."

"Thank you," I said, my voice barely a whisper. Then he just turned around and walked away.

I blinked a few times, the hard pressure on my chest increasing as his broad back disappeared out of the house. *Crap.* What had I done?

Ari... Finn started.

Don't. I don't want to hear it. Luckily we could speak mentally, because there was no way I'd have been able to speak out loud around the lump in my throat.

I needed to shove this painful searing in my chest way down and not think about it ever again. I needed to move on and focus on what was important – fixing the mecca and taking care of my people. After taking a few measured and deep breaths, I slowly walked out into the back yard. Monica and Violet were standing with Gerald. All three of them wore neutral expressions, but I kind of knew they'd heard everything.

I cleared my throat. "Where's Kade?"

Gerald showed none of his usual warmth as he addressed me. "King Kade shifted and went for a run. I'll escort you home now, Your Highness."

Just like that I was no longer welcome here, no longer allowed to be on friendly terms with the king. It was an uncomfortable drive back to the vortex. No one said a word. I'd upset Kade. I accepted my part in his ire, but we still needed to fix the mecca or we would both be screwed. Besides, when he had a chance to calm down, he would realize that what I had done was for the best. We'd been skirting around this stuff, flirting with disaster, letting the lines get blurred. It was time for one of us to make a stand.

Before I knew it we had arrived at the vortex and Gerald was escorting me out. When we reached the door, I wanted to say something, anything, to ease this uncomfortable situation that I had created. I opened my mouth but Gerald spoke first: "King Kade will meet you tomorrow morning at your estate to work on the fae issue," he said, and then bowed slightly before walking away.

My lip quivered a little and I wanted to cry all over again.

"Your Majesty?" Monica called out to me. I turned to find her standing with Violet and Finn at the vortex.

My best friend stepped closer to me, slipping her hand into mine. My aching heart clenched; her support was enough to send me over the emotional cliff again, so with one final squeeze I let her hand go.

Straightening my shoulders, I took a few deep and steadying breaths. It was time for me to be the queen shifter I had been born to be, time for me to get over my heartache, over the subtle but distinct rejection from Gerald.

Life was hard. Not everyone liked you. That didn't mean you had to let it ruin your day. Shaking off the drama with the king, I traveled back to Manhattan to do what I was meant to do since the day I was born. Be a queen to my people.

Chapter Seven

Love is like magic, volatile, beautiful, and scary.

AFTER WE ARRIVED back at Manhattan, I called a private formal meeting with Calista. If I was going to do this, I needed to dive right in before I chickened out. I remembered my mother telling me at a very young age that sometimes the best queens made the most sacrifices. When you died, your legacy only lived on in rumors and history of the time you ruled. The Red Queen's history was already beginning to be tainted by her rumors of a fae affair and love gone wrong. I didn't want that happening to me, to the red line.

Calista tapped lightly on the door.

"Come in," I called out, my palms sweating from nerves.

Calista walked through, clutching her tablet to her chest. "Your Majesty, you called for a formal meeting?" She was dressed in black slacks and a silk top, wearing her nice leather loafers.

"Sit down." I gestured to the large overstuffed chair in my office.

She sat and stared at me, probably wondering what the hell I was doing calling a formal meeting with my own advisor and close friend. I'd never done anything like this before, but protocol was important to the wolves, and I wanted to be seen doing all the right things.

I tried to keep my voice strong but it shook anyway: "I'm ready to take a mate."

Calista's face lit up with joy and surprise. "Oh! I wasn't expecting that. Wonderful!"

She hunched over her tablet and began typing notes. A queen declaring she was open to a mate was a formal process. It would be documented on this day, and preparations would begin.

"Yes, I think it's best that my people know once and for all that the King Kade rumors are just rumors. I am loyal to the wolves." There was no waver this time. My words rang true.

Calista nodded, smiling like a sixteen year old given her first car. "This is wonderful news, Arianna. A queen can be strengthened by a strong male at her side. Have you chosen someone or would you like me to open introductions?"

I paused. I hadn't chosen anyone. Opening introductions would be a long and tedious process, but I could see no other way.

"Open the introductions. Bring me only the best candidates."

It wouldn't be long before pictures and bios from around the world landed on my desk. I'd find all of them to be the strongest, most loyal, and fiercest males that the wolf shifter race had to offer. Calista, and likely the council, would sort through them and then bring me the top candidates. It was dangerously close to an arranged marriage, but I would have final say, and only after a few months of courting. I hoped that in this process I would genuinely fall in love. That was still hugely important to me.

Calista was up now, her eyes bright, cheeks pink. She would be a whirlwind of activity for the next few days.

I stopped her before she could leave. "One more thing, Cal." She met my eyes. "Tell me about Sir Baladar."

Sorrow blossomed out of her, then it was gone just as suddenly. "What about him?" she said, sounding cautious.

"I asked him how you knew each other and he said you were the love of his life."

Her shoulders hunched, and now there was no mistaking the pain on her face. "He did?" She forced out a strangled chuckle. "He's always so honest, to a fault."

I waited, but Calista just picked her cuticles, not speaking. After the last few days, and all the Kade stuff, I understood how hard it could be to talk about strong emotions.

"Calista? What happened?" My voice was softer now, and I stood, crossing around my large desk to stand before her.

She took in a deep breath and then met my eyes. "I was never the type to go out to parties or clubs or anything of that nature."

I envisioned the younger Calista as a bookworm who played mecca chess and studied. "So when my roommate came home with a key to an exclusive party, I wasn't interested at first. She finally convinced me, telling me that the key would expire the next day and that the party was so exclusive we may never be invited in our lifetime again."

I nodded. That would have gotten my attention for sure. "So what happened at the party?"

Calista smiled. "Baladar happened."

I noticed she didn't refer to him as "sir."

"He was greeting people at the door, handing out those magical drinks, which I of course refused, and, I don't know ... there was this spark when we locked eyes. It was like ... magic. That's the only thing I can liken it to."

I smiled, envisioning a young Calista falling in love. "Sounds like love."

She chuckled, wistfulness in the tone. "I wasn't prepared for him. He was so charming, so funny. He abandoned his own party and we talked for hours and hours." She stared off into the distance and I could see why he'd fallen so quickly for her. Calista was strikingly beautiful, super smart, and sure of herself. "We were together for two years, but then work got in the way and we had to spend longer periods apart and it just didn't work out. Duty calls, you know?"

My heart pinched. "Cal, was I the reason you guys finally broke up? My birth?"

Calista grasped my hand and squeezed hard. "Arianna, you and Winnie are the best thing that ever happened to me. I would not change one second of my life with you."

For the second time today I felt my throat tighten and tears prick my eyes. She didn't exactly answer my question, but I understood her meaning. Yes, my birth tore them apart, but she wouldn't have it any other way. Sometimes duty trumped love and that's just the way it was. A good queen knew that.

Calista stood with a big smile and clutched her tablet. "Enough of this sad talk. You're queen, and now on the verge of being mated. I couldn't be any happier!" She winked and I laughed. I believed that. This was what made Calista happy. Seeing my success as a queen, it reflected her good teachings.

"I'm glad you're happy," I said to her, and she bowed lightly before leaving the room. I stared at the door for a long while, trying to convince myself that this was the right thing to do, that one day I'd look back and be happy I chose this path.

The next morning I showered, had breakfast, and was dressed early. Kade was meeting me this morning to help me try and fix the mecca, and after our awkward conversation yesterday, I was dreading seeing him. I had made such a fool out of myself. Crying and running off! Declaring I was taking a mate. It felt like I was in high school all over again. Kade knew his duty; he knew we couldn't carry on with the flirting. He probably thought I was some crazy hormonal woman. Besides, probably after one night together we'd be over this attraction. Surely it was only this strong because our relationship was forbidden.

Right?

As I paced the secret library room that led to the mecca stone and tried to burn off my nerves, I startled at the light knock on the door.

"Come in," I called out with an unsteady voice.

The door opened to reveal Blaine. "Your guest is here, Your Majesty." He bowed deeply before letting Kade enter.

My legs felt weak as the huge bear entered, his molten eyes clashing with mine. He didn't say a word, he just stared at me, waiting for me to make the first move. His eyes did do a quick perusal of me. I was far more casually dressed than usual. My hair was down, and I was wearing tight yoga pants and a loose shirt.

Blaine was still waiting behind Kade with the door slightly ajar.

"That will be all, Blaine. Thank you." I gave my friend a brief smile, and he nodded before slowly backing out of the room and shutting the door.

"Thank you for coming," I said to Kade, forcing strength into my voice. I needed to make up for my loss of composure yesterday.

He nodded. "Despite the fact I would rather not be in wolf territory right now, I also don't want the Winter Court to rise up and wipe all of us out, so here I am."

His coldness hurt, but I understood and respected his feelings on this. If I was going to declare that it was time for me to take a mate, I needed to own the fallout.

Breathing deeply, using my meditation techniques, I calmed my racing heart. "Well, let's get right to it, then," I said as I walked over to the bookshelf, pulling the book down to open the secret wall and reveal the crystal room.

I felt his presence at my back. My awareness of Kade had not gone anywhere. "What's your plan?" His gruff voice washed over me, and I hated that he was close enough for me to smell his outdoorsy scent. He smelled like the first fresh pine needles at Christmas, or fresh cut grass in summer. Damn bear.

The wall opened and I had to take a few deep breaths to calm myself as the mecca energy slammed into me. "I don't have one. We're going to wing it," I said.

He exhaled lightly. "Great plan, Your Majesty."

I had to grit my teeth. Kade was in a nasty mood, and I could already tell he was going to have me ready to kill him more than once today. He was testing my trigger temper. I wasn't sure where my temper came from. My mother had been gentle and reserved, but I often lost control of my cool. The Red Queen had been like that though, so I just figured it was my royal right to be a bitch when I felt like it.

Picking up the pace, I stepped rapidly through the short hall and into the secret mecca stone room. Trudging through the heavy magic was the same as always, although there might have been even more resistance than last time. I stopped when I was close enough to touch the stone.

Kade stood beside me, arms crossed, staring at the crystal. I stared as well. Not speaking. The air around us was heavy with energy, and many other unspoken things. I couldn't remember our relationship ever being uncomfortable like this. There had been an ease between us even at fifteen.

"I'm sorry," he said softly.

I shook my head. "Uh ... what?"

He dropped his arms, a low groan rumbling his chest. "We shouldn't be experimenting with the mecca while there's anger and distrust between us. It might get us killed. So, I'm sorry, I've been stressed lately, and yesterday ... it was just a bad day. Let's forget about it, okay?"

If only it were that easy. I talked the talk ... said I was taking a mate. Acted like I was fine with it all. But no matter what I did, I couldn't forget Kade. The fifteen-year-old scrawny boy I had kissed on the Island was now a king and he was even more amazing than I remembered.

But he was right about messing with the mecca while angry. "You're right. I'm sorry too for being so blunt yesterday. And personal. It's all forgotten now."

He nodded and focused back on the crystal. "It's even more powerful than last time."

We both took a few extra minutes to let the strong energies settle into us, to allow the royal power we already owned mingle with the stone's power.

"So we just touch it and see what happens?" It was more a statement, but came out like a question.

Kade grinned. "Let's do it." He grabbed my right hand, placing his other hand on the crystal.

Energy sizzled up my spine as the mecca power rolled into me. Kade swiveled his head to see me better. "Now you touch it. Don't let go of my hand. I'll filter it if it starts to overpower you."

I nodded, trying to even my breathing before placing my left hand on the crystal and keeping my right firmly in Kade's strong grasp.

I sucked in as the crystal pulsed, nearly throwing us both back. I was so focused on the purple hue of my arms and the power coming through the crystal I didn't notice anything else. This was at least twice as strong as it had been during the Summit. The energy was everywhere, smashing against my wolf, against my alpha blood.

"What. The. Hell. Is that?" Kade's confusion broke me out of my spell and I looked up, following his gaze. Before me, on the far wall a … mirage had appeared. The wall was gone and a field of green grass now stood a mere six feet from us. The edges of the mirage were fuzzy but the picture inside so clear, so real. In the distance seemed to be huge mountains, lots of vast wilderness, and colors beyond anything I'd seen before. Everything looked like I could reach through and touch it. I had seen images during my Summit task, but nothing like this. This was almost … real.

"*Beware!*" That familiar mecca voice echoed within the room and I froze, chills running up my arms. It sounded like my mother – I would swear it was her – but my instincts were telling me it wasn't. Kade looked at me with one eyebrow raised.

"Did you hear that?" I asked him, unsure of what to do now. No one else had heard the voice before so I was astonished when he nodded.

"Yes," he said. "And I'm not liking this."

The image shifted slightly then, and a figure ran into view. My eyes were locked on, drinking in all the details. He was tall, wearing tan, fitted leather pants, a vest made of something similar, and tall soft looking boots. He held an intricate bow in his hands, ivory colored, looking like it was carved from bone. There was an arrow nocked in it. The male was looking away from us, his head turned to the side, which gave me a perfect view of his slightly pointy ears.

"Is this a memory, or something more?" Kade said, his voice low. He was doing that thing again where he tried to step in front of me.

At Kade's whisper, the hunter went still. His body going rigid, he whipped his head around and looked right at us.

"Not a memory," I said in a rush. *Holy heck!* This was an actual portal into the Otherworld.

The fae's brow furrowed, and before I could even think, he released the arrow.

"No!" Kade ripped his hand off the mecca crystal, and in a move almost too fast for me to track, thrust his arm out to intercept the projectile. It shredded through his hand, coming out the other end to rest against my chest. That bastard fae had been aiming straight for me, without thought or remorse. He had wanted to kill.

I tore my hand from the crystal, stumbling backward, and the mirage winked out in an instant. Finding my feet again, I rushed to Kade's side. He was just standing there, blood dripping from his hand, staring at me.

"Are you okay?" I tried to see his wound better. He was still staring at me.

"Kade! We need to get a healer to look at this."

He finally snapped out of his stupor, wincing as he looked down at his hand. "This is no normal arrow. It is laced with something that hurts like hellfire." Gritting his teeth, he reached with his uninjured hand and gripped the tip of the arrow. In a quick movement, he snapped the head off and then pulled the arrow out. As soon as it was gone, blood spurted out of the wound and flowed easily as I rushed to apply pressure.

"It's not healing!" I said.

Kade shook his head. "It's doused in something ... magic or poison." His eyes darkened then. "You would have died, Ari."

Finn, get Violet and have her come to the mecca crystal room. Kade's hurt. No matter how far in the world I was from my familiar, I could always call on him. I could have called on Violet too, as her queen alpha, but it would have taken too much time to sort through all the pack bonds within me. Time I didn't have right now.

I leaned in closer, my voice shaking as I said, "You saved me. Again."

My hands were pressing hard, sandwiching his injured hand, trying in vain to stop the bleeding. Kade was right. This arrow would have eviscerated my heart and kept it from regenerating.

He lifted his uninjured hand and cupped my face, those stunning eyes swimming with emotion. "Don't take a mate. It would be a mistake."

It got even harder to breathe than normal, but before I could do anything or reply, Violet was with us inside the room. She started toward us but couldn't make it all the way.

"Let's get out of here!" she shouted, her face crumpling as she fought the energy. In my panic over Kade I'd forgotten how strong the mecca energy was here. Either I'd gotten used to it, or Kade was shielding me from the worst of the effects.

Definitely Kade. He was always protecting me.

Keeping a tight hold on his hand, we waded through the magic to reach the tunnel and make our way out. Violet was already gone, no doubt waiting for us on the other side. Once we were all in the library room, and the pulse of mecca shut off behind the now closed door, Kade took a seat in one of the large reading chairs. The magic born wasted no time examining his hand. The first thing Violet did was smell it, her delicate nose crinkling prettily. Then she ran her palm over the top of it, hovering about half-an-inch from the wound.

She whistled low, her head coming up so she could see me. "Nasty old magic. I can fix it though."

She produced a bottle of liquid that resembled molten gold. Sometimes my friend was a walking apothecary; she almost always had the right elixir on hand – part of her extra-sensory, see the future thing. She focused on Kade. "You ready, King Kade? This is going to hurt like nothing you have ever experienced before…"

He looked at me. "I doubt that."

My heart clenched and ached. His meaning was clear, and so was the sorrow between us. Duty came first, for us both, but that didn't mean it wasn't painful. Our moment was broken when Violet poured the molten gold onto his palm and it began to smoke and sizzle. The bellow out of Kade's mouth had me and the magic born taking a big step backward; it had been the deepest bear roar I'd ever heard. My guards rushed into the room with weapons drawn, but upon seeing Kade, gritted teeth, rumbling chest, and bloodied hand, they lowered their weapons.

Violet looked impressed. "The last guy I did that to cried like a baby and passed out."

Kade took a deep settling breath and turned his hand over to see both sides of it. There was a shining gold filling the hole, and after a few moments the gold faded, turning into fresh pink skin.

"I cried a little on the inside," he said with a wink. Violet and I laughed at the same time, a nervous yet relieved sort of cackle.

"Okay, let's never do that again," I said.

Kade shrugged. "Not the most pleasant experience, but we might have just found our greatest weapon, and possibly a way to fix the mecca."

His meaning hit me then. Holy crap. We had a way into the fae lands. Could we fit soldiers through that mirage portal? If an arrow came through to our end, then surely we could send things into their lands. But why would we want to? Unless he meant...

"So if we could figure out how to manipulate the mecca, we might be able to use the stones to send the energy back to their side of the veil?" I asked, not sure if that was his way to fix the mecca.

As Kade nodded, Violet clapped her hands together. "I was in the newly unsealed magic library when you called," she said, her voice trilling with excitement. "I might have actually found some information to help with that."

She took off. I was right behind her, and even though he was quiet and graceful, a two hundred and fifty pound male couldn't follow without making some noise, so I knew Kade was there too. My guards fell in next to him, all of us chasing the magic born. Violet's hair whipped around her as she ran, and more than one surprised face turned in our direction. When they saw me in the midst, most of them averted their eyes, but some couldn't seem to turn away. Couldn't really blame them. We were an odd bunch. Especially the blood-spattered bear king.

Violet let us up three flights of stairs, past the late queen's private storeroom and into the small room filled with magical tomes, most of which were unreadable for all except magic born.

Jesabele and Seamus were already in the room, both of them with their heads bent over studying books, white hair reflecting off the magical light they must have all created. The room was very well lit, much brighter than the lighting originally in here. Everything was actually really clean too, which had to be their doing since this room had been sealed under the Red Queen's reign and only just now was opened. Walking deeper in, the room was much larger than I originally expected. At least ten by ten foot, shelves lining each wall from floor to ceiling. There were thousands of books. Some small, others huge. The moment I crossed into the room I felt a heavy pulse of magic; these books had old magic hidden within their words, I could sense it dancing across my skin.

"Are all of these about the Otherworld?" I asked, my voice breathless. "All fae magic?"

Violet shook her head. "Not directly. Most of these books are the long lost magic of the witches, but many of those spells are still fae in origin."

"Not so long lost after all," Blaine said, staring around. He'd fallen back with my other dominants near the doorway, all of them peering in to get a better look.

Violet's expression went dark then, shadows crossing over her. "It annoys me greatly that they have kept all of this information hidden. This is the rightful domain of magic born shifters. We're the descendants of witches."

The gene which triggers a magic born shifter to be born runs in a few specific family lines. They were the long-ago children of shifter and witch couples, and even though witches have not been seen since the dark war, random magic born continue to be born. Genetics are a funny thing.

"So tell me everything of importance you've learned." I took control of the room; the other two magic born were on their feet now, staring at me. "I want to know absolutely everything which might help us defeat the fae in battle."

Seamus crossed in front of me, and I wondered what he was doing as he disappeared behind a bookshelf. He was back in moments, dragging this huge white board across the room so we could all see it. I focused on the writing, recognizing my friend's messy scrawl. The words *Operation Nuke Fae* were up the top, underlined five times. I shook my head at Violet; this was typical of her, completely not-politically-correct. Beneath the title were dozens of bullet point notes. I started from the top:

- *Tuatha de Danann are thought to be immortal. They do not age and die, but can be killed by magic and by weapon. Never underestimate them, they're very difficult to kill.*
- *Weaknesses – they can burn out on mecca if they are forced to absorb too much of it or if they have too little of it at their disposal. Their magical objects of power are tied to all of their lives, and having one in your possession can control the mecca power of the court it originated from.*
- *They cannot lie, but do a very good job of telling half-truths.*
- *They struggle to produce young. Their long lives have slowly lessened the amount of Tuatha young that are born.*

*   *Their magical essence can be trapped during a special binding process, weakening them considerably. Iron can hurt them, as well as some manmade plastics and metals.*
*   *The five boroughs when divided are weaker. They must be joined to be at full power.*

This point gave me a moment's pause. What did that mean? Could Kade and my friendship, the first royal alliance in hundreds of years, actually be a thing that helped us in this battle? Did we just have to figure out a way to join our powers? How did we do that? Shaking my head, I read a few more points.

*   *The mecca is a blanket of energy which zaps constantly between the many mecca stones, on both sides of the veil. It flows between the two sides, keeping balance.*
*   *The mecca can easily move between both sides. All of the stones are joined.*

Holy crap. I stopped reading at this point; this was information which could be vital in our battle against the fae. Kade, reading over my shoulder, his heat wrapping around the back of me, moved closer as he said: "So if all of the stones are joined, it stands to reason we should be able to move the energy between them." He had reached the same conclusion as me.

Violet jumped in then. "Yes, so now that you know you can tap into the mecca energy, see and feel it through the stones, we just need to figure out how to move it around. Visualize where it needs to go and restore the balance."

"When I touch it, I feel this massive consciousness," I said slowly. "Almost like there are thousands of different facets to the stone's energy, but maybe it's the other stones I'm feeling. How did the energy move here in the first place though? What did the Red Queen do to make that happen?"

Had she used the mecca stone to start this pull of energy? It was too big a coincidence that the mecca energy changed the night she died. We already knew she'd done something to it. Now it was about figuring out what.

Jesabele was still holding her book, clutching it tightly to her chest. "It's almost as if the Red Queen had some sort of trigger in place. Upon her death the mecca would shift toward the Earth side. It has to be a spell, but so far we haven't found anything with that sort of power."

I let deep breaths calm me. Not only was the queen's death upsetting, the mess left behind for me to clean up was getting harder and harder to crawl through.

"Keep researching, I'm going to go and speak with someone who might be able to help."

I'd been thinking since the night I found myself in the brownstone across the city, that there was another reason Calista had sent me to the secret house with the special key. Like she wanted me to know there was someone with vast knowledge who I should be utilizing. Sir Baladar. After all of these years, he had to know some information which might help us.

Chapter Eight

All that glitters is a gold mine of information.

CALISTA AND MY dominants would not let me go to Baladar's on my own, so I promised them they could accompany me there, but that Kade and I would go inside to speak with him alone. We were the king and queen of the Earth side mecca, the only ones who could really fix this issue, and I wanted privacy if we were to speak of such sensitive things.

As Kade and I stepped out of the car and approached the door, I realized my palms were slightly damp. Nerves were getting to me. Glancing back, my guards spread out around the blacked-out SUV, arms crossed. They had their hands aloft, ready to grab weapons if needed.

Calista was inside the vehicle with Violet. My advisor was no doubt nervous about being back here, close to the shifter who called her the love of his life.

Reaching the door, I pulled out the special key before pausing and looking at Kade. "So this guy is ... different ... and his place is very magical. And possibly dangerous." I didn't know how to prepare Kade for the onslaught of loud music, glowing flowers, and dancing shifter socialites. Not to mention the random fae who seemed to show up there.

Kade gave me a sideways grin. "Don't worry. I'll protect you."

With a shake of my head, I worked hard to not roll my eyes at him. This damn bear certainly knew how to push all of my buttons. I stepped forward and slipped the key into the lock. The second it clicked, an eerie calm swept over us. I could no longer hear the street noise, or any noise really. Just the sound of my own breathing.

"Hmm," Kade said behind me, sounding a combination of intrigued and annoyed. I pushed the door open. Instead of being assaulted by loud music, black lights, and a long hallway, we were standing in a beautiful foyer with dark hardwood floors. Soft classical music was playing in the background. I stepped inside and Kade followed, shutting the door behind us.

There was no one in sight and I could not scent any shifters nearby. "Hello? Sir Baladar?" I raised my voice, stepping further into the room. I was astonished at the elegant beauty surrounding us; the inside was completely transformed.

How powerful was this magic born? He could create more than illusion, he could literally shift his entire space around to suit his mood or his guests. Kade tapped my arm and pointed across the open foyer to a hallway, where a stunning indigo blue and yellow butterfly was flapping its wings. As soon as we noticed the insect, it took off down the hall.

Kade and I shared a look. "Let's go," he said, stepping in front of me.

Gritting my teeth, I didn't argue. For now his ego could rest easy thinking it was the big protective, macho male. The hallway we traversed was extra wide, with tall ceilings and a rich maroon-patterned wall paper, gold flecks spattered across the bold color. Kade was huge enough that despite the width of this hall, I couldn't really see around him. Where was the butterfly now?

"God, how big are you? I can't see!" I grumbled.

He spun around quickly, too quickly for me to stop before I slammed into his chest. My breath escaped me in a rush as I put my hands on his biceps to steady myself. Kade's eyes went from subdued amber to molten fire in a millisecond.

"I've never had any complaints about my size before."

I swallowed hard, reminding myself to breathe. Of course breathing just meant I was inhaling his scent in large gulps, and that drove my inner wolf crazy. *Dammit!* I wasn't going to play into his flirting games any longer. Growling lightly, I stepped sideways and kept walking.

"Come on."

When I looked back he had a smile on his face. That damn bear knew exactly what he was doing. Picking up the pace I turned the corner, moving through a set of open double doors that led out into a ... *wow!*

I was standing in some type of butterfly atrium that was half inside and half outside. The entire room was screened with mesh and filled with hundreds of stunning and colorful butterflies. They flittered about, landing on the greenest and most vibrant flowers I had ever seen. The space was huge, maybe sixty feet long and twenty feet wide.

"Well, this is unexpected," Kade said, his eyes just a little wider than usual as he took in the beauty before us.

A streak of white caught my attention. Sir Baladar was walking toward us wearing casual white linen pants, a white tunic, and a little bowlers hat. He was beaming from ear to ear. "Your Majesties. I'm so honored to have you in my home." He opened his arms wide and bowed deeply.

I smiled and stepped forward. "Sir Baladar, the pleasure is all ours. This is King Kade of the bear shifters."

Baladar nodded. "We are well met."

Kade looked a combination of impressed and intrigued. "Well met indeed." He then gestured around to the butterflies. "Are they real? Or magic?"

Baladar got an extra twinkle in his eye then. "Isn't magic real? Can we ever truly tell what is real and illusion?"

Annnd now we were back to me having no idea if this was all a deception or if Baladar was the most powerful magic born. Ever.

A medium size, circular table appeared out of thin air before us. Atop the white table was an assortment of teas, including a steaming teapot, milk, and a variety of cookies. There were three chairs already waiting for us to fill them.

What. The. Hell?

"Please ... have a seat." Baladar gestured, his tone magnanimous.

Kade looked at me and raised an eyebrow and I knew immediately what had that wary look in his eyes. Sir Baladar was very powerful, and that clearly unnerved the king a little. Me too, if I was being perfectly honest.

Of course, since we needed Baladar's help, we had no choice but to play the part here today. We both sat, and I waited until the magic born was across from me before I leaned forward. I was done wasting time on pleasantries.

"We need your help in fixing the unstable mecca."

Sir Baladar nodded as if he'd expected this. "Magic born are fascinating creatures," he said randomly. "Did you know they hold a particularly close bond with the mecca? They can actually see the energy. Violet especially. It speaks to her."

I raised one eyebrow. "Yes, Violet is amazing, but what does that have to do with the help we need? Can she just speak to the mecca and tell it to move back to the Otherworld?"

I was confused, which was not a place I found myself often. Usually I was quick to figure things out. Of course, he did seem to be a shifter who erratically jumped around topics with ease, so it was probably not all my fault. Either way, I needed to know what he was talking about.

Of course, the more he was silent, the more I thought about his weirdness. Like why did he refer to magic born as if he wasn't one? Seriously, he had the white coloring and magical abilities, so what else could he be?

He leaned forward, peering into my eyes with his crystalline blue gaze. "You should know that magic is never that simple, Your Majesty."

It took me a minute to realize he was answering my question about Violet telling the mecca to return.

"The point I'm trying to make is that a magic born can temporarily share powers with their queen."

Kade sat up straighter. "So Arianna can temporarily see the mecca with Violet's help? But that doesn't tell us how we get the energy back into the fae lands."

Baladar shifted his gaze to Kade. "The truly fascinating thing here, King Kade, is that Queen Arianna just needs a little more vision, some more control over the energy, and she'll be able to call forth the mecca. And then you, with your affinity, can help her contain it, direct it even. It's almost as if your powers were always meant to be used together."

My cheeks burned as his suggestion settled over us. He was right. Kade had this rare affinity for the mecca and I was more linked to it than any queen before me. Neither of us really knew why, but facts were facts.

The bear king narrowed his gaze on Baladar. "How do you know I have an affinity for the mecca?"

The eccentric male just waved his hands. "Oh, people talk. That's my gift, King Kade, ferreting secrets from others."

Kade looked slightly uncomfortable. "My people don't talk," he stated with confidence. Then his expression grew a little uneasy. "Do they?"

Baladar bestowed the king with a broad smile. "Every Wednesday night I host a bear shifter night. Your people definitely talk."

My jaw dropped open. "Bears come to Manhattan?" I said loudly, letting my surprise and annoyance leak out.

Darkness crossed over Kade's features, and I knew his people were going to hear from their king about this very soon.

Baladar waved his hands in the air. "Let's focus on what is truly important here. You need to open a portal to the Otherworld. Get Violet to lend Queen Arianna her gift of mecca sight, then the special affinity inside of the queen will allow her to grab hold of the mecca. Then, with King Kade's help, you'll be able to funnel a large portion of the energy back to the stones within the fae lands. Assuming there is no foul magic at play here."

"And what if there is foul magic at play?" I asked. Knowing my luck, I could guarantee something foul was afoot.

He shrugged. "Then it gets more complicated."

Kade stood and I followed suit. We had our information, there was no time to linger. "Thank you, sir, for your wise council," I said. "We'll get Violet and do this at once."

Baladar put up a finger. "Not so fast … Violet can only lend her power during a full moon."

Of course it couldn't be that easy.

"The next full moon is the summer festival," Kade said.

We would all be on the Island partying the night away.

Baladar nodded. "After the festival, before the sun has risen, you must open the portal and give it a try."

Okay. The festival was two weeks away. I just hoped the Summer Court could wait that long, but this was our best chance as far as I could tell. I nodded to Baladar.

"We must go now. Thank you for everything."

He frowned, his expressive features turning somber. "That's a shame, I have so many stories to tell you."

I froze, my hand falling back to my chair as I tilted my head toward him. No queen was going to turn down an opportunity to learn more, and I sort of knew he wouldn't have stopped me if he didn't have important information to share.

I sat back down. "What kind of stories?"

He smiled. "How about I tell you one important story every time you visit?"

Okay, now I felt like a child being coerced into visiting a beloved grandparent.

"Alright." I was agreeing to his terms.

Kade said nothing, but he did sit beside me again. I wondered how much Kade actually knew about Baladar. He seemed reasonably surprised by everything he'd seen here today, but I knew him, and he wasn't ever really taken by surprise. He could probably sense that Baladar was one of the oldest wolves alive, and that he was our people's history keeper. If he hadn't known before today, he'd probably figured it out now.

"How about an origin story?" Baladar offered. "I'll keep it short."

Kade nodded and I did as well; I was all about origin stories lately. A butterfly landed on my shoulder and I smiled. Their beauty brought a little joy and lightness into the world. Baladar's entire posture changed when he morphed into storytelling mode; his expression took on a whimsical quality, and I almost thought I saw some rosy red in his pale cheeks.

"In the beginning, there were three races connected to the mecca: the humans, the Tuatha de Danann, and the witches."

I leaned forward, feeling my brow wrinkling. The origin story was not new, but ... this was different. Where were the shifters?

"The oldest of the races were the Tuatha, strong and powerful. Born of magic and energy, they controlled the mecca. Witches were humans that had a genetic affinity for the mecca, and were next in the power structure. Humans were last. They had very little connection or control to the magical energy which governs this area. For many years these three races existed together, but also very apart – they lived in separate but amicable worlds.

"The drama started with a forbidden romance, as most true dramas do. A high priestess of a powerful witch clan, Priscilla Cottington, fell hard and fast for a fae that lived nearby. They made love on the full moon, and nine months later had a beautiful pale, magical child."

Kade and I shared a look, the first magic born. I knew that magic born were descended from witches, but I'd believed it to be witches and shifters. So Baladar's story was a little different. I was most interested to hear where his account of the shifters was going to come in. As far as I was told, there were four races: human, fae, witch, and shifter. Shifters were evolved from humans, some sort of magical genetic anomaly which happened during the final days of fae on Earth.

"Then, one of the most powerful fae of all time, a dual animal-affinity male, named Wayland Lightmoon, who held the souls of both a wolf and bear inside, fell in love with a human. His human lover fell pregnant with twins. The children carried each a pure soul of their father's animals. One was a bear and the other a wolf. It was soon discovered that unlike their fae father, they not only had the animal affinity, but were able to actually shift into the form of their beast, and this was how the shifter race was born."

My face was pinched as I tried to sort this story out in my head. "Wait, so there weren't three magical races? We aren't evolved from humans?"

Baladar shook his head. "Queen Arianna, the shifters *are* fae. They are part fae, part human. The Tuatha never truly left the mecca, they just handed it off to their offspring. The full-blooded fae went back to the Otherworld because they are stronger on that side of the veil, but for all intents and purposes, you, Kade, and I are all fae." He leaned back in his chair. "That is the knowledge that landed me in here." He gestured around him.

Holy shifter. It was known that some shifters were descended from fae. This was the reason the Red Queen had so much power – she could trace her ancestry back to the fae. But the general gossip was that someone in her family had bred with the fae at some point. No one had ever stated that all shifters were actually descended from fae. This was much more than I thought. A fae with dual animal affinity was the creator of our entire race. And bear-wolf souls...

"Wolf and bear together..." Kade's voice was deep and deadly calm.

Baladar nodded. "In the beginning they were one and the same. Other bear-wolf fae began to mate with humans, and more and more shifters were born. For some reason that combination of animal-affinity fae and human are the only ones who produced children. Other fae tried to mate with humans but it never resulted in a child."

Geez, how many different types are fae were there?

"So magic born are descended from witch and fae?" My mind was reeling!

Baladar nodded, looking suddenly sad. "Only the bear-wolf shifter fae could mate with the humans to produce an offspring, but it was found that any fae could mate with a witch and create the powerful magic born. The dark Winter Court recognized early that the magic born were too powerful, and that's why they wiped the witches out. The few magic born we have left are descended from witches that mated with the bear-wolf fae and were smuggled into hiding."

Holy sweet shifter babies. I just sat there dumbfounded, thinking of what I would do if Violet didn't exist. Another thought came to me then.

"The heirs? The familiars? How?" My brain was buzzing with this new knowledge and also lining it all up with what the fae treeling had told me. It had been the truth. It all made sense now.

Baladar smiled. "The heirs are born from the royal line of the Tuatha de Danann. You're all descended from one of the four houses: Summer, Winter, Spring, or Fall Courts. You also have more fae in your genetics than most shifters. Once it was known that the fae touched with animal souls were mating with humans, each court wanted to have their own children represented. It's why you always have the four houses, Red, Green, Yellow, and Purple. One for each fae court. But you, Arianna, I must confess, you seem to me to be the most fae of them all."

I stood so fast I knocked the chair over. "I'm ... I'm going to need a bit of time to try and compute all of this information. It's a lot..."

Baladar stood and bowed his head. "Yes, of course, My Lady. I apologize. Before you go though, I do have one question to ask you ... when is your birthday?"

My heart was hammering in my chest. Why would he want to know that?

"December twenty-first," I finally said. It was no secret. Public records were available on the current queen for all shifters to access.

Baladar nodded like he'd expected me to say that exact date. "Yes, I'm starting to get a very clear picture now. That's an important date."

Yep, I was born on it, so it was pretty important to me. But seriously, how could that be more interesting than the fact that all shifters were fae? Part fae, anyway. It made me feel sick for some reason and I didn't know why. Hearing that we were bred like some prize or achievement for each court. Like animals. It was awful. I also had a sinking feeling in my gut that the House of Red didn't stand for the Summer Court, a court which I associated with the good guys.

Sucking in a few deep breaths, I forced myself to remember my training, to remember that we might have a powerful ally in Baladar, and I needed to be polite.

"Thank you for all of your help today," I said to him. "We'll pick this up another time?"

He gave me a small smile. "Of course, My Lady."

Kade had been very quiet for most of the story, although I could see a few veins bulging out of his forehead as he stared at butterfly covered plants.

When he turned and caught my eye, I almost stepped back. His copper irises were swirling, shadows visible in the depths of the molten color. He stood, and crossed over to stand behind me, closer than usual, his heat engulfing me and lessening the icy tendrils of shock coating my body.

"Well met," he rumbled toward Baladar, before we both turned to traverse the halls and find the exit.

Holy crap, shifters were fae. Like actual Tuatha de Danann mixed with humans.

I'd been so distracted I'd missed the fact that Baladar was walking us out, only noticing when we reached the door and his hand stilled on the knob. "Calista is here," he said, inhaling deeply.

My heart pinched a little. I could sense the sadness seeping from him. "When was the last time you saw her?"

He looked away; those pale eyes with lightning strikes through them were unfocused.

"We email each other every so often, but I haven't seen her in many years."

With that he ripped open the door. On the other side, hand raised, looking slightly flustered, was Blaine. Monica was on his right.

"You've been gone a while. We were starting to get worried," the commander of my dominants said, his huge body blocking the doorway completely. He stepped aside then, allowing us to walk out.

Baladar tsk tsked Blaine. "Your queen was perfectly safe in my home."

I noticed that Baladar stayed in the entryway; he made no attempted to walk out onto the front porch with us. He'd said he was banished here, as a punishment from the Red Queen; he literally could not walk out the door. There had to be a way to lift this banishment. It couldn't be true that now that the queen was dead, his only way of being released had died with her. Baladar was very powerful, though. If there was a way, surely he'd have figured it out. Which made my heart clench just a little tighter. It was a long life to spend trapped in a cage.

The car door opened, distracting us all. Calista stepped out clutching her tablet; she was wide-eyed and clearly a bit nervous. I could see her white knuckles where she held the small electronic device. The air around us charged as Baladar moved as far forward in the doorway as he could. They had their eyes locked on each other. Calista stopped at the first step and the intensity of energy zapping around increased. They stared at each other like nothing else in the world existed.

"Hi," Calista finally said. A simple greeting, but I could see the magic born's face crumble.

"Calista…" Her name on his lips was like poetry. The saddest poem you had ever heard.

A loud screech broke the moment, and Kade lifted his head to the sky. Nix was descending, her huge wings washing shadows across us all as she landed on the bear's arm. My line of sight dropped lower to where Finn was coming up the stairs. I reached out and ran my hand through his fur.

Where have you two been? I asked my familiar.

He nuzzled against me, his warmth so comforting. *We were scouting. I won't let the fae take anything more from you.*

The fae, right. I needed to tell Finn everything we had learned here today. *I followed along with the conversation,* he said before I could start. *Explains why the fae have familiars too. Clearly that is a royal trait, and those shifters strong enough are the ones who receive them.*

Yes, I said, digging my hands deeper into his fur. *So weird that we are both fae. You're from the Otherworld, and my ancestors and family are there now. It's all very different to the shifter history we're taught. Someone wiped this information from the history books. Someone didn't want shifters to know they are fae.*

I could sense that Finn agreed with me, but neither of us had any more answers about why that might be. Kade cleared his throat, and I realized that everyone was waiting for me to get into the car. Calista and Baladar were no longer Romeo and Julieting all over the place. They'd tucked their emotions back inside and were acting very polite.

Trying to follow their example, I turned to the magic born. "Thank you, I'll be in touch," I said to Baladar. He nodded, and I knew I would see him again very soon. After I processed the fact that I was part fae, I'm sure I would be hungry for more deep, dark secrets.

Violet peeked her head out of the car then. She hadn't bothered to get out. "This is cute but I'm starving, so…"

With a shake of my head, and a few chuckles, I strode back to the car. Stepping inside, and settling back into the rich leather seats, Kade's arm brushed mine when he dropped in next to me. Nix was too huge to come inside, so she had taken to the sky, Finn following her. Those two were fast becoming the best of friends. Which my familiar had never done with any others. Ragnar the Red Queen's lynx had been a friend, but still on a superficial level.

Kade and I were very close in the back seat; his scent wrapped around me, trying to cloud my mind and dull my senses. Shifting to see him better, my mouth opened, and before I could censor myself I said: "Want to grab some food with us?"

It was just Kade, Violet, and me in the car. Calista and the guards were in the second royal vehicle.

Kade's lips did that quirking thing where the dimple appeared and his eyes got all swirly. He was amused by what I'd said. Which part I had no idea. I wanted to ask him, but I was afraid of the answer.

Finally he said: "I can manage a quick bite, then I must get back to my people."

It was good that he was staying a little bit longer. We needed to fill Violet in on the plan for the next full moon. That was very important. This was what I was telling myself anyway. It had nothing to do with the fact that I wasn't ready to part company with him yet.

Hitting the intercom for the driver side of this beast of a car, I told Blaine about our plans to grab some food at the local pizza place.

There was a slight pause. "Are you sure we should go with such little guard? You and the king in one public place ... you're making it very easy for the fae."

"Blaine, you stress like an old woman," I said, trying to inject some humor into the situation. He was so serious lately. "We'll be fine. We won't stay long. I promise."

I heard his sigh and then the comm cut off. Seriously, we had some guards, plus Finn and Nix. We were strong. A couple more guards wouldn't make any difference if fae attacked en masse anyway.

Blaine chose Vinnies, which I had expected. The owners were wolf shifters and they had a special private party room in the back that they allowed me to use. Not only for my own privacy and safety, but also because humans frequented their restaurant and us sitting close to them for a long time would make them sick.

It was kind of ironic that for the most part the queen's security measures were in place to safeguard against a bear attack, and I was about to dine with the bear king.

Once Kade, Violet, Calista, and I were inside and seated around four large triple meat pizzas – Blaine, Monica and the other guards stationed about the room keeping watch – I started to tell everyone what we had learned from Baladar, focusing on his plan to try and fix the mecca. Violet leaned over listening intently, which was good, because she was a fundamental part of this plan.

The magic born was nodding. "Yes, that makes sense. If you and Kade can both see the mecca, then you will be able to work together to send it back! You'll know exactly how much to send and how much to keep so that we don't give the fae more power than is fair."

I picked off a huge chunk of sausage and popped it in my mouth. "You make it sound easy, Vi, but I'm sure tons can go wrong."

Kade, who had to be on his seventh slice of pizza, met my gaze. "I won't let anything go wrong."

The usual flash of mecca surged between us, and before I could say anything Calista pulled out her tablet and said, "I have your first batch of potential mates ready for viewing, Your Majesty. Would you like to cull some of them now?"

My stomach clenched; she had done that on purpose. She'd picked up on this ... thing ... between Kade and I and she had acted to bring it to a screeching halt.

My wolf howled, and my trigger temper went into overdrive. I didn't want to shout at my advisor in front of everyone, so I stood abruptly. "Excuse me. I have to use the restroom."

Violet stood as well.

"Alone," I clarified. She nodded and sat back down, not arguing; she understood.

My gaze swept over Calista, who I expected to look mortified, but instead she was wearing her look of stubbornness. I knew she thought what she was doing was best for me, but it was not her call to make. I had already taken steps to distance myself from Kade, so all she'd done was make things very awkward.

Needing to calm down, I blasted past Monica; her blond hair whipped around as she followed, but I held my hand up. "Bathroom. Alone." I attempted to smile at my dominants, but wasn't sure it was very convincing.

Letting the doors slam behind me, I did a quick room check. There was an old woman washing her hands. She'd jumped when the door slammed shut, scowling at me.

"Sorry," I murmured, deciding I might as well use the facilities while I was in here.

Stepping into the stall, I practiced some deep breathing, trying to clear the red haze from my mind. Of course, with a shifter's sense of smell, deep breathing in a toilet was so not a pleasant experience.

Why was I so angry? I felt like I was on an emotional rollercoaster when it came to all things Kade. I had agreed to take a mate, but after our fight the other day when I told him about it, it felt crass to just bring it up like that, to basically throw it in his face. No doubt everyone there knew Calista had done that deliberately.

After finishing up, I opened the door ready to head for the sink, when I came face to face with the old woman again. She was standing there peering at me with eyes that were not of this world.

Oh crap.

"Mon—"

Before I could finish shouting for my guard, the woman threw her arm out and slammed me back into the wall behind the toilet. Then she raised her arm, dragging me upwards using her powers, tight tendrils of magic choking the oxygen from me.

I tried to be calm, tried to think, but it's amazing how easy it is to panic when a dark fae has cut off your life-giving air.

Finn! I need you. Dark fae in bathroom of Vinnie's. Hurry.

I just had to survive long enough for him to get here and help me. Allowing myself a moment of stillness, I focused on my training with Kade. This woman was using mecca magic to hold me in place, and I was queen of the Earth side of the mecca – the stronger side now.

Taking hold of the electrical essence of my power, I let it crash out of me. With that one push, I broke the magical binds that held me and sent the woman flying backward into the sink, breaking it off the wall.

She was on her feet in milliseconds; her old-lady illusion dropped and I was face to face with a snarly female fae. She was taller than me, at least six feet tall. Her hair was blacker than death, her skin tinted with a greenish hue, and she had wide fae eyes and pointed ears. Not to mention the small nubby horns atop of her forehead, which told me all I needed to know. Not that I had much experience with it, but one would think horns were never worn by good people.

On my way, Ari! Finn's message blasted through my mind and I could feel his anger.

Monica was banging on the door now but it wasn't opening. Looked like I would need to get out of this one myself. My wolf was rattling my human body like a cage, trying to break free. We hadn't shifted for a while, which had my control shot. She was not going to take no for an answer, and I liked the idea of letting her fight the fae.

I dashed into another one of the toilet cubicles, sending my energy out to bar the door. I channeled as much as I could, pulling from whatever mecca was inside of and around me. A heavy thump slammed into the door but it held. I ripped my clothes off and let the energy of my wolf wash over me. Another thump on the door, but I couldn't lose focus. Shifting took time, but I needed to be quick today. The third rattle squeaked the door open a little, but my mecca binding pushed it back.

"You can't escape from me, Princess." The bell-like voice brought bumps across my skin. It was oddly singsong and creepy. "We'll end this before you end us all."

I wanted to care about what she was saying, but I was too busy having my body crushed into pieces and rebuilt. When the shift was almost over, I lost control of some of the mecca shield I'd erected; the fae crashed into the door and nudged it open a few inches. My energy didn't shut it again, so she managed to get her arm and leg through, inching the rest of her body through the gap.

She screamed out a war cry and lunged for me, her hands wrapping around my wolf legs. She then tossed me back out into the main part of the bathroom, and I yelped as I crashed against the wall. My side ached for a few moments as I shook off the hit. Water was pouring from the busted sink behind me, coating my fur.

I got to my feet. My shift was complete now, which meant I could tear this bitch limb from limb. This was why I wanted the wolf. She was animalistic in a way I could never be. She would not stop.

My wolf bared her teeth and the fae did the same. These fae kept coming to Earth, expecting I was an easy kill. Yes, I had guards. Yes, I was under constant protection, but none of that was because I weak. I would prove that right here and now.

With blinding speed she launched at me, just as I sprang up to meet her halfway. I called the mecca to me, building up a shield so that when she reached for me her hands were blasted backward. She'd done the same thing with mecca, shielded herself, but in her case it was weaker than mine, which meant I was able to reach her.

My jaws opened and I sank my teeth into the delicate flesh of her neck. Her blood hit my mouth and I wanted to recoil. It was like oil, a chemical taste. Mix that with the coppery floral smell coming off her and I wanted to vomit. But I held firm and shook her neck like a ragdoll, tearing through skin, bone, and muscle. Her razor-sharp nails slid down my back and I wasn't able to maintain any shielding; she cut through my fur, peeling back layers of skin. My instinct was to detach from her neck, but I forced myself to hang on. I had no true idea how to kill a fae, besides what the magic borns had written on the board, but I figured it was similar to how to kill a shifter. Our regenerative power was in our blood, so I was going to drain this fae.

My back was on fire with searing pain, but I kept ripping at her neck, trying to pull out the mecca energy I could feel inside of her – pull it into me. Draining her of power and blood seemed like a good fight plan. She'd surely need one or the other to survive.

She fought with everything she had; my back had to be torn to shreds by now, but at least the mecca energy inside of me was only growing.

That gave me the strength to fight the pain and hold on. It seemed to take forever, but eventually she slumped. Needing to make sure she wasn't trying to trick me, I held on until I could no longer hear her heart beating.

All of the fae who had attacked us so far, held vastly different levels of power. The ones who had struck at the vortex on the night of the Red Queen's death had been the weakest. The dark fae who killed Derek was still the strongest so far. Both he and this female before me tasted of old, powerful magic. Hence the reason I was lying in pieces on the floor right now.

The pounding on the door was louder now, rattling the hinges. "Arianna!" Kade was bellowing, very bear-like. An action I was pretty sure had been going on for some time, but I'd been too occupied to notice.

Focusing back on the fae, I remained diligent. Her heart might have not been beating, but it took a few more minutes for the magic to fade from the fae. I felt the last of it drain, and in that same instant the door blasted off its hinges.

I tried to shift away from the fae; I kept slipping in her nearly black blood, which was already coating my muzzle and body. It was thick, like oil, and I wondered if I'd ever get it out of my fur. Kade and Violet took in the whole scene, from the mangled horn-headed fae to my shredded wolf back. The bear king was partially shifted, in his massive form, clawed hands and bushy beard.

"Damn, you go, girl," Violet stated, and I gave her a weak but wolfish grin. I was pretty sure my best friend was incapable of being serious.

I could sense Finn charging his way through the crowded restaurant.

I'm safe, I told him, as I sucked up the pain and began to shift back to human form. This was the quickest way to heal my injuries and get back to fighting form. Of course I didn't think about who was in the room until I was standing stark naked in front of Kade. *Uh oh.*

Shifting in front of other wolves was no big deal. We had grown up doing it since we were babies, but shifting in front of the bear king after slamming on the brakes to our flirting was stupid. It was almost as if my wolf wanted him to see me like this. Kade's eyes caressed my body for a second, barely long enough that I could even be sure it happened. There was a flicker of heat there, but then it was gone as he let his body change back from his partial bear to his fully human form.

Violet stepped up to me, snapping her fingers as she walked. She now held a long white robe, which she tossed to me and I slipped into quickly. Finn's power brushed against me as he barreled into the room, moving to my side. Sinking my hands deep into his fur, I let his calming presence wash over me.

My eyes burned and my throat was tight, but I definitely couldn't fall apart now. We had to deal with this situation and make sure there were no other attacks on my people.

"Violet, get this body back to the castle and put it on ice. Calista!" I yelled. She poked her head in the bathroom door.

"Please pay for the repairs to have the bathroom fixed and find out if there were any other attacks in the boroughs," I said, my tone hard. She nodded, her tablet out, fingers flying across it.

Kade took a step away from me, his face unreadable. "I should get back to my people. Make sure there wasn't an attack there as well," he said.

There was so much wrong right now, not just with the fae attacking us, but also between Kade and me. Unfortunately, I had no time to deal with that. Neither of us did, so I simply nodded.

"Be safe," I managed to choke out.

"You too, Ari." His reply was soft, and then he was gone.

The moment his bright energy drifted from the room, my body caved in a little. I realized then, in a flash of clarity, that it wasn't possible for me to be just friends with Kade. There was so much more between us. Baladar's story had only made it worse. In the beginning, bear and wolf were one. A team. Stronger together. Somewhere along the line we had broken apart something that was whole.

If I were any normal wolf shifter I'd say screw the rules, I was taking what I wanted. But I was the queen, and selfish actions by me could bring down both of our races. Kade and I had to stop all of this, all the training; it was just asking for trouble. After fixing the mecca on the night of the summer festival, that would be the end of Kade in my life. Our people came first. The past was going to stay exactly where it was, in the past.

Chapter Nine

Summer fun. Summer love.

THE NEXT TWO weeks passed in a blur of organizing, training, and endless searching through the Red Queen's personal stores. I couldn't help my magic born with the fae magic library. Only a handful of the books were written in English. If I really concentrated I could understand the language of magic, of the Tuatha de Danann, but it was too hard to do it in larger texts. I was thankful to have Violet in charge of this research. I trusted her implicitly, and she was the next best thing to me being able to oversee it myself.

Of course, so far they hadn't turned up anything of importance, although as more and more fae magic and history was uncovered, more and more it seemed that Sir Baladar was correct. Shifters were not evolved from humans, we were the offspring of fae. Wrapping my head around it was still difficult. Especially since they kept trying to kill me and my people.

Since the day I got attacked by the dark fae in Vinnies, I had only seen Kade once, very briefly for a training session. We had planned to examine the dark fae's body together, but somehow it had disappeared before we could get it to my royal home. I couldn't figure out if I had a traitor in my mix, or if the Tuatha were becoming more paranoid about us finding out information on them. It felt like they'd spelled their assassins' bodies to return home after death. Probably we wouldn't have learned anything from the body, but it annoyed me that someone had snatched her away before anyone could check.

Tomorrow Kade and I would kick off the summer festival on the Island, then together with Violet we would send the mecca back to the Otherworld. I had a million things left to organize, but it was lunchtime, I hadn't eaten yet, and I desperately needed a break, so I snuck off. Some of my stress lifted as I wandered through the massive courtyard garden of the royal home;

crossing into the world of green had a calm descending over me.

Taking a good look around, I decided right then that I should spend more time here. The warmth of nature soothed my soul. In my opinion, the design and plant choices weren't as beautiful as those in Kade's garden, but it was still an amazing area, filled with large potted trees, rows of lavender, and other herbs. There were also long manicured rows of flowers, and a small duck pond near the back right corner. A few of my shifters kept the plants thriving and healthy. Kade took care of the garden in his own home, which was probably why it was so perfect.

Kade...

Dammit. He was distancing himself from me, and even though I should be happy about it, I found myself missing him. His wise council. His strength and kindness. It was often lonely as a leader, a life filled with responsibility, always having to hold yourself back from others.

As if she had heard my thoughts, a sweet voice shrieked my name, and I spun to find Winnie barreling toward me, her familiar and harassed looking advisor trailing after.

"Sissy!" she yelled again, her brown hair streaming out behind her, and the pure joy on her face lifted my spirits.

Despite my queenly outfit and heavy mecca crown, I took off toward her, reaching out to scoop her into my arms. We hugged for many long minutes, which was eventually too much for a five year old. She wriggled out of my arms, and with a cheeky grin reached out and tapped me on the hip.

"You're it!" She took off then, shrieking as she ran. I was right on her tail.

Eyes turned toward us as we dashed through the gardens, more than one person surprised to see the queen threatening her sister with tickle monster fingers. My heart felt light, free. It had been too long since I had these moments with Winnie. There was an uncomfortable feeling in my chest when I thought about things I was going to miss by being so busy. It was my duty, and growing up I had felt that distance from both my mother and the Red Queen, but I didn't want that for my sister. I wanted her to feel so much love that she never had a moment of loneliness. I wanted to protect her from the harsh realities of life for as long as I could.

Picking up my speed, I caught Winnie and proceeded to tickle her until she couldn't breathe. Which is what big sisters are for. Afterwards we both lay in the grass staring up at the cloudy sky. There was a smogginess to it, typical of the city, but that didn't bother me.

"Can you see a crow?" Winnie asked, pointing toward a fluffy white cloud. It had wisps spanning off of it, which did look a lot like wings.

"I see it," I said. "And look, there's a boat."

Winnie followed my pointed finger, and her little face was so peaceful as she stared up, snuggled in next to me. Rhett, her fox familiar, scampered across then and lay by her side. Then a heavy warmth and strong burst of energy dropped beside me.

Finn.

Hey, friend.

He nuzzled into my side, and then his mind went soft and fuzzy, like he was on the verge of sleep.

"We go on the boat tomorrow, Ari. I can't wait."

Winnie was coming to the summer festival; it was her second time, but her first time as a true queen heir. Rhett had appeared for her just before her fifth birthday, in October. She now wore similar teeth marks to me on her hand, the moment of their bonding.

"I can't wait either." I turned to my side, facing her. "It's going to be so much fun, you'll be able to play with the other little heirs, and see all the festivals. Lots of food. Lots of fun. Plus you can wear your costume."

Winnie was going as a mermaid; she had her fake tail and long red wig. The movie was her current obsession.

"I hope I meet a bear friend like yours," she said, her little hand snaking out to hold mine. "I like Kade. He's very nice."

I froze then, my hand tightly gripping her tiny fingers. "What do you mean? How do you know King Kade?"

With all the innocence of youth, she giggled. "Last time he came for your training session, he took a break outside and Rhett fell into the duck pond. I went in after him and almost drowned. He saved me and told me to call him Kade. Said he was your friend. He smelled like a bear but I liked him very much."

Damn Kade, even winning over my sister. And saving her from drowning and not even telling me! "You need to call him 'Your Majesty' or 'King Kade,' Win," I said as gently as I could. "You know how important protocol is."

She was silent then, just for a moment, before she burst out with, "I hate protocol, it's yucky."

I tried to hide my laughter behind a cough, before I pulled her in for another hug. You and me both, kid, you and me both. Protocol would probably be the death of me.

At least ten thousand wolf shifters made the trip each year to the Island. They came from the three boroughs, and also many from around the world. Calista had warned me there would be even more this year, with a new queen and all. Most of them had already landed and were setting up. There would be tents, motor homes, and all of the rental houses packed full of shifters. The Island's normal residents were aware of the summer festival; they thought it was a longstanding popular music festival with super exclusive tickets. None of them minded though, they usually left and rented out their homes to make money. Any stray humans that caught sight of any weird goings on would be compelled by a magic born to forget.

Nerves had me all tangled inside, for more than one reason. First summer festival as queen and the fae were probably trying to figure out how to kill us en masse. And here we were gathering together to make it easier. Hopefully the Summer Court's Prince Caspien was managing to keep his army strong. Violet had recently used the flower to let him know that we had a solid plan for fixing the mecca and that it would happen tonight. He'd been thrilled and passed on the news that they'd managed to retrieve his people's object of power, which was helping a bit, but that circumstances were still dire.

So much rested on this ritual tonight under the full moon. We were placing so much faith in Sir Baladar and his theory, so much faith in mine and Kade's abilities to manipulate the mecca. I knew I couldn't fail – I wouldn't fail my people. But I would be lying if I said that I was supremely confident about our success.

Being queen ... no one told me how hard it actually was. How many ways my time and attention would be scattered. Not only did I have to make decisions that affected all of my people, I had to anticipate things going wrong and make sure they never happened. Easy, right?

I was making my people proud in one way, a way I wished was not part of my life. Word of my taking a mate had gotten around and shifters everywhere were rejoicing. I had exhaustingly gone over the many possible candidates with Calista and narrowed my choice down to three men. They would all be flying out for the festival. Over the next month they would stay in the city so I could take turns getting to know them. I should be excited, I should be thrilled, but I wasn't. I was depressed. It felt like I was living a lie. One of the men, a very handsome and successful dominant from London had called me on the phone last night. He was polite and had a good sense of humor, making me laugh several times, but … there were no growly undertones to his voice to clench my belly and send the butterflies fluttering. He wasn't Kade. I shook my head to clear those thoughts when a knock came at my personal door.

"Come in!" My costume seamstresses were right on time. They peeked their heads into my sitting room before wheeling in a large cart with a huge dress lying on top. It was covered in white silk so I couldn't see the details. They had been over two times in the past week for fittings, but Jenny, the stocky golden-haired one, and Christy, the strawberry blonde, would never let me see the complete finished product. The pair were fun and lively, and we'd become friends in the past few visits, but no amount of friendship or cajoling had convinced them to show me the dress in any of the fittings. They'd even gone as far as to blindfold me.

They couldn't hold out any longer though. Today was the day.

"Oh, come on, girls. It's the day of the summer festival. Let me see it!" I pointed to the white silk.

Jenny shook her finger. "Not yet, Your Majesty. Let us put it on you and then you can look."

I groaned but obliged. Not only did they make me wait until they put it on, but I also had to wait for my full hair and makeup to be done. "Come on, it's been an hour. Let me see," I begged as my makeup artist sprinkled some glitter in my hair. It wasn't the summer festival if you weren't covered in glitter.

"Okay, Your Highness, you can look now."

I had no idea why I was so excited. Going crazy over clothes was not my normal personality, but there was a magic to the summer festival. It had always been my favorite time of the year.

Spinning around, my breath caught in my throat as I took a second to stare at my reflection in the full-length mirror. The upper bodice of the corset was a soft baby pink, laced so tight my breasts were pushed up high into my neck, but because I was naturally small breasted it didn't look slutty – just made my B's look like C's. The gown then fell out into a large bell shape from there and slowly went from light pink to a deep teal that matched my eyes. As if this weren't breathtaking enough, I was wearing teal glittering wings, and a mask of shimmering pink had been painted around my eyes, and streaks of my hair were coated in teal glitter.

I was a faerie – ironic, really, considering the war we were fighting, and the information Baladar had spilled about the origin of shifters – but there was no denying that Jenny and Christy had done an amazing job. I couldn't have chosen better if I'd tried.

"You're breathtaking," said Calista from the door, and I turned to meet her gaze. I felt my body relax, and realized I was no longer angry with her. After reprimanding her for talking about my potential mates in front of the king, things had been a bit awkward between us, but seeing her now, her pride as she gazed at me, I put it all to rest.

I turned to my two costume designers. "Thank you."

They both curtsied. "We will see you tonight, Your Highness," Christy said as they left with the hair and makeup artists. Then it was just me and Calista. I finally noticed her festival outfit. I had to smile at how amazing she looked in her deep purple mermaid silk gown. She had a fake tail across the bottom of her dress, and shells woven into her hair.

"You look fantastic, Cal," I said, knowing she'd probably let Winnie choose her costume for her.

She caught me off-guard then when she crossed the room and scooped my hand into hers. What had brought on this sudden break in protocol and show of affection?

She leaned into me. "You're happy, right, Ari?" I startled when I noticed that her eyes were dancing with tears. Where was this seriousness coming from?

She was just standing there, waiting for my answer, so I thought about her question. Really thought about it. Generally, I'd just answer with an affirmative. Most people didn't ask that sort of question really wanting to know the answer. It was a throwaway, an attempt to show that you cared without actually having to care. But I knew Calista wasn't careless with words like that, despite some questionable actions of late. She genuinely wanted to know.

Was I happy?

I was the queen of the wolf shifters, about to be honored at one of the greatest festivals we had, and afterwards I was going to fix the mecca and save everything. All happy things. All things I'd strived for my entire life, successes I could count as my own. But was I happy? A deep part of me shouted "No!" There was a hole inside of me that I feared could never be filled. If I were to fill it, my kingdom would fall into chaos.

I didn't want to lie to Calista, so I said: "No, but I hope I can be someday." Then I squeezed her hand and fled from the room before I could cry. This was the summer festival and I would not ruin it with my sorrow.

The boat ride to the Island and following drive up to the royal home was beautiful. It was around noon and the sun shone high in the sky, illuminating all of the breathtaking party décor. People ran out of houses and tents to greet my entourage, and I was so humbled. A new queen and the summer festival – it was a happy time for my people.

Despite the select few alphas I had chosen to share knowledge of the fae with, most shifters didn't know the true extent of the fae battles being fought behind the scenes, and I would do everything in my power to make sure they never had to find out. I waved until my arms ached, and even leaned out the window to brush against the children's outstretched hands. People's smiles were infectious and I couldn't help but feel my spirits lift. I was causing this happiness in them, my presence. What an amazing thing. I realized then that maybe I had not been completely truthful to Calista – there might be an empty spot inside of me, a sorrow I couldn't shake, but there was happiness too. My people made me happy, and being their queen was an honor. Maybe there would always be this void inside of me, but I could live with it if I brought such joy to their lives.

As we reached the royal home, my happy glow dulled at the sight of Selene standing on the porch with Torine and a few other council members. She was decked out in a full gold dress with draping tulle and glitter. She also wore a diamond tiara. Looked like she'd come as a queen. Typical Selene.

I wasn't exactly surprised to see them all. The royal Island home was spacious and could accommodate Selene and the entire council, but I'd been hoping they would choose to stay elsewhere. As my car drove down the long tree-lined road, we passed half a dozen large motor homes and I spotted Blaine grilling hot dogs with Ben. The guards would stay in the motor homes and surround the property to ensure I was safe. I used to camp with them. We'd never stay in one spot for long, driving our motor homes around the Island, parking in all the best places for the festival. A huge part of me missed those days.

The vehicle pulled up in front of the royal home. The council and Selene bowed in greeting as I exited the SUV. When I was standing before them, my full costume on display, Selene's eyes narrowed on me. Her features darkened and it was clear she was regretting her costume choice, wishing she was the queen, with access to my amazing seamstresses.

Never going to happen.

"Greetings," I said to everyone, and I was pretty proud of my sincerity. I actually sounded like I liked them all.

Making my way up the large staircase, I was pleased to not see Selene's familiar around. She had not forgotten my threat to turn him into a fried snake delicacy. Torine stepped in beside me, taking a look at my gown and smiling. As much as the council was driving me crazy lately, the summer festival was a time of merriment, so I returned his smile.

"How is security?" I asked.

The council was responsible for the security of the event, tasked with keeping the two shifter populations at peace, and keeping prying human eyes from seeing anything otherworldly. They would keep the four magic born close by in case of any incidents. Violet, Sabina, Seamus, and Jesabele were on their way right now. My best friend had my crown in her possession. I'd need it for later when the official ceremonies kicked off.

"Security is top rate, as always. We have no incidents to report, and the bear king has already paid his respects." He waved a hand as if that was that and I didn't need to hear anything further.

All I could think about was the fact that Kade was close by. I forced myself to focus.

"Did Violet spell the water?" I asked, wanting the council to know I was staying on top of things. No longer would they be pulling my strings in the background. Not to mention they were stupidly unconcerned about a fae attack during the summer festival.

Torine's face creased into a look of such arrogance that I wanted to punch him in his straight teeth. "It's all fine, Your Majesty. Go out and mingle with your people."

Hah! Just like that I was dismissed, no more useful than an ornament on a Christmas tree. Just hanging around to pretty up the place. Bastard.

Selene was looking rather smug, but that look fell when I cut her with a glare. A blast of warm wind, ancient power, and familiarity trickled in across the porch and I calmed. Finn was near. Turning, I saw him galloping toward me. He reached me in seconds, his warm body brushing up my side.

Fancy meeting you here, I teased.

Interesting choice for costume, Ari. Freudian slip on the seamstresses' behalf, I think.

Always one step ahead of everyone else, I wasn't surprised that he'd noted the fae nature of my costume. No one else had yet. Thank God for Finn. I would literally be curled up rocking in a corner without him.

Calista crossed over to me. She'd been organizing all of my things out of the car and into the royal home. "Time for you to mingle, Your Majesty," she said to me. "The official opening ceremony is in a few hours, but for now you need to be out with the people, reassure them with your presence."

"Okay, please send Violet to me when she arrives." I made a point of saying this loud enough for the council to hear.

Calista nodded, and started typing away on her tablet. Within seconds I had a royal contingent of dominants around me. My five inner circle were the closest to me, and at least twenty others streamed out around us.

I shook my head. "I won't greet my people with a wall of security between me and them. I will take my five, and they can call for backup if anything happens."

Torine shook his head. "It's not safe. You're queen now. Think what would happen if you were to be hurt, or even die here. We cannot allow it."

Well, that sounded an awful lot like an order.

I stood straighter, a few specks of glitter flying off my arms. "I am the queen, you allow nothing. If you want me to allow you to remain on the council, you will not question me in such a manner. I am neither rash nor stupid. I consider each and every decision. The shifters need reassurance right now, not only because of the death of the Red Queen, but also all the new security measures we have had their alphas implement. They are rattled. Seeing me striding around with more security than the president of America and the queen of England combined is not a great way to reassure them that everything is okay, that we have things under control."

Before they could utter anything more, I turned and strode off. By the time I was halfway out of the long drive, Finn, Blaine, Monica, Jen, Ben, and Victor were the only ones at my side. My declaration had been heard, and my reasons found sound, since not even Calista argued with me. It was the right decision to make. I hoped so anyway.

You're a good queen. You put your people first. Don't question yourself. The council has served their own purposes for too long.

I ran my hand along Finn. He already had on some of his harnesses and glittery adornments. Later he'd be saddled so I could ride him for the opening ceremony. Kade would join me, his familiar Nix by his side. This was how we maintained peace during the summer festival, by showing unity between the two leaders. I tried to remember if I'd seen Kade and the Red Queen last year.

I turned to Blaine. "We missed the opening ceremony last year, right?" Jagged snippets of memory were hitting me. Calista had blasted me because I was an heir and should have been front and center.

"Yes, Selene spiked our punch. We ended up half-naked on the south side of the Island. We were lucky we didn't drown."

"Crap, that's right. I'd forgotten she did that."

Flickers of memory were coming back to me. I'd woken up with a massive hangover the next day and Selene had been the heir of honor for the rest of the festival; the Red Queen had refused to speak to me. I hadn't thought about that for a year, but it was one of the many reasons I hated that redheaded harpy. She'd been a pain in my butt for too many years. I couldn't believe she was the backup queen.

It took the masses of wolf shifters many minutes before they realized I walked among them. It was only as I started to send out waves of warm mecca energy that faces turned toward me. I took my time, smiling, waving, sharing the energy of our mecca with them all. Blaine and Monica remained on point, each to one side of me. The others were a little further back, which made it seem like I was almost without security. Which is what I wanted.

My shifters looked happy; their children ran and played with abandon. There were no bears on this side of the Island yet. That would come later.

"Greetings, Your Majesty."

"Queen Arianna."

"The Red Queen lives again."

Shouts and choruses of words washed across the entire area. Then a boy of ten rushed over and grabbed my hand and silence descended throughout the tree-filled field. Faces drained of joy and I could feel urgency in the air. Everyone was waiting to see how I would deal with this child who had broken one of our golden rules and grabbed the queen without permission. I knew how the Red Queen would have dealt with him, but despite being from her line, I was happy to be nothing like her.

"Craig!" The frantic voice of a mother in distress reached me as she rushed forward. She fell to her knees beside her son, who was still clutching my hand. "I am so sorry, Your Majesty. He did not mean to break protocol."

I glanced around the crowd once, before lowering my gaze to smile at the pair before me. I then surprised everyone by dropping to my knees so I could be on the same level as them. "You need not worry for your son," I said. "I know the difference between harm and a happy little boy." I then kissed both of them on the cheek, before pulling my hand back and getting to my feet.

"Go!" I shouted out to the crowd. "Go, have fun, and be merry. This is the summer festival, and we will know nothing but joy!"

Noises and laughter started again, and I felt the warmth and love that I had showered out being returned to me. A true leader knows that respect and love are not given freely. You must earn the respect and love of your people, and I was determined to be a queen worthy of both.

Chapter Ten

For just one moment, time stood still.

IT WAS OPENING ceremony time. Calista had spent the last thirty minutes making sure I was versed in my duties. I was already perched on Finn's back, his strength comforting as always. My hair and makeup had been touched up, dress adjusted, mecca crown now atop my head. I was a wolf shifter queen, dressed as a faerie queen, about to stand next to a bear king. This was like the start of a bad shifter joke.

I had no idea what Kade was dressed as, or if he would even honor the tradition by dressing up at all, but I couldn't wait to see him. I stood off to the side of a recently erected stage, two throne chairs perched upon it. Not my mecca throne from back home, just one that was used during the summer festival. I could see the crowds out there waiting for us, a veritable sea of shifters spread out across a massive cleared hill in the center of the Island. Bear and wolf together ... well, sort of. There was still a divide, but the mingling energy was strong. The mecca was loving the closeness of the five boroughs, and it danced with abandon beneath my skin. It was hard to tell under the glitter and body paint I wore, but my skin had a fine purple glow about it, which seemed to be happening more and more lately. The pull of mecca from the Otherworld to Earth might have slowed, but the imbalance remained, and it was clearly starting to affect those of us closest to the power.

An influence which should be over after tonight. I let my eyes linger on the bright beams of the full moon. It could just be seen in the setting sun. Our special fae ceremony, the one in the mecca room at the castle to call on the fae portal, would take place at midnight, the time of the fullest moon.

"Time for you to take your throne, Ari." Violet leaned in and gently brushed her lips against my cheek, careful to not really touch me, for multiple reasons – my glittery makeup and her ability to read the essence of anyone she touched being two of the biggest. "If we lose each other during the night, I'll meet you at the boat docks just before midnight. I won't let you down."

I blew her a kiss. "You've never let me down. Now go out and have fun. I'll see you later." I let my eyes linger on her costume. She was in Renaissance garb, of course, so it wasn't really a costume, but she'd gone much more detailed than she usually wore. Tonight she was in a bright, vibrant pink, her hair elaborately up-styled with small ornaments woven into it. She had on some body paint that glowed against her white skin and hair. The glitter was sprinkling everywhere and mecca energy was oozing from her very pores. This was going to be one hell of a night, that was for sure.

When the music started Finn began to walk us into the massive crowd of thousands of gathered shifters. We were on Apple Hill, a breathtaking open field that was high enough to look out onto the ocean, almost directly in the center of the Island. Both bears and wolves were on this hill, and I was pleased to see a few talking to each other rather than standing with their own kind. At the base of the hill was a cherry tree grove, and beyond that grove a little empty cabin that few knew about. It was there that Kade and I had kissed over five years ago.

Faces turned to greet me, and I was pleased to see most of them smiling, only a few scowls.

Every queen knows you can't please everyone; the former Red Queen went out of her way to please no one, but I believed in catering to my people. At least a small amount.

Behind the stage was a beautiful adornment of hundreds of flowers that had been strung up. As Finn brought me out of the crowd and up to the stage's steps, I saw Kade. That damn bear. It felt like forever since I'd seen him, and as I found my gaze glued to his tall frame, my heart began to pound in my chest. My palms grew sweaty and my stomach was in knots. I knew there was no point denying it any longer. I had fallen for the bear king.

He was dressed in a worn pair of jeans, a red and black checked flannelette button-up, which was open at the neck, displaying a lot of bare, muscled chest, and he had an axe thrown over his shoulder. Add in some rugged black boots and ... hot damn. He'd just brought my fantasy to life. He was a huntsman.

Heat shot through me and I wanted to fan my face. He could have literally come to the summer festival naked and it wouldn't have been as hot as his woodcutter outfit. Okay, maybe not literally naked. Naked was the clear winner. I was a fan of naked. But seriously, did he somehow know I thought of him as a sexy woodsman? Maybe Violet told him? I wouldn't put it past her to start matchmaking behind the scenes.

I knew my cheeks were pink as I stepped off Finn and ascended the steps. Kade outstretched his hand to help me up the final few. Pushing aside naked thoughts, I took his hand, and as I looked into his warm golden eyes, everything else melted away. In this moment I forgot that thousands of shifters were watching us. I forgot that both of our lives and crowns were on the line. It felt like we were the only two in the world. Suddenly the crowd began to cheer, and like a swift kick to my clenched stomach muscles, I was reminded of where and who we were.

"Kade," I breathed now that I was a mere foot away from him. I finally noticed Nix on his shoulder, and I realized how single-focused I had been on the king. How did one miss a massive eagle?

"Arianna," he murmured back. God, the way he said my name made my stomach clench again, the desire heating even more within me.

I cleared my throat. "Happy summer festival."

His eyes narrowed the slightest bit, as he turned his head, assessing me. "Are you actually happy, Ari?"

I realized then my hand was still in his, so I pulled it back, rubbing it quickly across my face. A lame attempt to mask my shock. Breathing deeply, I tried to suppress my very strong emotions. It had been a huge, overly emotional day already, and I was having trouble containing myself.

Finally I said: "You're the second person today that's asked me that."

Why did shifters keep asking me this? Making me examine my feelings. I was much better with the suppress-until-I-had-to-deal-with-it type of existence. Was it that obvious that I was miserable inside?

Before either of us could respond further, howls rose up, followed by bellowing roars. Our people wanted a speech. Kade gave me one more long look, a look that said a thousand words, before he turned to the crowd.

"We have gathered here today, just as our ancestors before us, to honor the peace between our people and bask in the beauty of this season. I think I speak for both Queen Arianna and myself when I say that we wish you health, prosperity, and love on this blessed day."

His voice held such strength and sincerity. Despite his confession to me on the night of my coronation that he had never been meant to be king, it was clear that this was the role he'd been destined for. I nodded in agreement and let my voice be heard.

"For a long time we feared and even hated each other, but let tonight be a clean slate. Let us come together and drink, eat, and be merry. Let us make new memories for generations to come!"

The crowd went wild then, throwing their fists in the air and screaming as the music picked up. They all began to dance. From my previous years here, and the sight of many lifted beer mugs, I knew that at least half the crowd was already drunk, but that didn't matter. My people were happy, and that made me happy.

Kade and I both turned then and made our way across to our thrones. Just before I took my seat in the high-backed, jeweled piece, I turned to Kade and looked him dead in the eyes.

"Yes, I'm happy." Right now, in this moment. I wasn't sure if I'd just lied to Kade, or to Calista earlier.

The bear king's eyes turned dark as he nodded. It must have been the wrong thing to say, because over the next hour we drank, ate, watched dancing and fire throwing, and Kade uttered not one more word to me. Finally, when the sun had long set in the sky and it was dark, he turned to me. His stare was ... it was dark. And a part of me broke as I returned that gaze, helpless to tear myself away.

"What?" I finally managed to ask.

He reached out as if he was going to touch me. His huge hand stilled inches from my face, and I was struggling to breathe, struggling not to sob. Emotions were ricocheting through me, and I knew everything was about to change. I could feel it in the ache that had spread all the way into my soul.

His voice rumbled out. "I'm not happy."

Then he stood and walked off the stage, making his way through the drunken partying crowd. I was frozen to my seat, my hands clenched at my sides while I tried to pull myself together. How could he do this to me? At the summer festival where every eye was on us. Why wait until now to burst the bubble on the "just friends" world we were living in?

I stood, angry that he had this effect on me and that he thought it was okay to leave me up here alone. I mentally called for Finn, and as soon as he made his way to the stage, I got onto his back again.

I ran my hands across his fur. *Can you follow Kade's scent? I need to speak with him.*

No problem. One moody king coming right up. Finn took off into the crowd, and I forced myself to wave and smile, all the while both fuming and dying inside.

If I'd been in wolf form I'd have been able to follow Kade myself, but there were way too many wolves and bears here for my human nose to differentiate smells. As we made our way to the outer parts of the crowd, Finn turned in a familiar direction and I knew where we were going.

The king had gone to the abandoned cabin beyond the cherry grove, the place of our first kiss. When we were almost to the cabin, I hopped off Finn.

Wait here for me, buddy, I said, leaning down to kiss him on the nose. *I shouldn't be long.*

Go speak with the king. It's been a long time coming. I'll keep watch here.

I sent my familiar an exaggerated glare. *Anyone would think you're on Kade's side.*

He butted his head up against my side. *Never. Always yours. But you deserve happiness.*

If only it were that easy. I patted him one last time and walked the rest of the way through the trees to the alcove. I saw no shifters, but laughter, music, and voices could be heard behind me. The party was in full swing and there would be some growly shifters come tomorrow morning.

Once I broke into the clearing, I saw the king's massive form sitting on a flat rock, the same rock I had been sketching on when we first met. I swallowed hard and decided I needed to get to the bottom of this. Soft emotions were what made you weak, so instead I went for anger. Anger would get me through this.

"What do you think you're doing, leaving the party? We're here to show our people unity and you just bail on me?" When he spun to face me I could see he was also angry; he stalked toward me so fast I almost took a step back from him.

His eyes were burning as they nailed me with a glare. "You expect me to sit around and watch you take a mate and just act like everything is fine?" His voice could cut glass and his question shocked me. I had no reply. This entire time I didn't realize how much that had hurt him; it was almost as if I could feel his pain through the mecca, to which we were both connected.

"Kade..."

"Don't, Ari! You made your choice, but that doesn't mean I have to sit by and watch you live through it."

The tears came then. Dammit! Damn this bear and all of his charm. Why did he have to be the king? Why was I the queen? For a second I wished we were just those two fifteen year olds again. Where the only thing holding us back was the fact our parents would kick our butts for slumming it with the enemy.

Lifting my head, I said as calmly as I could: "Sometimes I think I hate you." Glitter-coated tears fell down my face. I wasn't bothering to hold them back. I couldn't if I tried.

Kade's big body looked frozen, but his eyes were heating up like fiery coals. When he didn't respond, some of my calm fell and the hot pierce of anger had me charging closer to him.

"Did you hear me? I hate that you kissed me when I was fifteen! A kiss I haven't been able to get out of my head for five years! I hate that you kissed me again in your garden. I hate that you're so sweet and loyal and kind. I hate that we can't be together! I hate all of it, Kade!" My fists were balled now and I had completely broken down all of my walls.

Still he was silent as he stepped closer to me, eating up the distance between us until his body was pressed up against mine. When there was no more space between us, when I could hardly breathe because Kade was doing that thing where he stole all the oxygen from around me, he leaned in and whispered, "I love you."

The world stopped. Nothing moved. For one brief second I was in a bubble of emotion, and then it exploded. Right then I made a choice, a choice that would forever change my life, but there was no way to deny it any longer. Leaping up to my tiptoes, I leaned forward and kissed that damn bear like my life depended on it. Because I had just realized that it did. He was *mine*, and if my people couldn't handle that, then I wasn't sure I could be their queen. He *loved* me.

Kade wrapped me up in his arms; he was so huge that I was completely surrounded by his heat. His hard body pressed to every part of me. The kiss started off hot and heavy and didn't ease up for a moment. His chest rumbled beneath us and I knew his bear was happy. My wolf was practically dancing a jig inside. She'd always been a Kade fan. As he held me even tighter, I found myself wrapping my legs around him. I needed to be closer. I needed more. This just wasn't enough.

Kade swung us around, and I was pressed against one of the huge trees surrounding the cabin. Somehow my hands found their way into the gap of his button-up shirt, and then just as suddenly those buttons were gone. I had dreamed about touching him like this for so long, running my hands across his body. He wasn't as hairy as many bears, but he still had a decent spattering of hair across his defined chest and down his abdominal muscles...

So many chiseled abs.

The kiss eased slightly and he pulled back so he could rest his forehead against mine, our lips inches apart. My hands were still pressed against his hot skin, the heat between us enough to start a forest fire.

Ari!

Finn's urgent call cut through my hazy mind.

There is someone sneaking around the bushes. They are cloaked with magic. I can't get a read on them, but you need to get back to your dominants.

Kade straightened then, and with one final kiss on my lips, gently dropped me to my feet. "We have to move," he said. "Nix is picking up some strange energy. She's with Finn."

He'd gotten the same warning. If both of our familiars were worried, we probably should be also. The crunch of undergrowth had me spinning, but thankfully it was only Finn and Nix. My wolf galloped up, the giant eagle perched on his back. Nix did a little jump-swoop thing and landed on the king's shoulder. But before we could move out, another figure appeared from the shadows and Kade reacted in an instant. He lunged forward and scooped up the smaller shifter with ease.

A flash of mecca shot him back and Violet fell to a heap on the forest floor. The magic born was back up and on her feet in an instant. She brushed herself off, throwing a cheeky smile at Kade. "Got to get up earlier than that if you want to bear-handle me, friend."

He shook his head, some of the bear fading out of his features as he calmed a little. He'd partially shifted the moment he grabbed at the "intruder."

"What are you doing here, Vi?" I asked, stepping closer. She seemed to be examining me with great concentration and I wondered how disheveled I looked. Probably I was a huge mess, looking exactly like a queen who'd just cried and been kissed all in one heartbeat.

"Vi!" My voice was sharper than I intended, but we were on a time crunch here. If it was fae wandering around these woods, we had to make sure our people were safe. We also had to get back to do the ritual. Until we could return the mecca energy, they were going to keep coming for us.

She smiled at me and it was a look full of knowledge. She knew exactly what Kade and I had been up to. Thankfully she wasn't going to tell anyone. She valued my head, and would likely hope it stayed attached to my neck.

"I was just coming to find you all so we could head back to Manhattan for the fae ceremony. We don't want to miss the peak of the full moon. But then I smelled a magical cloak and went to investigate."

My heart was already hammering in my chest from my heated kiss with Kade. News of a magical cloak didn't help with it at all. "Finn detected the magic too. It wasn't you?"

Violet shrugged. "No, wasn't me. But I've done some pretty crazy stuff with the other magic born when we were drunk off shifter wine two festivals ago. It's probably a prank to steal your thrones or any number of stupid tricks."

I relaxed a little. She was probably right. Shifters got pretty crazy under the full moon. Throw in alcohol and the magic of the summer festival … all kinds of mayhem could happen.

Kade stepped to my side; his hand brushed across my back, and I knew he was offering me comfort. Everything had changed between us – his declaration, the kiss. We could never go back, so now it was about figuring out how to do this. Together. Whether we hid our relationship, or whether we fought to destroy the prejudice that had lived for far too long between our people. We might be bear and wolf, but we were all shifters. We were the same. My heart was telling me it was time to stop the divide and bring back what once was.

I would have to be very careful with my council, but I felt like it could be done. Something for us to worry about tomorrow, after this ritual. In this moment though, I had never felt so at peace, like the thousand pound weight which had been sitting on my chest suffocating me had finally been lifted. That hole in my heart, well … it felt a little more filled.

Violet was just staring at me with a big lopsided goofy grin. My best friend knew exactly what was going on and she was happy for me. We walked out of the clearing and my mind was so fixated on Violet and the king that I didn't notice anything weird until the smell hit me.

That distinct floral smell.

"Fae!" I shouted, and ran through the last section of the cherry grove to come upon the base of the hill where our people were partying the night away. Except they weren't partying, they were fighting for their lives as fae descended upon the hill.

I turned to Violet. My best friend was glowing with mecca; she looked lethal and pissed as hell. Kade was fighting the shift, his growls rumbling across the hill and into the valleys. Now we knew why there was a magical cloak. Someone must have seen Kade and I leave the main party zone and used that moment to strike. The cloak hid their scent and the scent of bloodshed.

"Stay and fight, or flee and try to fix the mecca?" Violet asked me, her voice low and wispy but somehow still slamming mecca energy into me with each word.

"I will not leave them to die," I said, baring my teeth. My wolf was fighting against my hold; these were her people. Our people. We would never abandon them.

Violet clapped her hands together, sticky tendrils of purple energy forming between them.

She had that smile on her face, the one that usually meant get the heck out of her way – she was out for blood – and it was equally awesome and disturbing.

Bending down, she placed her hands over two thick fallen branches. "*Transformato,*" she whispered as a mist leaked from her palms and saturated the branches.

Mecca wrapped around them, coating their thick crumbly bark, and then as Violet pulled her hands back they had turned from simple broken wood to deadly blades. She tossed one to Kade; he caught it and sent Nix to fly the skies. Violet handed me the other one. Its weight was solid and fit my grip perfectly. This sword would kill many a fae tonight.

"Don't you need a weapon?" I asked my best friend.

When she stood, her eyes were set on the slaughter before us; her face looked ghostly.

"I am a weapon."

And with that we all charged up the hill to meet whatever fate the gods saw fit. As I neared the battle, my heart fell when I saw that more shifters than fae were dead on the ground. This was a huge attack. Hundreds of fae had descended on us, and our drunk, unarmed people were being crushed.

Finn nudged my side and I knew he wanted me to ride him. In two swifts movements I tore the costume wings from my back and leapt onto his saddle.

Kade, Violet, and I were all battle trained, and we knew on instinct to split up. Violet branched off to the right. After a moment's hesitation and a lingering look, Kade branched off to the left. I could tell he didn't want to leave me to battle the fae alone, but I was a queen. We did not cower on the sidelines. If I died tonight, I would die protecting my people. I would die with a happy heart.

Use the mecca, Ari. You're more powerful than any on this hill. Prove it.

Finn was right. I was linked to the most powerful energy grid of magic ever in existence. There was a lot more energy on our side of the veil, and I would utilize it tonight. I might not be the expert Kade was, but I was trained in calling the energy and using it as a weapon. The only thing I was having trouble with was cutting the magic off so it didn't suffocate me, but there was no time during combat to worry about that. As Finn galloped into the fighting crowd, I took a deep steadying breath and felt for that live wire deep inside of me, that electric pulse that was always a distinct current within my body. The mecca was always within me, just waiting for me to shape it, use it.

Some of the fae had noticed me. One of them came at me, but I easily cut him down with my sword, having the height and speed advantage of riding Finn. Despite the distance between me and my friends, I could make out Kade to my left fighting hard, using mecca and sword. There was a pile of fae at his feet. We were lucky the Tuatha attacking us now were far less powerful than the dark fae who'd tried to kill us all at Kade's Staten Island home. It felt like they were around the power level of those who hit the night of the queen's death. Which gave us a chance.

A flash of white to my right was Violet. She was blasting fae and taking them to their knees. Forcing myself to focus, I channeled the energy from my center and drew it in one fast motion to the surface of my being. I'd never pulled so much, so fast, and it brought with it a hot, sharp pain.

When my body felt like it was literally going to be torn into two, I screamed and thrust my hands out, directing it at the brutal mob before me. The mecca was clever; it knew who I considered friend and foe. It bypassed my people and followed the sickening floral scent.

I let the mecca flow from me as I lifted the sword and started cutting down fae, one after another, never stopping, not even to wipe the blood from my face. They had attacked us, hurt my people, and I would destroy them all even if it killed me. A few of them managed to land blows on me, but Finn was always right there with teeth and claws, tearing through them. Together we were a formidable weapon. Add in the mecca and it was even more. My blasts of mecca were bringing many of the fae to their knees, blood trickling from their eyes and noses and ears. This gave the shifters the opening they needed to pick themselves up and strike. Bear and wolf worked together, shifters united against a common enemy. For this moment, we were no longer divided.

I swung my sword in figure eights. My head was beginning to ache and my body starting to sway, but I kept pushing energy. Purple coated the hilltop, turning the fight in our favor.

"Ari, no more!" I heard Kade bellow. I registered his words, but not fully. I was almost too far gone to realize what I had done. There was no way to stop it. I was in a car going a hundred miles an hour down a hill and my brakes were cut. The momentum was too great. There was no way to save myself.

A spark of clarity hit me. Finn had paused and I could sense him trying to speak with me, but his words weren't getting through.

Finn!

I shouted in my head, but the mecca was a purple haze that couldn't be penetrated. It had become this huge living thing, moving on its own now, using me as a channel. I tried to stuff that live wire back down but nothing happened. The entire hill was coated in a purple mist and now I could see just at the top, just ten yards from me, near the stage, a portal had opened. Two fae magic users were using energy to hold it open, one on either side, as the remaining unharmed fae were escaping.

My legs began to violently jerk as I struggled to stay on Finn. I had gone too far this time. I might have saved my people, but the mecca was going to rip me in two. Then, as if this moment couldn't get any worse, Violet's scream cut through the dark night, forcing chills up my arms. I could only watch in horror as the two fae who had opened the portal wrapped some type of glowing magical bands around my best friend's arms and legs and shoved her through the portal just as the hole closed.

It all happened so fast I couldn't be sure it was true. A cavern of sorrow opened inside my chest. Kade reached me then; his huge hands came up to either side of my face, tearing my gaze from where my best friend had just been.

I looked into his eyes, those deep molten copper eyes, and the pain threatening to destroy my body eased the slightest bit. I tried to gasp for small breaths; I wasn't sure if the mecca or the loss of Violet had robbed me of oxygen. I couldn't think straight. Kade's eyes suddenly flared with spikes of purple and my legs stopped shaking, but his forehead broke out in sweat.

"No!" I tried to rip my face away from his. I couldn't lose them both. No one could control this amount of mecca, not even Kade. It was everywhere in an inexhaustible supply. But his hands clamped down harder and I watched in horror as his amber eyes went purple. Both of us were buffeted by a huge gust of wind, and I realized Nix was there. Her ten foot wingspan stole the moonlight from around us, and the next moment happened so fast I had no time to process it. Nix flew at Kade's face, landing on his head, and something snapped so hard I was thrown backward, and everything went dark.

Chapter Eleven

Fire can reduce the strongest tree to ash.

CONSCIOUSNESS RETURNED AND I floated in a sea of calm for a few beats, but as awareness filtered in, so did the memories. *Violet!* I forced my eyes open, trying to lift my head from the soft linen pillow beneath it. A sharp stab of pain rocked through my body, settling into my brain. It was like a migraine on steroids, and I wasn't sure I could sit up without throwing up.

I finally got my eyes open, and was in a half sitting position. "Violet!" I called out as I tried to take in my surroundings through the pounding pain. I was in my room at the Island mansion.

Movement from the couch off to the side caught my eye. Calista crossed to stand at my bedside. Her face was haggard and streaked with blood. Her eyes were red-ringed and puffy.

"Violet's gone. A lot of them are gone." Calista's voice was broken, a hollow shell.

Pushing through my pain, I attempted to leap from the bed. Calista caught me as I stumbled, but I made it to my feet.

"What do you mean, a lot of them? What about Winnie?" Warmth brushed against my leg and it was Finn, pressing himself against my comfortable night clothes, supporting my weight.

Calista's chin was trembling. "Winnie is fine. She's already on a boat back to Manhattan. Violet was taken, maybe more. We haven't accounted for everyone yet. And Ben is ... dead. He was ambushed by at least a dozen fae. We lost more than five hundred wolves and three hundred bears."

I sagged back into the bed at her news. *Ben.* No, it couldn't be true. Ben and Derek both killed by fae. Violet snatched into their world. My heart was breaking, I could feel the fissuring cracks as my body bled for my loved ones. Drawing on the strength of my crown, I searched the pack bonds, filtering energy around the alphas as I tried to sense my people.

Calista was right. Where Ben's bright shining energy used to be, there was only emptiness. Emptiness everywhere. Over five hundred lost on the night of the summer festival. Our celebration would now go down in the history books as the most awful battle we had endured since the dark days.

Fighting through my shock and pain, I forced myself to stand. On my own. No support from Finn or Calista. "Okay. I need to know exactly what happened last night. How the fae appeared, and if anyone was around. We'll need to interview the wolf and bear shifters..."

"You have no time for that," said Calista. "The council and Selene are waiting for you. They have called a trial for dissolution of crown." This time my advisor couldn't keep her composure. A single tear trailed down her cheek; her sorrow was palpable.

"Based on what?" I asked, my voice surprisingly steady.

"Unfit to rule." Another few tears trailed along her cheeks.

I let her information process. The council and Selene had decided I was unfit to rule and now they would challenge me. It wasn't an easy process, and without hard evidence they wouldn't succeed. Nope. This was a show of their strength, pushing me back for my display of dominance yesterday.

"Calista, listen to me..." My voice remained strong. The petty annoyances of the council and

Selene were so far down my list of things to worry about. I had no idea where Kade was, my best friend had been kidnapped by fae, and another one of my most cherished friends was dead. Everything else paled in comparison.

Calista swallowed hard and met my eyes.

"We'll get through this," I said to her, and she blinked a few times, before wiping at her eyes and nodding. My strong, clever advisor was back.

There was a knock at the door and my gut clenched. An unfit trial was a low blow after the shifter world had just lost so many people. The moment I was declared innocent, I was firing the entire council and killing Selene with my bare hands.

"Enter!" I shouted through gritted teeth.

It was Sabina, which only served to further piss me off. "You're wanted for questioning," she said, her white hair billowing slightly around her. They had sent the magic born to make sure I showed up and didn't use mecca to create a scene.

Striding from the room, I made a point to step out in front. No one was leading me to trial. Once I descended the steps from the opulent second floor, I made my way into the formal living room, my head held high, pain buried deep inside. None of them would know how much my heart ached at the sight of the entire council, Selene with her familiar on her arm, and six of the lead alphas from the boroughs, all preparing to strip me of my crown.

Calista, Finn, and Sabina, who had followed me into the room, remained at my back as I addressed the group. "How dare you? How dare you declare an unfit trial as we all grieve the loss of our people? We're at war, there's no worse time for a coup."

Selene seemed to have taken extra care with her hair and makeup today. Her red locks were pinned up in a mass of loose curls, her clothes very formal. She strode over and took center stage, just where she always like to be. She pinned me with a glare.

"Where were you when the fae attack began, Arianna?"

I growled. "That's 'Your Majesty.' You haven't stripped me of my crown yet."

The council did turn slightly disapproving looks on her, but none of them said anything. It was like the decision was made before I even heard the reasons.

"Where were you, Selene? I didn't see you when I blasted the entire hill with mecca magic and ended the attack! Saving thousands of shifters."

Three of the alphas smiled, before being cut off by glares from the council. Maybe I could count on some of them to be on my side. A declaration of unfit to rule had to be unanimous.

Selene touched her cheek. "Where was I? Hmm, good question." Suddenly she gestured to the large flat screen TV on the wall and I noticed there was a remote in her hand.

With one click the TV flared to life and I was looking upon the broken-down cabin, two figures on the screen. One was Kade and the other was me. *Oh crap.* I knew exactly what she had filmed here. It was the moment just after I had told him I hated him. Selene had been in the bushes watching us, recording us.

"I love you," Kade said on the video, and just about every person in the room gasped. I even heard Calista huff from behind me. Finn snuggled closer to my side, both for comfort and because we both knew that we might have to fight our way out of this room.

The next images on the video recording sealed my fate. It showed me reaching up and kissing Kade with a ferocious intensity. A kiss of passion. A kiss of love.

Selene paused the screen so that it stopped on us mid-kiss and turned to me. "Arianna, of the red line, you are unfit to rule the wolf shifters. Your affair with the bear king has blinded your judgment and allowed a war with the fae to brew and seep over into our lives, costing us greatly. I call for a motion to dethrone you and banish you from the boroughs. From the mecca. All in favor say 'aye.'"

"Wait!" I commanded, stepping closer to Selene as realization hit me. "It was you who cloaked the energy so I wouldn't sense the fae attack. You and Sabina..." I shot a look at the magic born, who remained expressionless.

My protests were pointless, completely ignored as the ayes began rolling in. One by one the council and alphas agreed with Selene's motion. Right up until there was one alpha left.

It was Roger, a diehard separate race fanatic. I realized now that Selene had only invited the alphas who were hardcore about the rules. I knew I was screwed, but I tried anyway.

"Don't do this. The mecca is broken, but I can fix it. I can fix it and the fae will leave us alone."

Roger just shook his head. "You took an oath." Then he looked at Selene. "Aye."

The people had spoken, and I was worse than a failed heir. I was a failed queen. Torine moved in front of me, sharp blade clutched in his right hand. "I must unbind the mecca to you and then tie it to Selene."

I saw the special goblet in his other hand. Selene had planned this entire thing, and she clearly had the council's approval. Calista stepped forward now, glaring at every wolf in the room.

"She'll never be fully separated from the mecca. Only in death. Arianna will always be the true queen. Selene is just a diluted replacement. I hope you're all happy with your choice. You may have doomed us all."

Torine growled before slicing my wrist and pouring my blood into the mecca cup. I just stood there in shock, trying to figure out a way to salvage this. When the cup was nearly full, he stopped and knelt to Finn, holding the sword out.

Finn crouched low and gave a deep growl.

"Cut him and lose your head," I warned.

Torine stood and backed up a few paces, handing the cup to Selene. "It's good enough," he said to her before he cut her wrist, allowing the blood to drain into the cup, mixing with mine.

The moment our blood touched I felt an awful invasion, a presence within my own body. Selene. As the cup drained, her presence washed away, but so did most of the mecca from within me. There was still a good amount there, but it was half what it used to be. Selene took a deep breath as the mecca power surged within her.

"Selene of the Purple Hearts pack, I now declare you queen of the wolf shifters."

The council faced the new queen and shouted, "Long live the queen!"

Just like that I had been replaced.

"Arianna, I cast you out of the boroughs. You may never enter the mecca again." Selene's banishment cut right into my soul. She'd just barred me from my home, from the one place an heir could feel the mecca, the power.

Well, since I had nothing left to lose, I might as well go out chopping that damn snake into a thousand pieces. Calista must have known what I was thinking, because her hand clamped around my upper arm in a death grip.

"Good luck," Calista told them all, and then with surprising strength yanked me backward down the hallway. My suitcase was at the base of the stairs, and I realized she'd brought it down with her before. She grabbed it and then we were moving, out of the mansion and through the open back door.

Once we were in the large open back yard, I turned to my advisor. "Why didn't you let me kill her!" Fury was riding my body in waves. This couldn't be happening. How was this happening?

Calista looked at Finn as if they'd shared some thought. "Because I want you to live," she said shortly, before she took off stalking into the woods behind the estate.

I ran after her. "Where are we going?"

Calista shook her head, ignoring my question: "Arianna, I raised you like a daughter. Why didn't you just tell me."

She was talking about Kade. "Because I was trying to fight it," I said, my voice filled with truth.

Calista paused so she could reach out and cup my face with one hand. "You can't fight love, baby girl."

My throat pinched at her term of endearment. She hadn't called me that since I was eight years old. Then she straightened her shoulders and took off again, pounding through the forest.

"Cal, where are we going?" I asked again as I ran to catch up, Finn trotting beside us.

Calista looked back at me. "If King Kade really loves you, then he may take us in, because as of right now we're homeless."

We were making our way to Kade's mansion, where he had kissed me in the garden. Life really knew how to come full circle.

Our journey across the Island was silent. I mourned for so much, but forced myself to deal with what I could. I needed Kade, whether I was queen or not, and this thing with the fae was not over. They had Violet, and I needed his help to get her back. Plus, we had to fix the imbalance. I still had a connection to the mecca. The council and Selene had made a mistake trying to rush this dethroning through under the noses of our people. A queen was about more than just a bit of blood in a cup, she was about the love of her people. It would take Selene time to prove herself, especially when she had usurped me in such a manner. Knowing her, she would try leak the video of Kade and me. The council would attempt to stop her though. The fact a queen could love a bear might just be enough to have some shifters questioning our ways. They would not want that. All it took was a little spark for a full-on fire to be fanned to life.

We'll be fine, Ari. You're a queen. You don't need a throne to prove that. And we will always have each other.

I dropped to my knees and buried my head in Finn's soft fur. Breathing in deeply, I let his familiar warmth, his scent and power drag into my lungs, into my battered soul. I let him soothe me for just a moment, and in return I poured my love back into him.

Thank you, old friend. I couldn't do any of this without you.

He licked up the side of my face, before gently nudging me to start walking again. Calista had paused too, and when I got to my feet she smiled at me. "We're in bear territory now. Weird that I'm strangely relieved to be off wolf land."

I shook my head. "I feel the same, but it's always been that way with Kade. Wherever he was, I wanted to be. Even when I was fifteen. I've never been able to stop thinking about him."

Calista grasped my hand. "I understand. All too well. We both spent our entire lives in the service of the crown and the council, letting protocol dictate everything we did. And this is how they repay you. They never even let you speak. They never even questioned that Selene and Sabina were working together, and in doing so actually allowed the fae access to our lands. Their cloaking was the perfect cover. What if it wasn't a coincidence and those two are working with the fae? For all we know Selene is going to let them slaughter all who oppose them, and the rest would become slaves."

I brushed my hand across my face. The headache had died off a little, but the loss of mecca had me off balance. "You're right. This could be far worse than we imagined. I need to get to the royal home in Manhattan and open the portal to the Otherworld. I need Violet so we can rebalance the energy. That might be enough to make the fae stay in their world."

"What happened to the Summer Court?" Calista asked as we started walking again. I picked up the suitcase this time. "Weren't they supposed to be keeping the Winter Court at bay?"

I shrugged. "Violet communicated with Prince Caspien just before the festival started and he said he was in a good position then. I don't know what happened after that to turn the tides." I slammed my hand against a nearby tree. "It's so frustrating. We were so close to ending this and Selene's need for power has put us all the way back to the beginning. It's even worse than it was before."

Calista nodded. "Yes, things are definitely bleak. My damn tablet is back at the mansion."

A burst of laughter shot from me. I'd barely ever seen my advisor without her tablet in her hands. We both stopped and stared at her empty hands, before we took a good look at ourselves. We were in our pajamas, dirt and leaves scattered about us, blood still on my advisor's face.

We lost it then. I collapsed on Finn as the laughter shook through my tired, sore body.

"We look homeless," Calista said between chuckles.

"We are homeless," I spluttered out as tears ran down my cheeks.

It wasn't funny. None of this was funny, but sometimes grief manifests in odd ways. And after we managed to pull ourselves together and cross the last of the Island to reach Kade's mansion, I realized that I felt just a little better. I might have lost my crown, I might be a failed queen, but I had Calista and Kade. Together we would get Violet back. For the first time ever I was not an heir or a queen. I was just Arianna of the red house. It was a scary thought, but an exciting one too.

Unlike when I sneaked into the bear king's manor during the Summit trials, this time I used the front entrance. Calista, Finn, and I walked right up to the guards on the gate. The bears eyed me, but weren't aggressive in their approach.

"Queen Arianna, we weren't expecting you," the slightly smaller guard – though still giant sized – said. He was eyeing my clothes, no doubt wondering why I was dressed in my PJ's.

"I need to speak with King Kade. Is he here?"

Please be here.

The other one whipped out his phone and hit a few buttons before lifting it to his ear. He turned away, speaking low, but my shifter hearing picked up the affirmative from the other side. It was Gerald.

"Go right on into the house." The guards stepped back and the huge gates opened for us.

Calista let out a huff of air and I swiveled to see her better, my eyebrows raised. A smirk of sorts crossed her lips. "It's kind of ironic that our people threw us out without a goodbye, banished us to never return, and here we are, welcomed into the bear's territory. Never thought I'd see the day."

I was about to answer when I caught sight of Kade. We were only halfway down the long drive, but he was clearly waiting on his huge porch, one arm resting against the wall. My body moved by instinct then. I dropped the suitcase and barreled down the path at a million miles an hour. I'd never been less dignified, less queen-like in my life, running toward him like my life depended on it.

Concern creased his features and he started moving toward me. As I ran I had to keep reminding myself not to touch him, not to throw myself into his warmth and comfort. The last thing I needed was his people to dethrone him too. Not before we sorted out this mecca and fae problem.

The distance closed and I could feel the energy that was always between us. I'd always thought the mecca was what made that pulse of energy so strong, but I'd just lost a lot of mecca and the connection was as strong as ever. A few feet from him I forced myself to stop. My heart was beating fast, breath coming out in short puffs – it wasn't the run which had me winded, it was Kade.

He didn't stop though, he scooped me into his arms and wrapped me up so tight that some of the leaking of my fissured heart seemed to ease. "Your people will see," I murmured into his chest. I was trying to find the strength to push him away, but instead my hands were tangled in his shirt, pulling him closer.

"Let them see. I already told my council this morning, and they have broken away to debate it. Last I heard, half of the council was in favor of us joining together. We defeated the fae together last night, and this division between our boroughs and packs is making us weaker." His lips brushed mine and everything was okay in that moment. As he pulled back he said: "Who better to join our worlds than the king and queen."

My eyes welled up then, the reality of what had happened hitting me hard. Kade's expression hardened as he took in my distraught features and my pajamas. He glanced behind me, where I knew Calista and Finn were waiting with my suitcase.

"What happened, Ari?" he asked as he turned back, still holding me close but allowing some distance so he could see my face. "What did those bastards on your council do?"

Chapter Twelve

A silver lining is sometimes black.

"I WILL KILL THEM," Kade said for the fiftieth time, his voice a bear rumble by now. We were inside his house and I'd just finished telling him everything that went down after the battle. He was one annoyed bear.

"They never healed you! They just left you in that room while they plotted against you? After you saved everyone and almost killed yourself in the process. If Nix and Finn hadn't intervened and used their connection to the mecca, it would have destroyed everyone. Once you lost control of it, it would have ripped through everyone in its path."

I hadn't known that. Information to consider next time I decided to jump in the car with no brakes.

Kade wasn't done trying to kill the council yet. "I trusted them," he said, his hands clenched. "I left you with your people to heal only after they assured me you would receive the best care. With Violet gone, I knew you were limited on magic born, but I didn't want to make things hard for you by insisting you come to my home."

Calista spoke up: "I never left her side, but I did think it was odd that no magic born was sent to us. Luckily, Ari healed quickly. Her natural shifter abilities and connection to the mecca helped immensely."

Kade finally sat beside me on the huge white couch; his body was like a rock, hard and unyielding. We were in that front sitting room with the huge windows and gauzy white curtains. It felt like a lifetime ago I'd climbed the cliff and made my way to try and steal his mecca necklace, a lifetime ago he had kissed me and sealed both of our fates. He reached for me, his hand brushing up my arms to cup my face. He did this a lot, and it was kind of perfect.

"What do you want to do now, Ari? You have the bear shifters on your side. We are forever grateful to you for saving us last night."

See, perfect. "We have to save Violet, and we have to fix the mecca. If we don't, the fae will keep coming until we're all destroyed."

Calista cleared her throat. "Except that we are banished from Manhattan, which is the only place you can open a portal into the Otherworld."

Dammit, Calista was right.

"We'll fight our way in, Selene can't stop me," Kade said, his lazy confidence back in full force.

I placed a hand on his chest. "Whoa there. I'm hoping to convince my people that a side by side existence with the bears is possible. That's going to be a touch harder if you attack them."

He grumbled, and I could see that he just wanted Selene's head on a stick, but acting on our base emotions would get us nowhere.

Calista raised her hand as if she was in school. "I have an idea..."

We stared at her, waiting for her to speak, but despite her hand-in-the-air-enthusiasm, she now seemed to be wrestling with some internal emotions.

"King Kade, do you swear to never harm Baladar based on the knowledge I am about to share?"

Kade's eyebrows furrowed as he assessed Calista. "Why?"

Calista set her best poker face. "Do you swear it?"

Just what the hell was my advisor up to?

Kade cleared his throat before saying, "I do. Now why?"

Calista exhaled slowly. "Because Baladar set up a vortex somewhere in Staten Island that leads right to his Manhattan loft."

"What?" Kade and I both cursed as we leapt to our feet. My wolf was rising inside, fighting my control. A hidden vortex, that was … impossible … illegal … dangerous.

Calista spoke over our ire: "If we can find the vortex, we can travel to Baladar's, and then sneak into the castle undetected." Her words were all rushed together, trying to defuse us.

Lucky for her it was a good plan. Selene would have the regular vortex discs crawling with guards now that I was banished. Sabina hadn't magically banished me, and I don't think it was possible really. I was still somewhat a queen, with mecca flowing through my veins, so if Kade and I could get into that crystal room we could open a portal and jump through … then find Violet.

"Where is the hidden vortex?" Kade looked livid that this had been going on under his nose.

Calista shrugged. "I don't know. I only heard of its existence. It's how your people get into his club."

Kade stood and reached out a hand to me. I grasped on without hesitation. "Where are we going?" I asked as he led me through the mansion and out onto the front steps.

"To speak to someone who I think will know where it is," he replied as Calista and Finn followed after us.

Once we reached the porch, Kade called to one of his guards. "Is Trixie on shift?"

The guard nodded. "She's on post at the water's edge."

Kade nodded and walked over to a golf cart. We all got in and Kade took off driving the cart out the front gate and down a steep side hill toward the shoreline, until the lapping waves came into sight.

"I've beefed up security all over after the attack," he said as he maneuvered around the natural terrain.

I wasn't surprised. If I had still been queen today, like I should have been, my first order would have been investigating the attack and making sure our lands were secure. Well, as secure as they could be. After seeing those two magic born just open a portal into our world like it was nothing, I knew without any doubt that nowhere was safe.

As we made our way through the dense bushes and out onto the sand, I took a moment to breathe in the salty air. Yes, my life sucked right now, and my best friend was missing, but I had always been soothed by the ocean. Violet had loved the ocean too; it calmed her energy.

Goddamn the fae.

"Why do you think they took Violet?"

The question burst from me in a short, angry eruption. I'd been so focused on the fact that my best friend was in enemy hands that I hadn't actually stopped long enough to question why. Calista and Kade were both quiet for a brief moment, neither of them answering until the cart came to a halt.

My advisor worried at her lip. "I've been thinking about it a lot. The attack was odd. The Summer Court was supposed to be keeping the dark fae at bay, and yet they managed to attack in the hundreds."

Kade interrupted her: "I'm not sure it was dark fae. They definitely weren't from the golden court, but the energy was different from the one who ambushed us on Staten Island. I'm not sure they are all from the same court."

Great! What was going on? How many of the courts were we fighting against now?

"So why do you think they took Violet?" Calista turned to Kade, nailing him with her famous glare. Her computer mind wanted to know everything.

Kade flicked his gaze across to me briefly, before throwing my advisor a mix of grin and grimace. "I think they want Ari. She has an unnatural affinity for the mecca. She can do what no queen has before, and she's closely related to the Red Queen. We know this all started with the Red Queen, and somehow it's not over yet."

"You think it has something to do with me now?" I said, my nails digging into my palms. "That my people died because some of the fae are trying to get to me." I forced myself to breathe a few deep breaths to calm myself.

The ercho, Finn reminded me. I let out a sigh. Dammit.

"Finn just reminded me that the ercho had been trying to drag me into the shiny water slick it came from. It was acting like it wanted me." I was starting to believe that Kade might be right. I needed to get into the Otherworld right away. Who knew what they would do to Violet. I was desperately hoping that if it was me they were after, they'd keep her alive until I got there. Give me a chance to save her.

"I'll never let them take you, Ari," Kade said as he switched off the cart. Silence descended across the stretch of beach we were on. "You're under my protection. Do you know what I do to anyone who touches those under my protection?"

The intensity and bristling anger he was exuding actually had the hairs on my body standing up. I didn't fear much, but right now Kade was all kinds of scary. He was holding my gaze with ferocity.

"What do you do to them?" I murmured, needing to know.

He leaned closer, his warmth and scent everywhere. "My bear takes them apart, piece by piece, and enjoys every second of it."

The urge to jump him then and there slammed through my body; my lower half clenched in need. I wasn't a shifter who had ever wanted to be protected by a man – I was expected to do the protecting, alphas and heirs were the strongest – but from Kade it didn't seem to take from my power. It felt like it built me up. We were a team and it made us stronger.

Before I could open my mouth and let all the emotions leak out, I noticed a beautiful female walking toward us. She was in full battle gear, all black leather and chain mail and holding a sickle that looked like it still had dried fae blood on it. Her skin was the color of caramel and her natural dark curly hair whipped back and forth in the wind. She was stunning, moving with the speed and grace of a shifter. But not wolf.

Kade followed my gaze, and we both watched as the female's long strides ate up the distance between her and our cart in moments. "My king?" she said, her brow creasing.

Kade exited the golf cart and approached her, placing a hand on her shoulder for a brief moment. "All is well, Trixie, but I need you to tell me the truth now."

She swallowed hard as if she knew she was about to be in trouble. "Yes?"

Calista and I exited also, stopping near Kade. Finn stayed in the golf cart, staring at the ocean. My familiar loved the ocean more than I did; it was a commonality he shared with Violet.

Kade's fierce expression darkened more, if that was even possible. "I know that some bears have been going to Manhattan to Baladar's club nights. I know you've been at the club, and now I need to know where the vortex is. I will not punish you if you tell me where to find it."

Her eyes widened and I could hear her heart hammering in her chest. It was clear that Kade knew she was the partying type and would have the answers he sought.

"Y-Your Highness," she stuttered. "I'm so sorry for keeping it from you. We figured it was innocent and—"

"Trixie, I don't care about what you've done. I have much bigger fae to fry. Just tell me where it is."

She chewed her bottom lip. "On the corner of Tennyson and Nelson, under the green bench."

Kade and I exchanged a single glance; he looked satisfied. Probably glad he didn't have to break any bones to get that information.

"Thank you," I said to Trixie, even though my wolf was growling inside, trying to force the change on me. She kinda wanted to rip this bear shifter's head from her shoulders for keeping information of an illegal vortex from her king. I also knew my wolf would be jealous of any female, even Calista, until we were properly mated and she had staked her claim on him.

"Are you going to shut it down?" Trixie asked Kade, and I could see her guilt. She knew she'd sold out Baladar and her friends, but she'd had no choice. When your king asks you for something, you give it to him.

"I'm going to use it," Kade said.

Trixie's brows furrowed, and she moved even closer, which really annoyed my wolf. "The vortex? When?"

Kade gave her a look that said he didn't like being questioned. She hurried on to explain: "I ask because the vortex only works on Wednesday nights after 9pm."

Crap! It was Saturday. I couldn't sit on my butt for four days while Violet endured gods-knew-what in the fae lands at the hands of our enemy.

Kade reached out and ran a gentle hand from the base of my spine up to the nape of my neck, his touch both soothing and frustrating. Growls were actually rumbling my chest now. I was losing the battle with keeping my wolf contained.

"Thank you," he said to Trixie. She bowed deeply and walked back to her station. I caught a few curious glances over her shoulder at me, but for the most part she remained professional.

"We'll find another way," Kade said as he turned to me.

I knew there was no other way without causing a war. I had played mecca chess enough to know that Selene would see any act of entering Manhattan as an assassination attempt. I was banned, and in her eyes Kade was the enemy.

It was a heavy silence as we walked back to the golf cart and I sank into my seat. "Four days. Violet could be anywhere by then."

Calista spoke up suddenly: "Didn't you tell me that time worked differently over there?"

I perked up. "Yes!" I turned to face her with a little hope in my heart. The Summer Court prince had told me he could buy me a few weeks in his time, which was a few seasons here. So four days here was probably only a day over there.

"Okay, Wednesday we get Violet back," I said.

Hang on, Vi. I'm coming for you.

Later that night I found myself at the grand dining table with Kade. We were back on Staten Island, and it was a relief to feel the mecca around me again. The council definitely had not separated me from it, although the dulling of the connection was there. I wasn't sure they could ever fully separate me from it now; it felt like it was permanently part of me. Like Calista said, until death.

Since this was the bear's territory, I wasn't breaking any rules, but I knew word would spread to Selene – we had spies everywhere – that I was back in the boroughs, and she would retaliate. I really didn't care though. I was surrounded by all the shifters I loved in the world: Calista, Finn, Winnie, and my four remaining dominants, Blaine, Monica, Jen, and Victor. They'd refused to go into service for Selene, and were now exiled with me. All of us mourned Ben, all of us angry we could not send him off in true warrior fashion as we had for Derek. But we were having our own private ceremony soon.

Victor in particular was stony-faced, darkness washing away his normally jovial expression. He'd lost two of his brothers now – not brothers in blood, but by a bond far greater: love. He had briefly spoken to me when we arrived here; his need for revenge was strong. I had to make sure he didn't go after the fae himself and die in the process. Anger and vengeance were terrible fuels for shifters; it made us hard and bitter. Changed who we were. Let the beast control us.

Victor's eyes flashed to me and I could see the wolf there. I'm not sure I'd ever get my friend back; in so many ways I'd lost all three of them now. Blaine was at his side, tense, not eating much, but he still looked like my beautiful friend, just with sadder eyes and a heavier heart. He was the only one keeping Victor together. Jen and Monica were doing what they could, but each of us were mourning and had very little comfort to offer anybody.

I wanted to kill the fae all over again. And make it more painful this time.

Kade reached across then and ran his hand up my thigh, comforting and hot, sending tingles of mecca through my body. I pushed down my sorrow as hard as I could, utilizing all my skills. As queen, my compartmentalizing was second to none. I focused on what was perfect right now. Kade.

Being with him like this had my heart overfull. There was so much pressure and emotion in my chest that it was hard to contain. Even though I hadn't said the words, I loved him more than any other in my world, and that was why I wasn't completely falling apart over the loss of my crown, the loss of Violet, and the death of my people. Kade was holding me together. It was as if his love was a balm, a glue. With him at my side I knew I could keep myself together long enough to save my best friend and deal with the fae. After that I'd fall apart – pull out these emotions and let them consume me. Until then I had to stay strong.

I loved the bear king. Holy crap.

It wasn't one little thing which I could pinpoint to tell me why, or how this had happened. There were a million of them – the way my wolf howled for his bear; the way his kiss stole my breath and had my heart beating fast; how kind he was, his protective instincts so different to wolf males. He was more dominant than me, and I was somehow okay with that. Most of the time.

Kade's copper eyes sparkled as that sexy grin lifted his chin. Dimples flashed at me through the scruff on his face, and I forced myself not to lean over and nuzzle into him. Gerald interrupted us by crossing to his king and whispering into his ear. I could have listened in, but I would not betray Kade's privacy like that. If he wanted me to know, he'd tell me.

His expression grew grim, the smile fading away, taking my favorite dimple with it.

"Everything okay?" I said as Gerald took his seat at the table. Yeah, so much for privacy. I wanted to know.

The hand on my thigh flexed slightly, before it relaxed and started running in slow circles over my leg. "Gerald just escorted most of my council from Staten Island. They're exiled out of the boroughs for now until I can decide what to do with them."

Despite the fact the bears were grateful to me for saving them, apparently learning I was no longer queen, and that I'd be shacking up with their king, had sent some of his council over the edge. As soon as we had arrived, Kade had made a public declaration of support and love for me. The council threw a fit, but I hadn't heard the outcome. Now I knew. He leaned over to Gerald.

"Spread the word. Those who are not okay with Arianna and I being together are welcome to leave New York City."

My jaw went slack. It was one of the hottest, craziest, most perfect things he'd ever done. I still couldn't believe after all we had been though, I was sitting next to him, his hand on my thigh, eating dinner with our friends and advisors, like it was no big deal.

I'd been content as queen, and the piece of me connected to my people would always ache at the loss, but if Calista asked me about my happiness right now, I would have no hesitation in answering.

My little sister twisted in her seat beside me and I glanced to her plate. She had completely devoured the BBQ chicken but hadn't touched her broccoli.

"Winnie, eat your vegetables," I said, grateful to have this moment to mother her again.

She looked at my plate, where I had the same pile of mini green trees. "You eat yours," she replied, with all the cheekiness of a five year old. I couldn't help but smile. Could I blame her? Unless Broccoli was covered in jalapeno cheese sauce, I wasn't touching it.

Kade watched our banter with a crooked smile. "How does everyone at this table feel about chocolate?"

There were a few chuckles. Come on, who didn't have the upmost love and respect for chocolate.

"I'm in a pretty serious relationship with chocolate," Monica said, and we all chuckled.

She had been a mixture of tense and somber for the entire meal – mourning Ben, worried for Victor, and, well, being in bear territory was an extremely unusual situation – so when she answered Kade with her normal sarcastic quip, I was happy. Then the double doors that led into the kitchen opened and two attendants rolled out a huge three-tiered melted chocolate fountain. All around the fountain were skewers with chunks of fruit and bread. Oh my God, was that pretzel bread?

"We do a chocolate fondue night here about once a week," Kade said, grinning at my sudden bright smile. Well, damn, I was starting to think Kade knew how to rule much better than the wolves did. We never had fondue night.

The next twenty minutes had talking at a minimum. We were all too busy devouring the warm melted gift from the gods. My favorite was the pineapple with chocolate. To die for. Chocolate was a great icebreaker too, slowly but surely my dominants began to warm up to the bears, conversing with Gerald and Kade. Maybe this was possible, a life where we all shared the same territory. It wouldn't happen overnight, but a change had started here, at this table.

By 9 P.M Winnie was slumping forward in her chair, her little face smeared with chocolate as she tried to lick the last tendrils from her fingers. "Winnie, come on, baby, let's get you to bed."

I stood and she hit me with a frown, her words slurred but defiant.

"I'm NOT tired."

With a shake of my head, I kissed her on the cheek. "Come on, little wolf, I'll carry you up."

I leaned down and scooped her out of her chair. She protested briefly, before she snuggled her head onto my shoulder.

Kade stood as well. "I'll show you to your rooms."

I followed him out of the dining room and into the expansive foyer. He led me up the staircase, and by the time we reached the next level I could feel Winnie's rhythmic breathing on my neck. She was already out. Kids. Why did they make it their life mission to fight sleep?

Kade took a left down a long hallway and then opened one of the bedroom doors. Stepping inside, I was surprised to see a child's room. A bunk bed rested against the wall to the left, and the other walls were painted with beautiful murals of the forest and animals. There was a reading nook filled with children's books and a bunch of toys.

I must have looked completely shocked because Kade laughed. "My cousin, Thane, has two children, and they often come visit us and stay here. He lives outside of the mecca in Connecticut."

Oh. For a second I thought he was going to tell me he had a kid or something crazy. There was so much we still didn't know about each other.

Which didn't bother me. We had forever to learn, but if he had a child he hadn't told me about, well, that'd be an issue for sure. Not because I couldn't love Kade's child, but because he would have hidden something that huge from me.

I lay Winnie down and tucked her into the bottom bunk, placing another kiss on her chocolate cheek. She really needed a bath, but if I knew anything about children, it was that you never woke a sleeping one. Following Kade out of the room, I was surprised to see Calista waiting for me.

"May I speak with you both privately?" she asked, her hands clutched in front of her, awkward without her beloved tablet. We'd have to get her a replacement. Right now though I had no idea if my private bank accounts were frozen, or what Selene was up to. All things to find out tomorrow.

"Of course." Kade led us into a study just down the hall from Winnie's room. Once we were all seated, my advisor turned to us, her movements a little agitated.

"It's my duty to protect the queen's reputation ... her public image ... and although Arianna might have been dethroned, she's the true queen. I intend to reverse her dethroning as soon as we get Violet back."

I was glad we were on the same page with that.

"There's a formal process to a royal taking a mate, and despite the wolf-bear thing, it should be no different between you two."

Ahh, that's what she was getting at. Kade nodded, no surprise across his face. "I'm not familiar with the wolf mating process," he said, "but I will adhere to whatever rules you see fit to protect the queen's image."

Calista smiled, relaxing a little. "Thank you. I think at this time courting is appropriate but no huge public displays of affection. It will take people some time to get used to this idea of a bear king and a wolf queen. Let them hear about it but not yet see it. Nothing indecent."

I gave a snort of laughter. "Jesus, Cal, what do you think of me? You think I'm going to grind on him on a public park bench?"

Calista simply glared at me. *Okay, so yes, that's exactly what she thought I was capable of.*

My cheeks turned red. Kade looked to be biting his lip to keep from laughing.

Calista stood. "Thank you for hearing my concerns." She bowed lightly as Kade and I stood.

As she reached the door, she turned back. "One final thing..."

"Anything," Kade said, and I was touched he was trying to please my dear advisor.

"Separate bedrooms until the mating ceremony," she said, and with that she closed the door and totally put a wet blanket over my plans to seduce Kade every night for the rest of my life.

I barked out a nervous laugh. "Wow. Yeah. I'm sorry about that. She's like my second mother, and ... I mean, you and I haven't even talked about mating or any of that, so this is just her being—"

Kade halted my explanation with a kiss, warm and passionate, and had the tension in my belly kicking into overdrive. When he pulled back, he met my eyes. "Don't worry about it, Arianna. I've been waiting for you for five years. Ever since that kiss you've dominated my thoughts. My world. My bear was determined to find you. Your fire, loyalty, and passion called to us both. Your wolf has always been a den mate to my bear." He caressed my face with his hand. "We will be mated."

And just like that Kade had declared his intentions. No hesitation. No worry for protocol. A man who knew what he wanted and would stop at nothing to make it happen

"What would have happened if I went through with my plans to take a wolf mate?" I asked, lifting my head up to see him better. "To mate for the good of my people."

Shadows washed over his features, darkening them further, and I found myself waiting with an unhealthy level of anticipation for his answer.

"Your wolf would never have let you, Ari. The queen in you wanted to follow protocol but our royal title is only one part of us. We're also shifters. We might look human, but we're ruled by so much more ... by instinct. I was just waiting for you to realize it."

"You'd have waited? Watched me date other wolves, experiment with the concept of a mate?" I had no idea why I was pushing him on this, but a part of me needed to dissect his emotions, his anger, his withdrawal ever since I'd mentioned my possible mate.

One of his hands wrapped around the back of my neck, the other slipping across my waist. His voice was a low rumble: "Anyone who touches what is mine, dies. Simple. Effective. You are mine, Arianna of the red line. You have been since I was a teenage bear rebelling against my royal life."

Holy shifter babies. He was channeling woodcutter and cave bear tonight. And why did my wolf and I like it so much? She was practically purring.

When his hand trailed up inside of my shirt, caressing my back, I decided one thing right then and there. There was no way in hell I was following all of Calista's rules. I was totally sneaking into his bedroom. Tonight.

Chapter Thirteen

Queen of hearts.

ALL OF MY people were on the same floor as me. I had my own suite and the others were in smaller rooms around me. Even though I was no longer a queen or heir, old habits were hard to break, and everyone thought they needed to protect me above all else.

I loved them, but I also knew it was going to be extremely difficult for me to sneak out tonight. But I was determined. Kade's floor was the one above, and I was getting there even if I had to scale the damn side of his beautiful brick home.

I wanted to speak with my dominants first. We needed to clear the air between us all. Blaine had been distant since the whole Kade and me thing came out – polite, but not like my best friend. A cavern of space was opening between us and I didn't know how to bridge the gap. Becoming queen had been one thing to separate us, and even though I hated it, I accepted that as my duty. But the Kade thing ... I felt Blaine's disapproval, but so far he had not voiced anything about it to me.

And Victor...

The box inside where I stuffed all those dark emotions started to rattle. I was worried about him, really worried. And even Monica and Jen, who were the glue to our group, as most women were, were fraying at the edges. I needed to make sure everyone felt their voice was heard, and I wanted to start with Blaine, privately.

After a soft knock he opened the door.

"Your Highness." His voice was low, without inflection, but I knew my old friend; he had everything bottled inside. Sooner or later he was going to explode. Might as well make it now.

"I wanted to speak with you," I said slowly. He just stood there, allowing me to wait in the hallway like a stranger. Why was he doing this? Acting so weird. The only thing I could think of was to proceed like I normally would, so I pushed past him and strode into his room. When

I was in the main part of the living area, I turned and crossed my arms, giving him a glare.

I'd totally pulled some queen moves on him, and I could see the smile fighting to break out across his face. Eventually he chuckled, shaking his head. "You don't change. Still a hothead. Still a princess."

The old nickname was soft gauze to the wounds rocking my body, like for a second we went back in time and were six year olds running in the boroughs. Back to simpler times. I couldn't hide in the past forever, though. Nope. Despite the fact I was no longer officially queen, I was still taking responsibility for my people.

Blaine shut the door, crossing to me. His height dwarfed me, and I realized this had been the first time in ages I'd taken a second to really look at him, to see the male he'd become. He was not as tall as Kade, but in the wolf world he was massive. Strong. His face had matured in the last year into chiseled lines. He was all man now, no sign of the boy that once was. Those light green eyes of his were boring into me, assessing, judging. Blaine was not going to take any crap from me tonight, and I for one was glad that we could hash this out.

"Just say it," I said. "Get it all out there. You disapprove of my relationship with the king and you're mad I've pulled you into all of this."

Those green of his eyes went murky as his features softened. He took a step closer to me. "Princess, the only thing I disapprove of is when you're unhappy."

My heart, which had felt oddly hollow since losing the crown – except for the Kade love – was suddenly bursting again. "I'm happy, Blaine. Despite everything else, happy is exactly what I am right now. You must see that, so why are you being weird? Kade is ... look, I know it's not conventional, but ... I love him."

There. I'd said it. To one of my best friends. Next step: say it to the man himself.

Blaine offered a small smile, but those fine creases that had suddenly appeared between his eyes told me he was hurting. "I know you do. I've known since the first time I saw you two together. I guess, knowing it was forbidden, I thought one day you'd be able to move on. One day you might somehow love me instead. It's okay. I get it now, though. Love doesn't work like that and I'll get over it. I just need time."

Oh. Oh crap! That's what I was noticing between us, Blaine had ... fallen for me? When? How? I felt awful and sort of uncomfortable being with him in this small room as he laid his feelings bare. Was this my fault? Sure, I'd been flirting with him on and off, which was what we always did, but I'd hate to think I gave him the wrong impression. I should have taken more care with my actions.

"Blaine, I—"

He cut me off with a wave of his hand and one of his killer smiles. "Just be happy, Princess, that's all I ask." I could tell he was done. "Thanks for checking in on me, Ari. It's getting pretty late, so I'm going to get some rest."

Hot, damp heat pricked my eyes, and I swallowed hard to relieve the pressure. I would not cry in front of him. I would not make him feel bad; he had done absolutely nothing wrong. This was just one of those impossible circumstances and I needed to deal with the fallout. Loving Kade was worth it, but I never wanted it to come at the pain of my friends.

"I'll see you in the morning, B. I..." I was going to say "Love you," as I had a million times before, but now I wasn't sure if that was just cruel.

Turning, I continued my deep breathing so I wouldn't break apart, which lasted right up until a large arm wrapped around me, spinning me and hauling me back into a hard chest. Blaine hugged me tightly, so tight it was almost as if he was trying to hold all the pieces of me together.

"We'll get through this," he said close to my ear. The swell of pain was rising, the heat like lava behind my eyes. "I will always love you, Ari, and it'll go back to just friendship soon. Don't spill tears over me. It's not worth it."

I hugged him back as hard as I could, before wrenching free and running from the room. Slamming his door behind me, I sank back against it, hot, silent tears dripping along my cheeks. My wolf howled inside of me and I knew she wanted to change, to escape some of the responsibility and emotions that came from being in human form.

Ari!

Finn called to me. He was off hunting. This had been hard on him too, and without lots of freedom he'd go crazy.

I'm okay, buddy. Just having an emotional chick moment.

His rumbling howl was soothing. *I can be right back if you need me.*

The tears were still running unchecked, but I felt slightly better. *No, you stay and enjoy yourself with Nix. I have a few more people to see tonight. I won't be alone.*

I love you.

He withdrew from my mind, and some of the ache in my heart eased. Turning, I pressed my hand against the door. Somehow I knew Blaine was right on the other side, standing there, feeling my sorrow as I cried for him ... for us.

Blaine was and always would be a part of me. When you know someone for so long, from childhood, they begin to define you, to take up so many precious memories. I needed Blaine to be in my life, always, just not like that. I was hoping what he said about getting over it was true and that we could go back to our old ways.

After pulling myself together, wiping away the last of my sadness, I went and knocked on Monica's door. She yelled out, "Come in," and I was pleased to step inside and see her, Victor, and Jen playing poker. That was a good sign, sticking together, playing poker like the old times.

When they looked up and saw me, all of them threw their cards down. "It's not the same without Derek and Ben."

Monica was always the one to cut right to the point.

I nodded. So not exactly like old times.

Victor grumbled, "I even miss Violet's cheating ways."

We all chuckled at that and I sat down next to them, our knees all touching. "I wanted to check in with you guys to let you know that I'm so sorry about the losses we've endured ... and that I plan to avenge Ben and Derek, and to get Violet back."

Victor's face suddenly looked haunted. "I want revenge, Ari. I want the faes' heads on a stick, and after that I don't want to ever see another pointy-eared demon for the rest of my life."

I understood his emotions. To a large degree I felt the same. The fae had proven to be cold, ruthless, and utterly relentless when they wanted something. But not all of them, right? We had some allies among the Tuatha, and I clung to this hope instead of letting the anger completely consume me.

One day soon I'd try to talk to Victor about it, to tell him that not all fae were bad, and that not all of them deserved to die. But now wasn't the time. I grasped his hand. "When we get Violet back, I will fix the mecca and make sure the fae never step foot in our territory again."

He nodded, and so did Jen and Monica.

I took a deep breath before speaking my last and most important point. "I know that being my guard while living with the bear king and fighting fae wasn't really on the job description when you signed up, so I want to give you all the opportunity to leave. Go explore the country or settle down somewhere safe. No hard feelings. I'll call often and—"

Monica was the one to cut me off and she did so in Spanish. Lord only knows what she said but she sounded pissed. Jen and Victor just stared at her. "I think she's saying that you're batshit crazy and we will never leave you," Jen said. "And if so, I agree."

Monica nodded. Victor just chucked one of the cards at my head. "You're not getting rid of us that easily."

My eyes had that hot, damp thing going on again. I was a regular fountain of emotion tonight. "Group hug," I called out, leaning forward and crashing into my friends. I was the luckiest dethroned queen in the world to have such a loyal inner circle.

After leaving my friends, I felt a bit lighter. Instinct was telling me that we would get through this, but only if we stuck together. Oh, and a bit of blood revenge wouldn't hurt either. As I turned the corner I saw Calista just about to step into her room, which was right next to mine.

"You doing okay?"

When Calista turned to face me, I saw a brand new white tablet in her hands and she was practically crying. "King Kade had this sitting on my bed! And guess what? Selene hasn't revoked my passwords yet. I'm going to get everything off before she thinks to lock me out."

I chuckled as her fingers flew over the tablet, no doubt checking in on everything she'd missed during her technology strike. That damn bear was thoughtful. Now I was really going to have to find a way to sneak in and thank him.

"Good night, Cal," I said, stepping into my room.

"Night," she called, closing her door.

Okay how long until she would fall asleep? I felt like I was fourteen again, sneaking out with Violet just to run around the city and be reckless. When I came upon my own bed, I saw a handwritten note and smiled.

Arianna,

I respect Calista's wishes ... but in case you don't, your balcony has a ladder that leads to my suite.

Kade

I grinned. He'd given me this room on purpose. That sneaky, gorgeous, sexy bear. Holy crap ... I was in love with a damn bear. Who would have ever guessed that was in the cards for me.

It had been a long day, so a shower was first order of business, in and out, no time to waste. The drawers in this room were already filled with brand new clothes and underwear. Calista probably gave Kade's people all my sizes. Lord knows I'd never had to shop for my own things before. I was grateful for all the thoughtfulness. After slipping on some underwear and night clothes, I opened the double glass doors to my balcony. Peeking my head around, I was happy to see that Calista's room had no balcony, and her curtains were drawn. The universe clearly wanted this to happen as much as me.

To my right was a stone ladder, built right into the wall. It led up and over to Kade's balcony, and I could see that his doors were open. *Here goes nothing.* I never in a million years thought I would be sneaking into the bear king's bedroom. Hah! A burst of laughter almost escaped at the thought. In all honesty, I had been dreaming of this day since I was fifteen. Kade had captivated me on that day, and his hold had been strong ever since.

I took each step silently until I had reached the top. The height, danger, and physical activity had my wolf prancing happily inside. She'd been bored. Okay, she was probably more excited about the Kade part; she already thought of the bear as her pack mate. I was right there with her.

After crossing the balcony, I hesitated on the edge of his room. The curtains were billowing out a little, the interior dark. My stomach was all tied up in knots and I wondered if I should just stroll in. Or should I knock? What would I say? This was pretty much a booty call. Maybe I should turn back?

"Are you just going to stand out there all night?" Kade's gruff voice came from just inside the door. He moved slightly and now a swath of moonlight bathed across him and I could see that he was shirtless. Keyword: shirtless.

I cleared my throat and stepped into his room, the same room he had placed me in after I passed out when fighting off that fae in his backyard. Now I felt bold, confident. This was Kade. He had been taking care of me since I became queen, and if I could trust him with my heart, I could trust him with my body.

"Thank you for getting Calista the tablet," I said, striding closer to him, my bare feet silent on his thick carpet. Our eyes locked together. His were fire and life and beauty. Somehow everything was wrapped in those swirling copper depths.

"You're welcome."

He stepped forward, eating up the final distance between us in two long strides. As if we were two magnets and I had no control over my body, my hands reached out and landed on his chest; his stroked my back.

"I have a confession," he said, that low rumbly voice echoing around the darkness. I tensed slightly; that sentence never ended well. Maybe he did have a kid somewhere after all.

"Okay…" I swallowed hard and Kade chuckled seeing my reaction.

"Relax, it's a happy confession."

Some of my tension eased, and a real smile broke across my face.

Kade continued on, his low voice weaving a tale. "After that kiss on the Island when we were fifteen ... I forced my father's palace magic born to cloak me and take me into Manhattan to check up on you."

My grin grew. "Check up on me? I don't know, Bear King, that sounds an awful lot like stalking?"

He gave me a playful glare. "No, I checked up on you. Had the magic born ask around and find out where you lived. I wasn't okay with never seeing you again."

His words stirred a deep, hot emotion inside of me; it was so strong and potent. I had pined over him for weeks after that kiss. Talked to Violet about ways to find him again. I even went back to that same place on the Island a few days later, but he wasn't there. So I figured it wasn't meant to be and he didn't feel the same, so I worked hard to forget about him. Hearing now that he had searched for me ... it confirmed everything I had felt at the time. We were meant to be together.

"What happened?" I asked, because I never saw him again until that day in his garden.

His face darkened, and I was confused for a moment until he said, "I found you in the park. You were crying."

Crying? I thought back to when I was fifteen, after the summer festival.

Oh. Yes. My mother died right after I kissed him. She gave birth to Winnie and didn't make it. I was distraught for weeks. He must have come in that timeframe.

Kade stroked my cheek as a tear I didn't realize was there began to fall. "I then heard about your mother's passing and knew the timing wasn't right. So I waited."

I nodded. "But then I moved," I finished for him.

He nodded as well. "You were an heir, I had found out. You inherited the Bronx and I couldn't travel there. Then my father discovered I was going to the city to check on you..."

"Stalk me," I said, and he smiled.

"After my brother disappeared, everything changed for me. Circumstances changed for both of us, but I want you to know that I intended for you to be mine back then."

My hands were curled around his biceps now as I pulled myself closer to him. The hot nub of emotions in my chest, all about Kade, swelled until it felt like mecca and energy and life was going to literally burst from me. His declaration was the full circle of our life together. It would be what I held on to no matter the fallout of our love. He had claimed me when I was fifteen, and even though it had taken five years for us to finally be together, it was worth the wait. It was funny how life worked, like no matter what, things would turn out as they should. It just took time and patience.

"I love you," I whispered. "I've been in love with a damn bear since I was fifteen years old, and even though I promised I would never sacrifice anything for the crown, you are worth that much to me. You are more than my duty. You are everything."

Kade's eyes were aged whiskey again, his hands on my face and tangled in my hair. "Say it again," he murmured against my lips. "Tell me."

He was awfully demanding tonight. "I'm in love with you, damn bear," I said, my voice growly.

He threw back his head and laughed then. "How long have you been calling me 'damn bear?'" he finally said, flashing all those white teeth at me.

I grinned back at him. "Not long enough. I think I have a few more years of insults in me."

The laughter eased and the flare of heat between us increased. "I'm very glad to hear that," he said. His hands snaked down to cup my butt, and then he was lifting me up. My legs went around his waist like they had been made to rest there. He held me with ease as our lips crashed together. A deep throbbing was clenching my lower half, my belly filled with heat and butterflies. The emotion of the kiss was everything, it was so much. I had never known this love before and somehow I knew I never would again. This was a once in a lifetime.

He sucked on my bottom lip and I moaned as he gently lay me on the bed. I breathed him in then: *wood, soil, home*. He was mine and I was willing to die for this love. I just hoped it wouldn't come to that.

The bed engulfed me, softness cushioning my body as Kade rested against me, his weight solid, his bare skin touching mine. Seriously, though, we had too many clothes on. I wanted to feel all of him. I needed the contact.

As if he'd heard me, Kade's hands slowly skimmed up the side of my body, then my shirt was gone. Pants followed soon after and I was clad in nothing but black lingerie. Not particularly sexy, but you'd never know it by the heat in his gaze. The masculine planes of his face were extra pronounced as he stared down at me, sending my body into a sexual-need overdrive.

I pushed back on him, needing to be in charge as I ran my hands down his bare chest. His eyes lazily following my movements, lips turned up a little in the corners. He was indulging my show of dominance. *Damn bear.* Reaching for his sleep pants, I drew them down in one easy movement, taking my time to brush against him. The smirk fell from his face, and now he was staring at me with bear in his eyes. Throwing his clothes to the side, he was naked. Holy heck he was naked. I paused, taking a second to stare, because as always, Kade was worth staring at.

"Ari, you're driving my bear crazy." Kade's voice was deeper than usual. Rumbly.

My wolf started howling inside, urging me forward. I needed no urging. I pushed him back down to the bed, straddling him, my hands running across his hard body, caressing his skin, touching wherever I could reach. He lifted himself slightly and cupped my breasts, curving his palms around to take my bra off. My underwear bottoms followed, and then it was nothing but heat and kissing. Hot, drugging, kisses.

Kade let me stay on top for longer than I expected, but as the heat built between us, as our bodies fought for more closeness, his dominance kicked in hard and he flipped our positions. He paused briefly, hands tenderly caressing my face, before he kissed me over and over, my lips swollen and plumped by the attention. Then

Kade trailed down further, across my jaw and along my throat. My hands clenched the bed sheets, my body wound up tight and ready to fall apart. We had waited five years to be together, we weren't going to waste one second of tonight apart. Ten minutes with him and I already could tell ... Kade had been worth the wait.

Chapter Fourteen

The best things in life are furry.

THE FIRST BRUSH of sunlight warmed the bed and woke me from my dozing. There was a heavy weight across my body, and on instinct I snuggled closer to the heat. *Pack. Mate.* Last night had been more than I could have ever expected. I'd had sex before. Great sex. But nothing like Kade. Bears did not love the same way wolves loved. Nope, they wrapped you up tight and caressed every part of your body. They were everywhere, touched everything, and ... holy crap, there needed to be a word greater than orgasm, because I had surely surpassed that multiple times.

I wanted a lifetime of loving like that. I would never be satisfied with anything less. I hadn't gotten much sleep, so it was easy to drift back into a nap, pressed tightly to the huge body beside me. Of course, that was right around the time I thought of my advisor. Dammit. Calista was going to kill me if she found out I was with Kade. I was going to have to sneak back in and pretend I was...

Kisses started trailing down my spine and all thoughts were gone. The scrape of his beard against my skin was literally the most erotic thing that had ever happened to me. I was completely at his mercy. He could have asked for anything in that moment and I would have agreed.

"Good morning." The rumbly voice was a close second on the erotic scale, and as I rolled over to see him, his amber eyes moved right into third place.

The way this man looked at me ... holy shifter babies.

"Waking with you is a life I'm already used to, Ari." Kade kissed me as he spoke. I arched my body like a kitten, shifting closer to him. "I'm not sure I'll ever let you go back to your own room."

"You can ... deal ... with Calista then." My breathless words had him chuckling.

"I like her," he said, and went back to kissing me.

I moaned and then there was a knock at the door. I froze.

"Go away!" Kade grumbled, pulling me tighter as if he sensed my instinct to flee.

A male voice spoke through the door: "It's your mother, sir. She's waiting downstairs."

The word "mother" was all it took to have me ripping out of Kade's arms and shooting out of bed like I'd been stung. "Crap, Kade, your mother's here. Does she know about us?" I had no idea how the bear matriarch felt about her son's relationship with a wolf shifter.

My eyes scanned the room for my bra and finally spotted it hanging on his lamp.

Kade was still sitting in bed, the sheets piled across his lower half, which was still very distracting. "She's been on vacation. Must have come back after learning about the attack, even though I called and told her everything was okay."

We couldn't use cell phones, tablets, or computers without short circuiting them, but landlines were okay. That would have been the only way he could have reached her.

I was fully dressed now, feeling much more in control. "Do you think she's angry about me being here? Do you think we should leave?"

What if she'd heard about him firing his council over me and was here to straighten him out? Why hadn't we just gone to a hotel. This was not the way to ease his people into the idea of a wolf-bear relationship.

Kade was out of bed now, the sheets falling away to give me a glorious glimpse of his body. All of a sudden I wasn't sure we needed to leave the room yet. Maybe I could avoid meeting his mother for a few more minutes. He strode across to me, his eyes pinning me in place.

"My mother knows all about you, Ari. She's excited to meet you."

Okay, then. My mother would have killed Kade on sight. And let's not even get to the Red Queen, although she'd been with a fae, so there was no room for her judgment.

I was having trouble concentrating on Kade's words with his huge body right in front of me. "Meet us downstairs for breakfast?" he said.

I cleared my throat. "Uh ... what ... oh, yeah, sure." With great difficulty I turned, ready to descend to my room. Kade stopped me, wrapping his hand around my wrist and spinning me around.

He pulled me back into his warmth, his lips gently caressing my own. My hands found their way to his hard stomach and my legs went all weightless as the kiss deepened. When he pulled away, he said, "Even if my mother didn't approve of us, that wouldn't stop me. You're mine now. No matter what."

I might have been an heir for my entire life. Queen for a brief period too. But I was still like most women and shifters, insecure, lost, searching for pack and home. Kade's reassurance wrapped around me, sank into the darkest recesses of my insecurities, to the place where my father disappeared and my mother was distant to me. It filled in some of the cracks in my soul. I had Kade now. Forever. He was my family, my mate, and I wasn't going to let anyone jeopardize that.

After sneaking downstairs into my room I quickly messed up my bed so Calista wouldn't suspect anything, considering I hadn't made my bed in my entire life. Heir perk. Then I showered and put on a nice dress. I was going to meet Kade's mom. I needed to make a good impression. Luckily I was pretty well trained in etiquette and small talk. I could do this.

I knew Kade had said that she was okay with us being a couple, but sometimes men don't see the truth. Especially sons. She might be secretly plotting my death. I would know after this first meeting. I could size someone up in about sixty seconds.

After throwing my long hair into a braid and finishing my makeup, I made my way downstairs. It was still early, just after 7 A.M, and Calista's door was closed. That was good. I would rather not have a crowd for this meeting, I was nervous enough as it was. Damn, I missed Violet so much. I wish she were here to calm my nerves, or at least make fun of me. *Three days.* Three more days and I could get her back.

I heard Kade's low voice the moment I stepped into the foyer. I was trying to walk quickly to announce my presence and not eavesdrop, but I picked up some of the conversation.

"How dare they dethrone her for this! We should march on Manhattan and make this right." The woman's voice was strong and deep.

Kade's reply was low: "We have to be political, Mother. Arianna's first priority is Violet. Then she can decide what to do about her crown when she gets her best friend back."

"Hmpf. In my day you couldn't just dethrone someone so easily. It took a fight to the death with just cause." Her voice was heating up; she sounded enraged on my behalf, which of course made me instantly like her.

I turned the corner then and cleared my throat. Sitting at the table was Kade and his mother. I wasn't prepared to see bright blond hair; she looked mid-forties, although with shifter aging who knew her real age. She had fine wrinkles around her eyes and mouth, which told me she smiled a lot, and she was wearing a dress that would make Violet swoon. Full Renaissance style.

She stood and I bowed deeply. I don't care if you're the pope, when you meet your king boyfriend's mother, you bow.

She greeted me with a smile and a deep bow of her own as she crossed the room quickly and opened her arms. "It is so nice to finally meet you!"

My body froze when she pulled me in for a tight hug. Quite quickly though my shock eased, and I was able to relax into her comforting embrace. She was tall. At least a few inches taller than me.

"You too, Your Majesty," I replied, unsure of proper protocol here.

"Oh please, call me Annette." She waved a hand and ushered me to sit beside Kade. I did so and then she took a seat as well.

"We were just talking about your dethroning. Honey, I'm so sorry, that must have been hard." Her tone of voice, the way she looked at me, this must have been what it was like to have a real mother. She reminded me of the softer parts of

Calista. I loved my mother, but she'd been duty first and all hard edges.

"Yes, it was very hard, but I'm not a quitter. Selene is not a fit leader for my people, and as soon as I rescue my best friend, I will take back what is mine." I hadn't really said it out loud to anyone yet. Weird that it was Kade's mom I was eventually confiding in, but I had never planned on letting my dethroning stand. I was going to fight that evil hag until my dying day. I would not allow her wickedness to taint our packs.

Annette patted my hand. It was ... nice. I felt more relaxed than I ever would have expected, so deciding it was time to address it straight up, I said, "So ... I need you to know that I love your son. Pretty sure I have since I was fifteen. We never meant to go against our packs like this ... but ... are you okay with us?" Kade hadn't said a word since I walked into the room, but his hand slipped in mine now and he squeezed.

"Oh, honey, didn't Kade tell you? Bears marry for love. Always. We don't do the arrangement thing like the cold wolves—"

"Mother," Kade said, a slight warning in his tone.

She waved a hand. "I'm sorry, but it's weird to me. Breeding for dominance, mating for pedigree..."

It was weird. I'd never been a fan of it, but the way she put it, so bluntly, it really struck me how odd it actually was. Why didn't we marry for love? Why didn't we teach our young that it was okay to do that? Lineage should come second, love first. But when you grew up knowing that was the way, it was hard to break.

"You're right. It is weird," I said, and she smiled.

"Yep, but then again, so is a bear and a wolf. It took some getting used to, but I knew you had to be a special woman. Kade's been talking about you since your coronation."

"Is that right?" I said, raising my eyebrows at the king.

Kade grinned then, and I could see that cocky confidence he was so well known for. He always owned his feelings. His gaze remained on my face, before he gave me the slightest of winks. Damn bear.

"So, Mother, how was Florida?"

Annette went with the change, starting out with a hilarious tale of a few bear cubs in the Orlando den.

Our breakfast was brought out then, huge piles of bacon, eggs, and sausages, fruit platters, small rolls and sweets. I might have lost my throne, but this morning I'd still eat like a queen.

Annette and Kade had huge appetites. For once I was the one eating smaller.

I realized that I had barely stopped smiling for thirty minutes. It was so warm and friendly at this table. I was starting to see where Kade's beautiful heart and soul had come from. I'd never known what his father had been like, but his mother was wonderful. And funny. She gossiped and told tales, all of it in good humor. Once we finished eating, Annette announced that she was going to head back to her house.

"It was so lovely to meet you," I said, standing and bowing into a curtsy.

Annette grabbed me and hauled me in for another hug. When she pulled back she kept her hands on my shoulders. "I've lost my husband and my eldest son, so Kade is all I have now. I want a big fancy wedding to help plan, and a couple grandbabies one day. You got it?"

A grumble rocked Kade's chest, but I just laughed.

"Yes, ma'am," I told her, and she winked, giving Kade a long hug before leaving the room.

Once she was gone, Kade turned to me. "Sorry, she's a little intense."

I smiled. "She's wonderful." It was refreshing to have someone so brutally honest, although Annette and Baladar in the same room might be too much to handle.

"What now?" he asked me.

My features hardened. "Now we make a plan to get Violet back. Starting with the tree in your yard."

Kade tucked a loose strand of my hair behind my ear. My heart rate picked up and I almost missed when he asked, "The old fae tree you can talk to?"

Kade had tried to communicate with the tree in the same way as me, but nothing happened. No voices, no energy. I really should ask the faeling why that was, but for now I was more interested in hashing out a rescue plan.

I nodded. "Hopefully he can give us the right information to help with our plans to rescue Violet."

Kade nodded, trusting me without explanation. I led him out onto the front lawn, both of us striding toward the huge, ancient, gnarled tree. By the time Wednesday arrived I wanted a map of the fae lands, names of the leaders of the courts, and any information that would help me get my best friend back.

The days passed quickly, and before I knew it, it was Wednesday morning. We were finalizing the plan to rescue Violet, armed with all the knowledge I'd managed to glean from many hours beneath the fae treeling. It'd had much to share, although most of it was outdated. The tree spirit couldn't be sure of the current leaders of the courts, only those who were in power when it was in the Otherworld. With their long lives, it was hopefully still the same leadership.

More importantly, the terrain and way of life wouldn't have changed. I had my rough map and some clues as to where the dark court would have taken a prisoner. *Prisoner.* That word was like a punch to the gut.

I stood before my inner circle, preparing to give everyone a job for tonight. Kade's job, which he'd only just learned, was to stay back here and rule the bears, keep everything calm while I was gone. I wanted a stealth sneak attack; a big party in fae land wasn't on the menu. I'd known he was going to fight me on it, but I had to try. It was the best thing for his people, and … I couldn't lose him too. Or be responsible for taking him away and then having Selene attack his people when she found out he was gone.

Of course, one should never argue with a bear; they were immoveable.

"It's not going to happen, Arianna. I will never let you go to that land without me." Kade wasn't even mad. He just crossed his arms.

Immoveable.

"Kade, I could be gone for weeks in Earth time. What will happen if someone attacks your people?"

His stance remained calm, but now his eyes were burning hot coals. "Gerald and my mother will wipe them from the face of the planet. I'm going, Ari. You need my help to control the mecca. That's the end of it."

I wanted to fight him more on this. My gut was telling me to push back, but my heart wouldn't do it. It was so selfish, but I didn't want to do this without him.

"King Kade has a point," Monica piped up. "What if you have to use the mecca in the fae lands and he isn't there to bail you out?"

Yep, that was a fair call. When it came to mecca things, Kade did have a wonderful, annoying habit of saving my butt.

Knowing I'd never win this argument, and since my heart wasn't in it any longer, I conceded.

"Fine, Kade and I will go to the Otherworld. The rest of you will stay here and make sure that the wolf and bear shifters are protected in case the fae attack while we're gone."

They opened their mouths to argue with me again, and I let out a growl that shut the conversation down fast. The Otherworld was dangerous, fae were dangerous. I was trying to save my people here. Why couldn't they see that?

Kade stepped up to my side then, from where he'd been propped against a wall. "I have a plan," he said. Nix was perched on his shoulder looking down at Finn. Our familiars were probably having a silent conversation.

"Arianna, Nikoli, and I will head east. The treeling said that was the quickest way to the dark fae lands from where the mecca stone would place us. Monica, Blaine, and Victor follow soon after, head a few clicks west of our trail, but start curving around to meet up with us eventually. It will look like two small traveling or hunting parties, but if things go wrong we can assemble quickly as a group. Jen and Calista can stay behind, taking two of the spare seats on my council, handling any affairs you think would be in the queen's best interest."

In that moment, the fae could have burst into the room and slaughtered us all. We were that stunned. It was one thing to try to form a mate bond with a wolf shifter, but Kade had just offered two of my wolves a seat on his council. Even if it was just temporary, it was still completely unprecedented.

Jen stood taller, her eyes wide, face lit up. I think she liked that plan very much. Calista would be absolutely ecstatic when she heard this news. She was currently off doing some sort of conference call with the alphas in the borough, keeping updated with the changes from Selene. I couldn't wait to tell her; this was a huge opportunity for her, one she deserved. The Red Queen's council hadn't changed in over a hundred years, so she had known she'd never have a shot there, despite her qualifications.

Outside of the council seats, I could see everyone else was more than okay with Kade's plan. I was the only one not happy with all my people coming to the Otherworld, but I would tentatively admit Kade might be right. My plan to go alone would put me at a greater risk. Bringing a magic born along was definitely a huge help. Teamed with Kade and me, we might have a shot at defending ourselves against a small party of fae attackers.

"Sounds like a plan to me," Blaine said. Monica and Victor agreed as well.

"Well, I guess it's decided. We all go together."

Unease rolled in my gut. This was the best plan, but it still wasn't a great one. There were no great plans when it came to traveling to the Otherworld and taking on the Winter Court. I made a silent promise to myself: if one more friend or loved one died at the hands of the fae, I was going nuclear and taking out as many of those pointy-eared bastards as I could.

Kade interrupted my murderous thoughts: "Time is of haste. Prepare your traveling packs. Make them lightweight and practical. Nikoli will give you each a healing tincture that may help against any fae magic or peculiar encounters."

Peculiar encounters. I didn't even want to know what that meant, but the ercho came to mind.

"Wear plain clothes, nothing branded or overly fashionable. We want to blend in," I added. No doubt we'd be attacked on sight if we strolled around the Otherworld in our designer Earth gear.

Blaine and Victor nodded and then they were gone. Monica and Jen said their goodbyes as well, until I was standing before Kade. His deep copper eyes were soft. He ditched his king mode now that we were alone, back to being my mate. *Mate.* That word held so much meaning in the shifter world. Even without a ceremony or rings we were mates, no one could deny that.

"You realize we could all die right?" I said, wishing that no one had to risk their life but me.

He stepped closer and brushed his fingers along my lower back, sending chills up my spine. "In bear culture, we take honorable deaths very seriously. What better and more glorious way to die than trying to save a beloved friend?"

I sighed and leaned my head against his chest. "Would you stop being so perfect."

He chuckled, rumbling deep in my ear. "It comes so naturally to me though."

Hah! I smacked his arm and was about to lean in and kiss him when Calista burst into the room.

She was dancing on the balls of her feet, clutching her tablet.

"What's up?" I asked, stepping back a few feet from Kade to bring the PDA down a notch.

She thrust the tablet in my face. "Operation reinstate Arianna's crown is in full effect!"

"Operation what?" I laughed, before sobering enough to read the long text before me. Kade and I were both careful not to touch the device. Even so, we were close enough that I could feel the static electricity. Stepping back a little, I read.

My dear beloved wolves,

As you may have heard, Selene and the council stripped me of my crown just after the battle on the Island, the same battle where we fought alongside the bears and defeated the fae who dared to come into our world and try and take our power – the battle where I used so much mecca to kill the fae that it nearly took my own life. I would have died if it weren't for King Kade.

Yes, the rumors about the king and I are true. I have known him since I was fifteen, and as much as I tried I could not deny my heart, as I would never expect you to. If you believe loving a bear makes me unfit to rule, then by all means I will go in peace and allow Selene to be your leader. But if you saw what I saw on that hill, bears and wolves fighting and dying together to defeat our common enemy, and a king that loved a queen so much he put his own life on the line to save her, then I insist you speak up and stand with me.

Selene does not see the fae as a real threat. She thinks she can beat them on her own, but I know we need to band with the bears in order for our races to survive. I am sworn to retrieve my trusted friend and advisor, Violet, from the fae lands, and when I return, if it is your wish, I will rule again. And I will take the life of every dark fae that threatens us.

Forever yours,
Queen Arianna.

"You wrote this?"

I wasn't surprised that she had chosen almost the exact same words I would have used; she knew me better than anyone else. But I was blown away by the heart in this letter. She really was okay with Kade and me, with bears and wolves working together.

Calista grinned. "I did and ... please don't hate me – I know I should have checked with you – but I couldn't wait to send it out to the entirety of the wolf shifters on my email list." She had hundreds of thousands of shifters in her contact list. Selene was a true idiot for not locking Calista out of everything.

"I'm not mad, Cal. I know I need to fight for my crown, but right now my focus is Violet. Thank you for stepping in and filling the gap. So what was the response?" My question came out tentatively. I would fight no matter what, but it would be easier if I wasn't battling everyone.

"The responses are pouring in, and the majority are with you, Ari."

Her answer nearly knocked me over, as a couple of tears spilled down my face. Kade placed his hand on my lower back, his other gripping my hand. My people had not yet given up on me, and that filled me with more drive and motivation than ever before.

I cleared my throat so I could speak. "Let's get Violet back and then take Selene and the council down."

Bears and wolves would rule the boroughs together, if it was the last thing I achieved.

Chapter Fifteen

There's no business like fae business.

WE SPENT THE next several hours going over our plan and triple-checking everyone's packs to make sure all the important stuff was in there, including the map I'd had drawn up based on the treeling's directions, and enough dried meat and fruits to last two weeks. Now it was almost 9 P.M and we were on our way to the bench that Trixie had spoken of.

We must have looked like quite the group, dressed in dark colors, lots of leather and natural fibers, all of us wearing backpacks. We had briefly debated leaving Finn and Nix behind, but neither of them would agree, and even if we insisted I knew they'd follow us somehow. So they were coming. We were stronger with our familiars, and I was glad to have Finn with me.

As Kade's driver pulled up to the bench, we all got out and I noticed two people sitting on the bench already, a man and woman. When we opened the door, they froze.

"K-King Kade," the man stammered, jumping to his feet. He was dressed in nice slacks and a button-down shirt.

"What are you doing here?" The woman was standing behind him, running her hands along her dress and looking nervously down at the golden disc at her feet.

As I stepped closer I could feel the pulsing mecca coming from the disc. We were at the right place.

Kade was angry. I could feel it simmering in his energy, but we had more important things to worry about. He'd have to deal with his people's tendency to borough hop at a later stage.

"I'm going to the same place you are, to Baladar's club," he said shortly. Nix landed then, in all her glory, on his shoulder.

The man and woman were frozen with fear, staring at Nix as if waiting for her to peck their eyes out.

"Ummm..." The man didn't know what to say.

Kade waved him off. "Come on, show us how it's done and I will allow you one more night of partying before I shut this down."

The couple seemed unsure, like this might be a trick, but after cowering under the steely gaze of their king for about twenty seconds, they caved.

Both of them sat down again and placed their feet precisely on the disc. They started to breathe slowly in through their nose and out through their mouth. "It's just like vortex," the man said between breaths. "Only not as strong, so most shifters can use it. We just have to wait until after 9 P.M for it to work." He glanced down at his watch and smiled. "It's time. Oh and this is a direct link, you don't have to tell it where to go. Just picture traveling along it." Then, in a surge of mecca, they were gone.

"This is a very public place to have a vortex." I turned around and noticed there were a few people in the park. Weirdly enough, no one seemed to be looking in this direction. If anything, their eyes skimmed over the spot like it wasn't even here, like there weren't half a dozen shifters standing around a golden disc.

Kade followed my line of sight. "I think it's spelled. The energy is off and it smells strange," he said.

Nikoli stepped forward and bent down, looking around the bench. "Yep, it is. The humans see nothing here but an old dirty park bench. Not the sort anyone would want to sit upon."

Interesting. Just how the hell did Baladar set this up, and how many more did he have?

"Arianna..." Kade reached out for my hand and I took it, sitting with him on the bench. Nix remained on his shoulder,

Finn settled into my side, placing two paws on the disc.

The swirl of mecca beneath my feet was just like a vortex, but I could sense there was only one path. The rest of the magical crisscross of lines were not available. With a deep breath, I focused on the one path, Baladar's brownstone in Manhattan, and we were sucked into the vortex.

Arianna, forgive me.

That voice echoed through my head. The mecca was still trying to tell me something.

Before I could concentrate or try to focus on it, I was spat out of the vortex and into a grassy park area, underneath a large tree with shimmering pink flowers. Music was blaring, lots of bodies moving to the heavy beat. Looking around, I recognized the landscape. We'd made it to Baladar's. This was his club night.

"Key?" The voice to my right had my head swiveling. Two beefy bear shifters were paused on either side of us. There was security on this vortex entrance as well apparently.

Kade growled then, and both of them about cried when they realized it was their king. Their knees slammed against the grass as they bowed deeply. "We're so sorry, Your Majesty. We did not realize you would be here tonight."

One of them was stammering out the explanations, the other seemed to be struggling to breathe. Kade's expression remained hard, and I could see that despite his generally easygoing nature, he could slip into king mode no problem.

"Find Baladar. Now." His command was low, no yelling, but the two guards shot up like he'd stabbed them in the heart. They took off, disappearing into the mass of bears on the dance floor.

Within seconds they were back, a flash of purple between them. Baladar. He wore a regal looking, deep purple suit, with a felt top hat. Opening his arms wide, he greeted us with a smile.

"Your Majesties, what an honor! Calista told me to be expecting you."

Kade's bear let out another low growl, and I stepped in front of him, drawing the magic born's attention. Yes, Baladar was kind of a rule-breaker, but he was also powerful and helpful, and seemed to really like me, so I wanted to keep him as an ally.

"Sir Baladar..." I nodded my head in greeting.

His face grew somber as he assessed my face. "I was so sorry to hear about the dethroning."

I gave him a small smile. "Thank you. It's temporary, I believe. Selene won't be queen for long. Right now what I need help with is getting my best friend back. Violet was taken to the Otherworld."

I heard a crackling noise. Behind me, the rest of our group was traveling in. Monica, Blaine, Victor, and Nikoli appeared, striding straight across to join us.

Baladar assessed the group, stopping on my huge familiar. "Yes, I heard she was taken. I fear you're not prepared for the unique and dangerous things you will encounter in the fae lands."

Why was he speaking ominously and staring at my familiar?

I tried to draw his attention back to me. "I'm not a queen or shifter, who would ever leave a friend behind. Violet is my best friend. The fae took what's mine and I will be getting her back."

"She's been spending way too much time with the bear king," I heard Monica whisper behind us, followed by a few chuckles. They weren't wrong. I was getting all bear-possessive like him.

Baladar nodded. "Yes, Violet is a special soul. I hope you can get her back."

Kade was still growling when he said, "We can and we will."

Baladar looked from me to Kade and back, tilting his head slightly as he examined us. "I was wondering when you two would realize."

And we were back to the riddles. "Realize what?"

Baladar grinned. "Come on, you haven't recognized it yet?"

I fought the urge to punch him, my wolf rising up, prepared to strike. We had no time for this, we had to move out of here and get this journey started.

Before I could say anything, Kade stepped into him, his voice flat as he said: "Just tell us, Baladar. We have no time for your mysteriousness."

Baladar leaned over, bringing his head closer to us as he lowered his voice: "You're *bonded mates*. Like the original shifters. You can speak into each other's minds, feel the other's emotions, sense when the other is in danger, no matter how far away. Haven't you felt it? I can see it."

I understood his explanation, but I wasn't sure I believed what he was saying. Modern wolves didn't have bonded mates. It was like an old tale from the origin of shifters, and no one knew if it was actually true or just made up.

Turning to Kade, I reached out a hand, feeling for that spark of energy that was always between us. The closer I got, the stronger the pull. Had this changed since we'd made love? For the first time I tried to speak to him using the same path I did with Finn – a bonded mental connection. As my energy expended, I realized my heart was hammering. I both feared the truth, and hurt at the thought that it might not be possible.

Kade? I focused the question, not sure if Finn would hear too.

Kade's arms went around me and he lifted me up into his body. *How is this possible?* His deep voice rumbled through my mind, and right then, as our thoughts mingled in our consciousnesses, our energy let out a deep gonging sound, like a bell had been struck. My body sank into his as mecca danced around the room. Both of us glowed purple, and some of the space inside, from where Selene had stolen my energy, was filled.

"I can feel you," I said out loud, still not used to speaking with him in my mind. "Your energy, your strength." My voice dropped to barely a whisper. "I can feel you."

Kade kissed me then, long and hard, the purple of our skin brightening. I could see it beneath my closed lids. Using our bond, he said to me: *I can feel you too. Everything. Your kindness, your heart, your loyalty and love for all your people. Your love for me. I am not sure I'm worthy, but I will never take this for granted. You are my bonded mate. My true one.*

My true one, I echoed back, losing myself in his embrace.

Eventually we had to stop kissing, but Kade kept me close to his side. He turned to Baladar, and I could feel the happiness and confusion within him. "It is true. We're bonded mates. But how is this possible? I thought bonded mates were a fairy tale? No bears have ever bonded in such a way. There are stories, but no evidence of it."

So it wasn't just the wolves.

Baladar shook his head. "They were very common back in my day, when wolves and bears inter-mated. You see, the combination is only possible with the opposite race. It's how things were meant to be. Yin and Yang. Balance. The reason bears have male heirs and wolves have females. The leaders have always been meant to be together."

Holy shifter babies. We had intentionally separated the races, and by doing so kept everyone from meeting their bonded mate. It left an awful pit in my stomach. Not to mention …

how freaking old was Baladar? Wolves and bears had not been together for hundreds of years, clearly since the time of the original shifters.

I could see that all of our people were affected by this revelation, by the knowledge which had been lost, knowledge which would have helped to strengthen our people. When did this all start, the division between us?

Nikoli cleared his throat. "Sorry to interrupt, but we must hurry if we're to make the changing of the guard."

Kade and I separated ourselves then, the purple mecca fading from our skin. *Never separated now, love,* he said, before a mental barrier fell between our minds. I could feel him there, but the thoughts weren't actively flowing between us. He'd done that, separated our thoughts, and I was grateful. It was going to take me some time to figure out how to isolate Finn and Kade in my mind, and how to only project the thought I wanted each to know. It wouldn't be long, though. All my years meditating and using the bonded connection to Finn had been good training.

Baladar led us across to the far side of his bear party area, and pointed toward a door that was discreetly hidden in a small alcove. "Use this exit. It'll drop you very close to the royal residence. Selene hasn't had time yet to incorporate too many new security measures, but she is actively keeping an eye out for you. Especially after Calista's letter."

I grinned. "You knew it was her. That she wrote on my behalf?"

The magic born threw back his head and laughed. "I could see my little spitfire in every word, but it was your words she used. She knows you better than anyone else. She knows what you'd want her to say to your people."

"I'd be lost without her," I said, injecting every ounce of my love for Calista into the sentiment. "She's been my rock for twenty years, and she has never given up on me."

Baladar surprised me then with a hug. I was so used to no one touching me without permission, I tensed for a second. But then it was nice. Just a light, comforting hug.

When he pulled away, he had a bright purple flower in his outstretched hand. "Take care in the Otherworld. Use this to stay in touch with me, and be safe. I would not see you lost. The shifter world needs you and King Kade."

He pulled away, and before I could say anything more he was gone, disappearing into the brightness of his prison world, leaving me with the fae flower communication device, which I tucked into my backpack. I needed to figure out a way to break the imposed imprisonment of him here. I still couldn't understand why it hadn't fallen with the death of the Red Queen. Somehow she had figured out a way to continue to rule, even from the grave.

Kade reached around me to open the door, his hands brushing along my sides as we stepped out into the dark night, bathed by the glow of the street lamps. *What the...?*

We were nowhere near Baladar's loft. We were only a block from the palace. That man had some serious magic up his sleeve. Kade wrapped one of his arms around me, offering comfort in the way of our people – touch. It hit me hard then. I wasn't alone. Sure, I'd never been fully alone, always surrounded by dominants, guards, advisors, but I had stood apart from them, always with the proper protocol, me being heir or queen. The only one who was my equal was Finn, and I'd clung to our bond with ferocity.

Now I had Kade too, another equal – more than equals, we were partners – and that gave me a sense of strength and happiness I'd never felt before. It also scared me to death. How did one go on without their partner? It was like my soul was divided again now, and I had twice as much to lose if this went badly. Crap. Going to the Otherworld was a really bad idea, but we had no choice. If anyone else was the third part of my soul, it was Violet. I couldn't lose any of them.

I would just have to pray to all the shifter gods that I was strong enough for this, that I could be a queen, friend, and mate, without losing any of my loved ones.

We moved silently toward the royal home as Nix took to the skies. So far we'd passed a few shifter patrols, but my dominants were familiar with the general walk line and shift changes, so we were able to avoid them. The closer we got, though, the harder it would be. Selene seemed to have doubled the numbers patrolling, and I wasn't sure if it was fae or me she feared. Either way, she was continuing her trend of being a pain in the butt. It was stressful to think of all the stupid and selfish energy she was probably filtering across our boroughs, and right when we were at war. It was not a time for that sort of weakness to be here.

"Three royal guards on my six," Victor whispered. "Turn into this alley. We'll wait it out here."

No one spoke or questioned his orders, even though he sounded a little uncertain. All of us were missing Ben right now; he would have had a million routes plotted out in his head, already have known which way to turn to avoid everyone. My heart squeezed tightly in my chest as I swallowed down my sorrow. There was no time for mourning, no matter how much I needed to grieve.

Nikoli stepped closer to Kade and me, whispering softly: "I can cloak three people, but not all six." Darkness surrounded us in the alley.

"Cloak, Monica, Blaine, and Victor," I said. "The king and I will meet you in the crystal room. They know the way."

He moved to argue but Kade interrupted. "Do it."

"But—"

"That's an order, Nik." Kade's voice could cut glass. We didn't have time for anyone to be second-guessing us. The truth was Kade and I together were stronger than everyone in this alley. We would be fine.

Reluctantly, Nikoli slowed his steps, squeezing himself into Monica, Blaine, and Victor's space. The alleyway was tight, and three wolves walking side by side left barely any room for the bear magic born. Before my dominants could ask what was going on, they vanished, as if they had just traveled on the vortex, but I knew they were still standing before me.

Kade, Finn, and I hugged the wall to let them pass us. A whoosh of air brushed across my face and then they were gone. I'm sure they had wanted to argue, but Nikoli had probably cloaked and silenced them, for their own safety.

We gave them a few minutes before Kade and I stepped out of the darkness.

The street was empty again, so we stuck to the shadows and moved with speed toward the royal home. I had no idea how we were going to get inside, but that was a problem I'd deal with once we got there.

The huge building dominated much of the sky in the area. I could feel the surge of mecca stronger there than anywhere else.

"Cloaked shifter to our right," Kade said with urgency. I felt it then: shifter energy. They had to have been cloaked and shielded so no one would notice. The only reason Kade had was because he was powerful and the shifter was basically right on top of us.

Too late to run.

"Don't move," a male guard growled.

Raising my hands, I swiveled my head enough to see who it was. A familiar face came into view: long amber hair tied back at the nape of his neck, lean corded muscles, and burning dark eyes. Mason. Now I understood how he had snuck up on us. He was the sneakiest of all border guards. His entire training had been in stealth and subterfuge. On top of that, he'd clearly been spelled to hide his scent and energy.

Kade growled, but I shut him down with a look.

I got this, I said, trying the newly formed bond between us. Kade's eyes still swirled, but he gave me a nod.

I slowly peeled my jacket hood back and Finn stepped out of the shadows to stand beside me.

Mason's face fell and he lowered the sword he had raised. Looking back over his shoulder, he called out into the dark alley. "Stand down!"

There must have been more guards, possibly with bow and arrows ready to take us out.

"Your High ... Arianna." He wasn't sure what to call me and I wasn't sure either. I was a dethroned queen. There was no title for that.

The two guards hiding in the shadows walked out slowly to join Mason. I looked up and saw Nix circling lower in the sky, ready to dive down here and join if a fight broke out. As the other guards stepped closer, I relaxed a little. I knew them all. Selene had not yet had time to switch out her entire staff.

"Mason, Garret, Gwen, I am not here to cause Selene harm. I know you're sworn to protect her now, and I give you my word as your former queen that I will not actively harm her today. I'm just here to get Violet back."

They all shared a look, and then Garret, the senior guard of the group, nodded. "It's good to see you again, My Queen."

Then they all turned and walked away down the alley and out of sight.

I exhaled the breath I had been holding.

"Come on." Kade grabbed my arm and we jogged the rest of the way down the alley to the back terrace entrance.

That meeting had been pure luck, and I knew it wouldn't happen again. Selene would put the least-trusted guards on the perimeter; her loyal guards would be inside and they wouldn't hesitate to take my head if they found me on the grounds.

"Plan?" I asked Kade, because we were running out of time to just wing it.

He tilted his head toward me, a glint in his eye and a half-smile turning up his lips. "I have a crazy idea."

That was usually Violet's line. "I'm okay with crazy right now."

Nix dropped from the sky and onto Kade's shoulder. I had to back up several feet so her wings didn't hit me in the face.

Kade was staring at his familiar, no doubt having a conversation. I knew now that I could probably link up with Kade's thoughts and listen in, but I would never do that. If he wanted me to hear he would share it with me, but I did sense some apprehension from him. His feelings were seeping into me and making me nervous.

"What's the plan, Kade?" If it made him nervous, I wasn't sure I liked it.

He looked at Nix. "A diversion."

Right before my eyes, Nix changed her appearance to that of a smaller, less-imposing black crow. Everyone would recognize Kade's large rare eagle, but a crow might be passed off as just another New York pest. I grinned. It was a good idea, but it did put Nix at risk.

"They'll never catch her," Kade said, either reading my thoughts or my expression.

He nodded to his familiar. As she launched off his shoulder, Kade snatched up my hand and we were running. Nix began squawking like a bird in mating season, and we slowed our steps, choosing to take the last few at a silent tiptoe. Finn remained by my side, now looking like his dog persona.

A door opened on the back porch. A guard peeked his head out to hear what the commotion was all about and Nix took the open door as her entrance, flying right into the back patio and entering the castle.

"She'll use her energy to keep the doors open, and make sure all the guards follow her," Kade murmured to me.

Sure enough...

"What the—"

Two guards yelled as she dashed past them. They then raced inside after the bird. I saw Nix circle around a few times, before heading upstairs, squawking the entire time. A few guards followed, but there would be more around. We'd have to be cautious.

The door remained open, as Kade said, so it was time to move. We crept across the back patio and slid inside. Nix's screeching was distant now, but still echoing across the many floors, no doubt waking the entire castle. Which could be an issue for us in the long run, but getting inside had been our first obstacle, and we'd managed it.

Even though my rule had been short, I knew the estate quite well. I led Kade and Finn to the elevator just off to the side of the entrance. This particular elevator was not used a lot. Most shifters preferred the grand stairs, so we slipped inside unseen, hit the button for the floor that the mecca crystal was on, and the doors closed.

"How will she get back to us?" I said, as soon as we were secured inside.

The plan worked to get us inside, but now we needed Nix back before we could enter the fae lands. Kade just grinned. "Don't worry about Nix, she's a wily familiar. She'll find us before we leave."

Trusting him, I focused on the elevator numbers. We were closing in on the floor, and I pressed myself to the side of the door. Kade did the same on the other side, preparing for the fact that there would probably be guards on this level somewhere. It was the queen's private floor after all – *my* private floor. I tried not to let my anger about Selene stealing my throne get to me now. That needed to be dealt with later.

With a barely perceptible ding, the lift doors slid open. Finn went first, scouting out the hall. Somehow we all knew this was the plan, though none of us had discussed it. This mental link thing was getting stronger. And even though I couldn't hear Nix now, I sensed she was near.

All clear.

Kade and I moved out of the elevator and straight along the corridor. The small library-sitting room that hid the entrance to the mecca stone was at the end of this hall. We passed no one in the first half, and I was giving myself a mental high-five when a door to the right opened and two people stepped out into the hall.

Selene and her lead guard.

Chapter Sixteen

The dance of life, one step forward, ten steps back.

AS SOON AS he saw the queen, Kade gathered me up into his arms, slamming us both back against the wall. We'd have barreled right into them otherwise.

"There has been no security breach, Your Majesty. You have nothing to..." The lead guard trailed off as he finally noticed Kade and me standing there. I recognized him from our time together in the Summit. He'd stuck pretty close to Selene's side and was a brutal fighter. He wore a spelled talisman that gave him mild magical powers and increased strength. Selene had always said she needed such a talisman to make up for the fact she had no personal magic born like me. Yeah, no bitterness there.

I should have known this initial infiltration had been way too easy. Of course we would run into the freaking queen and her most powerful wolf. The four of us faced off, and the redheaded wench stepped forward, dressed in a ball gown of all things, floor length with a mass of tulle and satin. Upon her head was a simple diadem, nothing like my crown of mecca, which was still in the possession of the council. Either they hadn't had time to make her crown yet, or the special covenant that the council used to figure these things out had run out of ideas. It was literally a few pieces of gold twirled around some greenish hued gems. So simple. And I was pleased to see she was sans her slimy snake familiar, although I doubted he was far.

"How the hell did you get in here, Arianna? The guards have strict instructions to remove your head should you step foot in Manhattan. I have all the vortexes being triple guarded."

Clearly not all of them.

When I didn't answer immediately, her voice went into a shriek. "What are you doing here?" She slapped out at us with mecca, but Kade easily absorbed it, filtering it out into the world.

My wolf rose within me, both of us letting out low growls. "I am here to rescue Violet, and any more of our people who might have been taken by the Tuatha. I will not let them die in the Otherworld. *I* protect my people."

My voice was low, each word resonating across the hall with a heavy and powerful tone. The mecca was so close here, it was filling up the gaps stolen by my dethroning. Almost like the power didn't like our joining not being complete.

"A queen's responsibility is to all of her people, not an individual few," her lead guard said, shifting around slightly. They were maneuvering themselves to attack from both sides. I recognized the procedure, and found it amusing they thought I wouldn't notice.

"Let us pass. I'm not here to fight you, Selene. But if you try and stop me I will be forced to retaliate." That was my best attempt at being political in front of the fake queen.

Selene's cackle ricocheted off the halls and I knew my attempt at peace was futile. She wanted my head.

Nix will be here in seconds, Kade said in my mind. *She'll attack them from behind. I can channel mecca through her, surround them with it.*

I will join with Nix from behind, Finn added.

Okay, then, confirmation that Finn could hear the conversation too. We really needed to work this mental link thing out. Another time, when we weren't about to jump into a shifter throwdown.

Let's attack now, I said, hoping everyone would hear. *They won't have time to call in more guards, and I sense that Victor and the others are close.*

Now! Three voices crossed the bond, and I had the first chance to hear the light, whispery tones of Nix.

Kade grabbed my hand, the two of us drawing in mecca energy. It was easy this close to the stone; there was so much it was literally seeping in from all directions. Our mated bond also helped. It was like the well of energy in my center was connected to Kade's, and holy crap ... his connection to the mecca was beyond anything I'd ever felt.

Selene shrieked before the skin on her hand and forearms shone purple. She blasted out again, running toward us. Of course she must have forgotten she was wearing a ridiculous gown. Her legs tangled in the hem, tripping her down flat onto the floor, and her shot went wide. Ignoring her, Kade and I advanced on the guard. The talisman around his neck glowed a purplish hue as he began to chant a spell that had the wind whipping up around us. Sabina must have made that talisman. No one else was powerful enough, save for Violet, and she never would have.

He's calling the guards and magic born," I said, loud enough to be heard over the whipping winds. "I felt the call go out."

Kade pulled me closer, his chest rumbling against my arm. *If I attack them, they could declare war on the bears. I can't let that happen while I'm not here to defend them. What's your plan?*

I shook my head. *They won't declare war on the bears. They don't have the manpower to fight both your people and the fae. Besides, their beef is with me alone. They're going to try and take care of this in-house, and probably hope your people think you were taken by the fae.*

I knew Selene. That was the devious path she'd take.

Kade grinned, his rumbles turning into chuckles. "In-house is perfect. That's exactly what I hoped you'd say."

He dropped my hand then and charged toward the guard, leaving me to deal with Selene, who was already back on her feet. I wasn't worried about Kade. The guard was powerful, and he had a spelled talisman, but he wasn't royal or magic born. He couldn't manipulate mecca like we could, and he stood no chance against an almost seven-foot bear king. I watched long enough to see him slam into the giant guard, knocking him back into the wall, breaking his magical call for help. The guard quickly stood, pulling a blade from behind his back with a menacing look in his eye

Kade winked at me before diving into the fight; he looked to be enjoying it.

"Figures you'd end up slumming it with a bear," Selene said, spitting blood out of her mouth as she advanced on me. "You always were scum. No idea who fathered you to even know if it was a decent lineage. All you had going for you was the Red Queen's lineage, and look at what a whore she turned out to be. She let fae into our world. She caused all of this, and I think the red line should be wiped out now, forever. No longer are you fit to be heirs."

Her dark brown eyes narrowed, her grin sinister, especially with some blood staining her teeth. Figures she would hurt herself so badly just from tripping over a stupid dress. Even though her shifter healing had kicked in, and the wound was closed over, the blood remained long after.

"Say goodbye, Arianna of the red line. You are a failed queen. A failed heir. And a true disgrace to all wolves."

She dived toward me, pulling a knife from her arm cuff at the same time. The dress was a hindrance for her, but she was still a shifter, so she made the six foot leap with ease. We tangled together, my back crashing to the floor as she plunged the knife toward my face. I raised my forearm just in time to deflect the blow, capturing her hand and stopping her from stabbing at me again.

She was strong, filled with energy, and we struggled for dominance, neither of us wanting to give in. "The royal guards will be here any moment. You have lost. Time to say goodbye to your freak of a friend. She's going to remain a fae plaything for the rest of her days."

I remained focus.

Nix and I are holding off the guards. Finn's voice was briefly there, then he was gone.

Take that, Selene, you bitch. I twisted my body to the side; her knife slipped along my arm, cutting through my shirt and slicing my cheek. I didn't worry about the cut, it'd heal soon enough, and she let me move enough so I could swing my elbow across her brow. It clipped her hard, the brunt force enough to open her face up right along her forehead and down her temple.

She howled, rolling off me. Larak appeared then, slithering out from wherever he'd been, and launched himself at me. I knew that damn snake would be nearby, and let me just say, there is nothing scarier than a massive anaconda throwing itself at you with both fangs bared.

"Ari!" Kade growled.

Ari! Finn was in my head.

I focused on the snake. My hand brushed along a metal object as I raised both hands to defend myself. I realized a second later that it was Selene's knife. I rolled out of the way of Larak's first strike, scooping up the knife as I went. By the time I turned, he was launching at me again.

I twisted to the side to avoid his fangs, throwing the huge body over my shoulder and using the knife to slice along his underbody as he went.

Selene started screaming then, these long howling shrieks, and I felt a hot surge of energy crash into me as she started throwing mecca bombs at me. Only been queen for four days and she already knew how to form the mecca into powerful little balls of energy. *Unfair.* Sabina must have trained her with knowledge she'd hid from me.

Knocked down by a particularly huge blast, Larak went with me, his dark-brownish blood splashing across my chest and neck. It burned a little, and I was hoping it wasn't poisonous like his venom. The mecca bombs had hurt, a lot – my side was bruised and aching where she'd hit me.

I had to get moving; she would keep trying to kill me if I didn't. But Larak's huge body was pinning me to the floor. I was strong enough to move him normally, but my current position had me unable to get enough leverage to heave him off.

Selene's face appeared above me, but she wasn't looking at me. She bent down so she could run her hands frantically along her familiar.

"Larak, don't you die on me." Tears ran down her face, smudging her makeup and giving her a goth clown look.

I had a temporary moment of insanity, feeling bad for Larak and Selene, but then I remembered how he'd almost kill Finn in an underhanded sneak attack, and my pity fled. In a flash the weight lifted off me. Larak was pulled away and Kade was scooping me up. Selene scrambled to where Larak lay bleeding freely; the snake had his glossy eyes pinned to his queen. Over the bear's shoulder I could see that Kade had knocked Selene's guard unconscious. A burst of mecca rocked down the hall and all of us turned to see what was coming at us now.

Sabina, in all her cloaked glory. Her white hair was already fanning out around her as she channeled mecca. She then dropped her cloak and rushed toward us.

Her pale eyes were glancing between Kade and me, then back to Selene and Larak, as if she couldn't decide whether to shoot a spell at me or to help the queen.

"Heal him!" Selene shrieked, so loud I was sure the glass sconces that lined the halls would shatter.

As Sabina knelt to heal Larak, Kade's hand slipped into mine and then he was pulling me down the hall.

Selene's voice boomed out around me as she screamed. "This isn't over Arianna! The next time I see you I will rip you apart limb by limb! You're dead!" The final two words shook the walls and I knew then that she wasn't kidding. And she was possibly powerful enough to do it. The mecca coursed through both of us. The next time I saw her it would be a fight to the death.

As we rounded the corner, I was beyond relieved to see the door to the sitting room that hid the mecca stone being held open by Blaine. A flapping of wings and a howl from Finn let me know the familiars were right on our tail. I didn't dare look behind me as we all raced into the room, Blaine slamming the doors closed after us. Just as the door slammed shut, thuds could be heard, and we all jumped back as the tip of an arrow pierced right through the wooden barrier.

The royal guard were here. Nikoli stepped up and started chanting, holding both hands out. A blue mist leaked toward the door. Blaine dived to the side to avoid being touched by the magic born's spell. The blue increased across the door, thickening until no more arrows were visible, but I could still hear commotion on the other side.

After a few seconds, Nikoli turned to us. "It should hold long enough, but we have to hurry."

Racing across the room, I pulled down the book that was the secret door lever into the mecca stone room. As the hidden door popped open, I was blasted with mecca. More than usual. The energy had increased again. Great.

I wished I could get word to the Summer Prince to tell him all that had happened, ask for his assistance traversing into the Otherworld, but that damn flower was in my old room.

Kade strode in behind me and the others followed. From what I could see of my people, Monica's right arm was injured, but otherwise she looked okay. The rest were pretty much unscathed. Blaine, Monica, and Victor were all grimacing as they tried to trudge through the mecca energy in the room.

"It's stronger," Kade yelled over the buzzing noise the crystal was emitting.

So much stronger. Touching it right now felt like a stupid thing to do. Who knew if any of us would even survive that much mecca flooding through our bodies, but ... I had to try for Violet.

She was my sister, present in almost every one of my memories growing up. Like the time she was seven and had had a rough day in the human world. Some of them had teased her for her peculiar pale looks, told her she was a freak. I'd been so mad, I told her that I wanted names and addresses so I could go beat them all up. She'd laughed through her tears, told me that it didn't matter, that our friendship was all she needed. It was probably that moment I knew we'd be lifelong best friends. We'd even decided to seal our bond with a blood oath. Violet was my blood sister, and I would literally do anything to get her back. Some people were just worth dying for.

I could tell Kade had been reading my emotions, if not my thoughts. He grabbed my hand and together we touched the crystal. That told me he was all in. He would also risk everything for Violet. For me. She was that important to me and I was that important to him.

The mecca shot into me so hard I let out a strangled cry. Somehow I managed to hold on. I could feel Kade filtering the energy so it wouldn't affect me as much, but it was straining him. We needed to do this quickly. Channeling the energy into what I needed, the portal began to open, the faint image becoming clearer by the second, trees and bushes appearing before us.

Someone gasped behind me, then Nikoli said, "I didn't believe you could actually do it. We've always been taught that only fae can open portals to the Otherworld."

Yeah, we're part fae, I wanted to say, but that was a whole other conversation for another day.

"Go! We can't hold it much longer," I shouted. Blaine seemed cemented to the spot, staring at the image, but at my command he grabbed Monica's hand and nudged Victor's shoulder.

"We'll head west before doubling back toward the east so we can meet up with you in a few days," I heard Blaine say, before he stepped through. Finn ran in after them.

I'll stick with them for now and keep in touch, he said. *That way we can communicate easily between our groups.* I hated being apart from him, but it was a good plan. He'd keep them safe.

Take care, old friend!

Nikoli and Nix went through next, and I noticed Kade's forehead had broken out with beads of sweat.

"Arianna, go!" he bellowed, letting go of my hand, his other remaining on the crystal.

"No way! We go together!" I shouted, snatching his hand back up. The mecca was buzzing so loudly now I wanted to cover my ears.

I heard the door in the sitting room crash open. Now or never. On the other side of the portal, Nikoli and Nix were waiting for us. The magic born had a ball of orange fire in his hands, gearing up for some spell, hopefully to help keep the portal open while we jumped through, or maybe to stop anyone else following us.

On three... Kade said. I readied myself and tried not to think of what would happen if the portal closed while we were halfway through it. Most likely it would slice our bodies in half.

Stop thinking!

"One ... two ... three!" Kade shouted and we pulled our hands off in unison, stepping around the mecca crystal and charging at the open portal. As we neared it, it began to shrink.

"Jump!" I yelled, both of us taking a leap at the same time. We hit the portal just as Nikoli's orange ball of fire slammed in from the side. The closing of the entrance slowed, his power keeping it open for us. As I passed through the portal opening, I heard that voice again, that familiar voice that had been in the mecca for weeks.

Arianna, I loved you dearly. Forgive me.

I hit the cold hard dirt with enough force to take my breath away, rolling a few times before coming to a halt. Lying there, I had to take a moment to catch my breath. Not just because of the fall, but because of that voice. It had been so clear this time. I knew who it was now. Without any doubt ... it was the Red Queen. All this time she'd been trying to communicate with me through the mecca.

Dammit! We might have gotten our answers if I'd known that. I could have tried harder to find out how it was even possible for her to speak to me from the afterlife. But I was in the Otherworld now, and there was no time for me to deal with the Red Queen.

Jumping to my feet, I was up in time to see the portal crush the last of Nikoli's orange ball spell. It was almost closed now, but I did see Selene running into the room with her guard. She took one look at me on the other side and screamed so loud I heard it in the fae lands. Then she was gone.

Earth was gone. We were in the Otherworld, and I had absolutely no idea how we were going to get back home once we found Violet. A problem to worry about later. For now we had a mission and I was focusing on that. Breathing in slowly, calming my nerves after the last thirty minutes of adrenalin, I let myself really see the land we'd arrived in, taking stock of threats and such that might be in the vicinity.

It was beautiful here, quiet and peaceful. I could sense energy in the land beyond what Earth had, a true natural force that quietly flowed beneath us. Rolling green hills, towering trees which seemed to expand out into the horizon – not to mention a plethora of flowering plants. It was pretty and it smelled good. And all of this beauty hid a deadliness which could get us killed.

In the distance, about five hundred yards away, I caught sight of Blaine and the others. They had wasted no time moving, and we needed to go as well. Thankfully, our travel bags had remained on our backs, even through the fight. We had everything we needed. It was time to go.

Nikoli and Kade started to stalk around, scouting the land. Nix was on Kade's shoulder, not wanting to fly up yet. When we traveled, though, she would be our first line of defense against any attack. Through the trees I could see a few small huts that made up some type of village, and farther beyond it a huge white-stone castle.

Kade turned to me, his face more serious than usual. "Does it seem a little less vibrant than the last time we saw this world? The plants are sick. I can feel their pain."

He was right. The last time the colors had almost been too much to stare at. Taking a much more thorough look around, I realized that many of the flowers were wilted, the trees and grass browning in some patches. The sky was also a sickly bluish green, which was different to what I remembered. The mecca was definitely affecting these lands.

A snarly voice came from behind us: "Announce yourself! You know protocol!"

I slowly turned, not wanting to startle them into an attack. I cursed myself for not pulling my hood up, but thankfully my long hair mostly covered my very non-pointy ears. No doubt I was a mess, covered in blood and dirt, which would not help alleviate suspicions.

When the fae came into sight, I was a little surprised, but managed to keep my expression from changing. I hadn't been sure what to expect, but the four-foot creature with thick brown, wrinkled skin and pointy ears was not it. He had a humanoid shape, but clearly was not one of the fae I was used to seeing. His face had the texture and structure of a brown nut, with two very green eyes that seemed to be one pure color, no pupil to break it up. I scanned down to his toes and saw he was barefoot, with wide hairy stumps for feet. Weird, coarse looking, brown tufts of hair sprouted out at various places on his body.

Let me know what you want to do, Kade said, waiting at my side.

Let's see if we can talk our way out of this before we attack.

Our conversation was cut off as the creature cleared his throat and took a small step forward. "Announce yourself," he said again.

He wasn't coming at us threateningly, but did hold a small knife in his hand, the blade beautiful and unusual. It had a twirled looking blade, the point sharp and glinting. The twirl of metals were a mix of steel and gold.

I had a pretty good idea of the type of fae we were dealing with here. The treeling in Kade's garden had spent a lot of time talking to me about the different races. He was a gnome. They were great with metals, and they loved food, which gave me an idea.

Keeping my voice low, hiding the New York accent best I could, I said, "Greetings! We're traders. We come with dried fruits, nuts, and meats in exchange for two nights stay and some finely crafted weapons."

His wrinkled face went even more creased. My accent was still going to be odd, no matter what I did to smooth it out. My heartbeat was picking up. I really hoped he wasn't going to attack, because we needed to sneak in without drawing attention to ourselves. We also needed weapons. We'd decided not to bring Earth-made weapons into the fae lands, for many reasons, but mostly because we would never be able to hide our foreignness with them.

The gnome studied us harder, and didn't say anything, which was disconcerting. He seemed to spend a long time staring at my feet. His mouth dropped open slightly, revealing some sharp, pointed teeth. He then turned to look at Kade, taking in his huge body, before finally Nikoli. On all of us he paid particular attention to our feet.

I looked down, wondering what had caught his eye. Did we wear the wrong shoes, or something? *Holy crap!* The grass all around me, in about a two foot radius, was a bright vibrant green. It was the same around Kade and Nikoli. All of us had brought some of the mecca with us and it was healing the land here.

The gnome's green eyes almost disappeared into his face folds as he shouted: "Ye ain't no traders!" He said a few more things as he jabbed at my feet, but I couldn't understand him. Finally he calmed a little and said: "Trader or not, we are low in food, so I'll take ye up on yer offer."

His accent was definitely an odd a mixture of Irish and something else. "Can I sample the foods to make sure ye aren't lyin'?"

I nodded and slowly swung the backpack off my shoulder. Kade did the same, and even knelt on one knee so as not to seem so tall in front of our four-foot friend. The moment I pulled a paper sack of cashews from my bag the gnome smelled the air and stepped even closer. I held the bag out for him to peer into.

"What are they? Look like nuk nuts but more curved."

I knew I couldn't say cashews, in case they had nothing like that here, so I just offered him two. He popped them in his mouth and moaned. "Splendid!" His entire demeanor changed now that he saw we had so much food. Part of me worried we might need this food, but it was better to make friends and sleep in the village tonight. Maybe we could get him drunk on whatever did that here and get him to tell us stories. Help us figure out where we were and were we needed to go. Despite the fact I was desperate to get to Violet, it would be a huge advantage for us to observe some fae and learn how to blend in.

Kade held out his palm. Upon it were two dried apricots. The gnome snatched them from his palm and popped him in his mouth. After a few chews he giggled.

"What are two high born from the royal courts and a magic wielder doing all de way out in these woods?" he asked, sniffing Nikoli's bag. Nikoli produced a dried piece of beef jerky and handed it to him.

High born, the treeling had told me, was their terminology for the tall, human-looking, pointy-eared fae.

I chuckled nervously. My trader story wasn't going to work. We had him enthralled with the food now, but it wouldn't last.

Kade called the gnome closer as if he was going to whisper a secret. The gnome stepped gingerly toward Kade, and I too leaned in, waiting to see what my mate would say.

"My lady here was a maid in the Summer Court palace, and I was a royal guard. We got caught … having a relationship, and were exiled."

The gnome's eyes popped open wide, but then he grinned. "Ah, she's quite a looker, ain't she?" He winked to Kade. The bear didn't respond, but I could see tension lining his jaw. Of course, we hadn't explained Nikoli's presence, who the gnome was eyeing wearily.

"What's his story?" the gnome asked, flaring his nostrils near my bag again. I dropped two cashews in his palm and he popped them into his mouth.

Nikoli pointed to Kade. "He's my best friend. I got caught trying to help them get out of the palace."

The gnome chuckled. "Two exiled high borns and a magic user in my woods? Frinnie won't believe this."

He began to walk away toward the village, then noticed we were still standing there.

"Come on, lads! Bring your food and I'll agree to your terms. Two nights stay and some fine weapons. But no longer. I don't need any more trouble with the Summer Court."

Kade, Nikoli, and I shared a look. He had trouble with the Summer Court already? Interesting. I had no idea where on the map we were, but I intended to find out. I intended to find my best friend, get the hell out of here, and then get my crown back from Selene. You know the saying: *All is fair in love and war*? Well, Selene and the dark fae holding my best friend captive had definitely declared war, and I intended to bring it to them.

Queen Fae – NYC Mecca Series #3 is available to pre-order now!

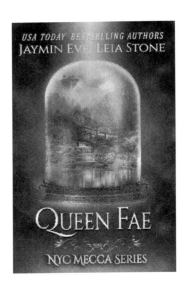

When the fae kidnapped Violet, they underestimated Arianna, Queen of the wolf shifters. There was literally nothing she wouldn't do to save her best friend. Which is why she sets out with her mate and pack of dominants to rescue the magic born from the fae lands.

As she expected the Otherworld is fraught with danger, but there is one thing which takes her completely by surprise. A dark secret which could rock her world to its very foundation.

Arianna must now save her friend and herself. Because the fae have been waiting for her, and she's just walked right into their trap.

Acknowledgements from Leia: We are so proud of this book. This book started as all of our books starts together. I email Jaymin with an idea and she took it and ran and I ran with her. We are so so proud of this book. Arianna is so different than our other characters and this story is so developed, we really poured our heart and soul into it and we hope you love it. Thank you to Lee and Patti for your eagle eyed editing. Thank you to the Enforcers for being down to read all books Jaymin and Leia. A huge thank you to my husband and kids for dealing with me running off and writing in the closet because this story just poured out of us. Jaymin, I never imagined a world in which I would write books with another person so seamlessly that it sounds like my own inner voice at times. Thanks for being my author twin. <3 To all our readers and my release team, we do this for you! Much love.

Acknowledgements from Jaymin: My biggest thanks is to my family. Thank you so much for all your support and love. I couldn't do what I do without you, and I never forget that. I love you more than words.

To my bestie Leia Stone. I love you, girl! Authoring would be a much lonelier place without such a wonderful friend to share it with. <3 BAFFs always. Big thanks also to my great friend Donna Augustine for keeping me sane, and offering countless advice on cover and many other things.

Next thanks is for my betas, who have shown so much love and enthusiasm for Queen Heir. You guys rock!! Couldn't do this without you.

Thanks as always to my release teams, the Nerd Herd, and Enforcers group. All of you are amazing, and I am so grateful to have found so many friends to share these worlds with.

Thank you to Lee for your wonderful and detailed editing. And to Tamara, our cover artist. You're awesome! We love every single thing you do for us, you bring our worlds to life.

To our fans. We love you. All of our books are for you. xxx.

Books from Leia Stone

<u>Matefinder Trilogy (Optioned for film)</u>
Matefinder: Book 1
Devi: Book 2
Balance: Book 3

<u>Matefinder Next Generation</u>
Keeper: Book 1

<u>Hive Trilogy</u>
Ash: Book 1
Anarchy: Book 2
Annihilate: Book 3

Stay in touch with Leia:
www.facebook.com/leia.stone/
Mailing list: http://goo.gl/0EX98P

Books from Jaymin Eve

<u>A Walker Saga - YA Paranormal Romance series
(complete)</u>
First World - #1
Spurn - #2
Crais - #3
Regali - #4
Nephilius - #5
Dronish - #6
Earth - #7

<u>Supernatural Prison Trilogy - NA Urban Fantasy
series (complete)</u>

Dragon Marked - #1
Dragon Mystics - #2
Dragon Mated - #3

Supernatural Prison Stories
Broken Compass - #1

Sinclair Stories
Songbird - Standalone Contemporary Romance

Hive Trilogy (complete)
Ash - #1
Anarchy - #2
Annihilate: #3

NYC Mecca Series
Queen Heir
Queen Alpha
Queen Fae (late April 2017)

Curse of the Gods Series
Trickery (28th February 2017)

Stay in touch with Jaymin:
www.facebook.com/JayminEve.Author
Website: www.jaymineve.com
jaymineve@gmail.com

Printed in Great Britain
by Amazon